Staff memo
From: Liz Otley, KSEA news director
To: All newsroom personnel

As you are aware, the incident at the Grand Hotel
ballroom on Saturday afternoon involved our station
meteorologist, Jennifer Winn, and her fiancé, Russell
Sprague. A small aircraft crashed into the ballroom,
killing the pilot and injuring Russell and a female friend.
Jennifer was unharmed.

I have just learned that Russell died last night and the
death is being treated as suspicious.

Although it is our duty to keep our viewers fully and
accurately informed to the best of our ability, I am
requesting at this point that all news reports on this
story avoid mention of the connection between the
victim and Jennifer. Obviously we will not be able to hold
back this info indefinitely, nor would we want to as
Courage Bay's premier television news station. However,
by doing this, we can buy Jennifer a little time to cope
with the shock of the situation.

Jennifer has been assessed by Dr Michael Temple, a
clinical psychiatrist on the staff at Courage Bay Hospital.
When she returns to work, we will offer her our support
and sympathy, but until further notice, KSEA will not
reveal Jennifer's relationship to the late Russell Sprague.

MJ Rodgers is a firm believer that whatever we put out into the world is what we receive back. That's why she chooses to write romances. Stories filled with the heartwarming magic of love are, in her opinion, the best kind of messages to both send and receive.

In summer, she and her family wake up to the song of eagles in a sunlit ocean inlet of Washington State, USA. When winter comes, they travel to southern Nevada, where they enjoy the warm crimson sunsets of the desert mesa.

CODE RED

ORDINARY PEOPLE
EXTRAORDINARY CIRCUMSTANCES

CRITICAL
AFFAIR

MJ
RODGERS

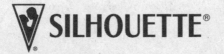

SILHOUETTE®

First published in Great Britain 2005
Silhouette Books, Eton House, 18-24 Paradise Road,
Richmond, Surrey TW9 1SR

© Harlequin Books S.A. 2004

MJ Rodgers is acknowledged as the author of this work.

ISBN 0 373 61293 1

156-1105

Printed and bound in Spain
by Litografia Rosés S.A., Barcelona

Dear Reader,

I'm honoured to be a writer on the CODE RED series. We live in a culture that is so quick to idolise actors and sports figures that sometimes we forget the real heroes and heroines living among us. The medical, police and fire personnel who respond to our emergency calls are men and women who have dedicated their lives to helping others. To my mind, there is no better definition of a hero and heroine.

In this CODE RED story, a new kind of medical professional makes his debut. Michael Temple is a psychiatrist at Courage Bay Hospital. When emergency psychiatric problems arise, he's the one called in to defuse life-threatening situations. After a decade on the job, Michael is a seasoned professional, confident he's prepared for any challenge.

Until his summons to the ER for an emergency psychological evaluation brings him face-to-face with Jennifer, the woman he lost his heart to five years before.

I hope you enjoy Michael and Jennifer's story. If you would like a personally autographed sticker for your copy of the book, send an SAE to me at PO Box 284, Seabeck, Washington 98380-0284, USA.

Warmest wishes,

MJ

This book is for Margaret Learn,
an exceptionally gifted editor
with a warm and generous heart.

CHAPTER ONE

IT WAS COMING BACK.

Jennifer Winn watched the gigantic black cloud gather momentum as it rolled off the Pacific Ocean, swallowed the sandy shore, the rocky bluff and every last ray of evening light. When its thick saliva began to coat the windowpanes of the Grand Hotel, she took an involuntary step back.

Storms, floods, droughts—these Jennifer took in her stride as Courage Bay's resident meteorologist. But this insidious fog, which robbed her of sight, upset her on a deep visceral level she could not explain.

"Isn't it perfect?" Russell asked from behind her.

Jennifer spun away from the blackened windows to face her fiancé's bright smile. She'd been so caught up in thoughts of the fog that it took a moment for her to realize he was talking about the ballroom.

Her eyes swept over the expansive space with its twenty-two-foot ceilings, sparkling chandeliers and shiny marble floors. Waiters in pristine attire prepared place settings of crystal and fine china on tables covered in white linen. According to the hallway banner, tonight the room would be filled with a prestigious law school's alumni celebrating their twenty-year reunion.

"Very nice," she said, "but big."

"Don't worry about filling the tables," Russell said. "My invitation list alone will do that."

"Yours will have to. Mine has no more than a dozen names." She hadn't meant the comment to come out with sadness, but it seemed to.

Russell clasped her hand, rubbed the large diamond on her finger. "Jen, you deserve a big, beautiful wedding, and I'm going to see that you get one."

He would, too. Russell was the cliché of every woman's fantasy—handsome, charming and more than ready to commit. From the moment they'd met the year before, he'd done everything he could to sweep her off her feet.

By all rights this should be the most exciting time of her life.

"I gave the hotel manager the deposit," Gina called as she came into the hotel's ballroom from the adjacent hall.

Jennifer found herself frowning at her approaching friend. "Why did you do that? We haven't decided yet."

"But Russell said—" Gina began.

"I told her to give him the deposit, Jen," Russell interrupted. "This place is normally booked at least a year in advance. The only reason they have an opening next month is because of a last-minute cancellation. I wouldn't have even known about that if the manager wasn't a patient of mine."

"This is the first place we've seen," Jennifer said. "There may be something else that—"

"Not at this late date," he declared. "The only other available reception halls are dumps. Mother's already checked them out. A reception says a lot about a couple. We want ours to say the right thing about us. This is the place that will."

Jennifer once again surveyed the elegantly appointed room. No doubt about it. Russell fit right in here.

He moved closer, circled his arm around her.

"I want us to be married next month, Jen, not next year. If we don't take this right now, someone else is going to. We can't let this chance pass us by."

"Russell's right," Gina said. "My group used to perform here. The acoustics are great. You're going to be able to hear the band's every drumbeat."

"What band?" Jennifer asked.

"The one Mother hired for us on Thursday," Russell said. "Eight-piece. Three vocalists. You'll love them. Their repertoire includes everything from classic to contemporary. She gave them a list of all the songs we like. 'My One and Only' will be what they play when we have our first dance together as man and wife. Great pick, isn't it?"

Of course it was. Russell and his mother had impeccable taste. So did his father and sister, for that matter. The Sprague family genes were positively oozing with the stuff.

"And now let me give you a preview of the coming attractions," Russell said.

He clasped her hand and whisked her on to the dance floor, waltzing to the music being piped through the ballroom. As with everything else he did, Russell was a precision dancer, each move executed with perfect timing. Jennifer concentrated on matching his steps.

"Can't you see us right here next month—me in my tux and you in your wedding dress—all eyes on us? We're going to have a great wedding. All you have to do is leave it to me."

A big part of her wanted to. Russell was a man who knew how to get things done. And what he didn't have time to handle, his mother would be more than willing to. Between them they would put together a first-class affair.

But this was her wedding. Shouldn't she be in the thick of the preparations? Wasn't that supposed to be half the fun? Why was she content to sit on the sidelines?

Jennifer began missing steps, no matter how diligently she tried to keep up.

Russell eased to a graceful halt. "Tired, darling?"

"A little." Until she said it, she didn't realize how much. It had been awhile since lunch. Maybe she needed to eat something. Maybe she was coming down with a cold. Maybe—

She felt a tap on her shoulder.

"Your relief is here," Gina said. "I'll drag his inept butt around the dance floor a few times and give your poor stepped-on toes a chance to heal."

Gina always did have a good sense of humor. Jennifer gave her friend a smile and moved aside.

As Russell and Gina whirled away, Jennifer looked around, to see that the waiters had finished their preparations and left. She headed for the nearest table and lowered herself onto one of its cushioned chairs to watch her fiancé and best friend.

They were something to watch. Gina shared Russell's dark coloring and height. She was a professional dancer, performing on stage throughout Southern California. Together they turned what proved to be a difficult beat for Jennifer into a flowing art form.

Maybe I should take lessons, Jennifer thought. *Russell loves parties and socializing. There'll be a lot of dancing in our future. Wish I enjoyed dancing more.*

Her gaze drifted to the blackened windows beyond the twirling couple. Whatever this strange mood was that claimed her, it seemed in some way to be linked to the unsettling fog.

For nearly a week, the coastal community of Courage Bay had been consumed each evening by the ominous cloud. It wreaked havoc on the roadways, as residents, trying to navigate through the unaccustomed gloom toward the light of hearth and home, found themselves in pileups and ditches and the hospital's emergency room.

And with every weather forecast she gave, Jennifer had nothing to offer but more of the same. The precipitating conditions of unseasonably warm air masses mixing with the cold water upwelling along the coast persisted.

It was as though the fog were a ravenous predator, rising out of the ocean each night to hunt its human prey.

Jennifer jumped right out of her chair as an ominous roar suddenly drowned out the music. Two gigantic eyes glowed out of the dense fog and stared right at her—giving shape to her darkest imaginings. Time stopped as her disbelieving eyes locked on those of the disembodied beast.

Then a private airplane materialized out of the black night and smashed through the windows, spewing glass everywhere, tearing the crystal chandeliers from the ceiling and crashing onto the floor in a cacophony of blinding light and deafening sound.

And beneath its rocking, twisted body were Russell and Gina.

Jennifer yanked her cell phone out of her purse as she ran into the wreckage. She darted through the broken glass, ducked beneath ripped and dangling electrical wires hanging from the ceiling, still emitting sparks.

A flurry of startled voices and stomping feet erupted behind her. She paid them no heed as she vaulted over a smashed chandelier. By the time she'd told the 911 operator what had happened, she'd reached Russell beneath one of the plane's sheared-off wings.

She dropped to his side, her heart beating high, fast. His eyes were closed and he wasn't moving. Broken glass and pieces of plane and other debris surrounded him, but she could see no blood to indicate a wound.

"Russell?"

No response. She groped for the pulse in his neck. For what seemed like forever, she felt nothing but the pounding of her heart. Then a steady beat registered beneath her fingertips. Relief left her light-headed.

"Ms. Winn?" the manager's voice called from somewhere behind her. "Where are you?"

"Over here," Jennifer answered. "Beneath the wing."

"Hold on. I'll be right there."

Jennifer heard the noise of glass crunching beneath shoes. A soft curse. Then the manager came into view and squatted beside her. He was a gray-haired man whose face got grayer as he looked at Russell's unconscious form.

"The pilot's dead," he stated. "Russell isn't…?"

"His pulse is strong," Jennifer assured him. "I called 911."

"Glad to see someone's keeping it together," he said, and she noticed his hands were shaking.

She gave him a brief smile. "I'll be falling apart later. Right now I can't afford to."

Jennifer started as she heard Gina groan.

"That's my friend," she said, wanting to go to her, but not willing to leave Russell.

The manager seemed to understand her dilemma. "It's okay. I'll stay with him."

She quickly bent to kiss Russell's cheek before jumping to her feet and scurrying off in the direction of the next groan. It took a frantic search through the rubble before she found Gina at the other end of the wreckage. Her friend was lying on her side behind the tail portion of the plane. A triangular-shaped piece of glass stuck out of her arm, the wound pulsing blood.

Jennifer dropped to her knees, whipped off her belt and wrapped it tightly around the top of Gina's arm to stop the blood loss.

"Jen?"

"Right here."

Gina blinked up at her. "You're fuzzy."

"Most of the lights on this side of the room are out," Jennifer said, hoping that was the only reason her friend was having trouble seeing her.

"I'm cold."

Jennifer wasn't surprised. They were on the very edge of the ballroom floor next to a yawning gap that had once been floor-to-ceiling windows. In the blackness beyond lay a two-hundred-foot drop to the sea. The chilling wet fog poured over them.

She pulled off her jacket, wrapped it around Gina, kicked away two large pieces of glass and sat on the floor. Propping Gina's injured arm against her knee, she settled her friend's head in her lap. "Better?" she asked.

"That damn thing came right at us. Did you see it?"

"Hard to miss," Jennifer said, working to keep her voice calm. She was shivering in her light sweater and didn't know how much of it was from cold and how much from shock.

"What in the hell was it?" Gina asked.

"A small plane. Did you see Russell when it hit?" Jennifer asked, trying to keep her mind focused and functioning.

"Hell, I was too busy diving for the floor. Where is he?"

"Other side of the wreckage. He was knocked out. How are you feeling?"

"My arm hurts like hell."

"How about the rest of you?"

"Okay, I guess. What's wrong with my arm?"

"Appears you got hit by a piece of flying glass."

Gina stared at her arm. Something must have been registering because after a succession of rapid blinks, a look of horror stole over her face.

"Get it out!"

"We'll have to wait for the paramedics," Jennifer told her.

"I'm bleeding!"

"Very slowly now. My belt's acting as a tourniquet, and I'm keeping your arm raised and supported. You're going to be fine."

"But all that blood!"

"It's not that much," Jennifer lied. "Now close your eyes. Try to rest. Help's on the way."

Gina's eyes remained open, darting about. "Jen, I'm scared. What if I lose my arm? What if I don't make it at all?"

"Don't be silly. You're going to make it."

"That's what they always say in the movies just before the guy dies."

"Aren't you glad this isn't the movies and you're not a guy?"

Gina's eyes steadied on Jennifer's face. "You've been a good friend to me. The best friend I've ever had. Do you know that?"

"You've been a really good friend to me as well."

"I feel so rotten."

The sound of sirens wailed up the road toward the hotel. "Hear that?" Jennifer asked, her voice high with relief. "Help is nearly here."

Gina closed her eyes and sank the full weight of her head onto Jennifer's lap. "It's too late. Everything's getting blurry. Jen, I can't die with this on my conscience. I have to tell you. I've been sleeping with Russell for the past six months."

DR. MICHAEL TEMPLE'S shift at the hospital had officially ended two hours before. He'd stayed on because of a deeply troubled young man.

Gary was twenty, a good-looking college sophomore on an athletic scholarship, with plenty of pretty girls interested in him and a shot at pro sports—until a few beers and some dangerous horsing around with his buddies resulted in his right hand being severed.

His scholarship had been terminated, and as far as Gary was concerned, so had his life.

A month after he'd been sent home from the hospital, Gary used his new artificial hand to apply a razor blade to his remaining wrist. His suicide attempt hadn't been successful.

The E.R. had stopped the bleeding. The O.R. had sutured his wrist. Now he lay in the psychiatric ward, both arms bound to the bed.

He'd turned away everyone who tried to visit him. Hadn't opened his cards. Kicked the vases of flowers and boxes of candy that arrived onto the floor. All his parents got were dead stares.

For the past three hours, Michael had listened as Gary finally opened up and let out the emotions seething inside him. He was full of rage, a sense of injustice, a roaring self-pity.

And a profound isolation.

Emotions Michael understood only too well.

But he had said nothing to Gary. The young man wouldn't have heard anything he had to say. Gary simply needed someone to listen to him today. Michael had listened.

And then he had given orders that Gary's bed be moved out of isolation and into the room where Leon, a twenty-one-year-old with osteogenic sarcoma, was recuperating after having the bottom half of his left leg amputated.

Leon was also at the point where he hated all well people and was ready to take out his anger on anyone who came within hearing range. But Michael saw the anger of both young men for what it was—a desire for change. They were fighting back.

Adapting to their new realities and healing their torn emotions would take more than time, however. It would take connection with someone who understood. They could help each other in a way he could not.

After finishing his case notes, Michael turned off his computer, stretching to get the kinks out of his shoulders and back.

The workout at the gym was going to feel good tonight. Saturday was always his favorite time—no competition for the weight machines or overcrowding in the steam room.

Out in the hallway, he was about to press the elevator button when Hazel, the senior nurse on the ward, scurried over. "They need a psych consult in the E.R., Dr. Temple. Can you take it?"

Hazel knew when his shift had ended. He also knew that she wouldn't be making the request if there were anyone else available.

"Who's the E.R. doctor?" Michael asked.

"Brad Winslow."

Michael nodded as he headed toward the stairs, always the quickest route down to the E.R. As he exited onto the floor, he found himself in the midst of a barely controlled frenzy.

A few nights before he'd been called down to the E.R. to evaluate a patient and had faced a similar situation. The emergency team's resources were taxed to the hilt because of the casualties caused by the dense fog.

Motorists refused to listen to the advisories being broadcast over the radio and TV about the reduced visibility. Slowing down wasn't something that came easily to drivers in Southern California. And they were paying for their folly.

Every trauma room was full, all curtains closed around examining areas. Patients lay on gurneys in the hallways. Even the waiting room was overflowing. Triage nurses scurried from patient to patient, taking vital signs, assessing injuries in order to prioritize the most serious.

The harried clerk at the desk had a telephone to his ear while trying to simultaneously answer questions being shot at him by two anxious family members on the conditions of their loved ones.

Michael located Brad in exam room 4. He slipped inside and stood at the door while the E.R. doctor worked on a young man with a knife wound to the stomach.

All the ravages Mother Nature could unleash still paled next to the damage human beings inflicted on one another.

"You called for a psych consult?" Michael asked as soon as the patient's bleeding had been controlled.

Brad didn't turn from his task. "Thanks for coming down, Michael. I haven't had time to start a chart on her. She's in the doctor's lounge. Only secluded place we had to put her."

"What happened?" Michael asked.

"Technically, she assaulted an E.R. patient."

Which meant that according to hospital policy, she had to be seen within one hour of being placed in seclusion.

"How's the patient?" Michael asked.

"Concussion but stable. He'll be spending the night with us in a bed upstairs."

The doors burst open behind Michael and a nurse's head appeared. "Dr. Winslow, we have a car accident victim who's gone into cardiac arrest."

Brad quickly finished with the patient in front of him, barking orders that he be taken up to the O.R. Twisting around, he ripped off his bloodied gloves and smock and raced after the disappearing nurse.

"Frank Keller witnessed the assault," Brad called over his shoulder to Michael. "He's in the waiting room."

Brad was out the door to attend to the new emergency before Michael could even ask him the name of the psych patient.

Back at the admissions desk, Michael noted that the beleaguered clerk was still tied up on the phone and being harassed by patients and family alike. Helping himself to a clipboard and fresh patient chart from behind the counter, Michael stepped into the waiting room.

"Frank Keller?"

A fiftyish man leaned away from the wall and headed toward him. Michael introduced himself. Since there was no place to talk privately in the crowded and noisy corridors, Michael beckoned his witness toward the exit.

Once they were outside, the din of humanity subsided. The evening was moist and pitch-black with fog. They made for a bench at the corner of the building, away from the flow of foot traffic and yet still within the lighted perimeter.

As they sat side by side, Michael studied his companion.

Keller had carefully clipped nails and wore a suit and dress shoes, all currently soiled. He'd washed his hands and face within the past few minutes. The smell of the antiseptic soap used in the hospital's rest rooms was unmistakable.

But there was a dirt smudge on his neck that he'd missed, and his fingers quivered slightly as he picked at encrusted debris on his trousers. The man was holding together, but something had shaken him.

"What happened tonight, Mr. Keller?"

Keller took a deep breath before he began. "I'm the manager at the Grand Hotel. About an hour ago, a private airplane crashed into our second floor ballroom, tore it to pieces. The pilot was gone before I got to him."

He paused, rubbed his eyes as though trying to rub away the image. "I guess I should be thankful that it was just the three of them in there. Thirty minutes later and the place would have been filled with lawyers."

Michael watched as the imagined nightmare of that scenario played through the man's mind, etching deep lines into his face.

"The three of them?" Michael prompted, to get Keller's attention back on track.

"Russell and Jennifer had just booked the ballroom for their wedding reception. Her friend, Gina, was with them. I was in my office, working on their menu, when it happened."

His hand gesture was one of irritation. "These last-minute things are always a pain. When he was fitting me for a crown last week, I warned Russell that he'd never pull off a decent wedding in a month's time. But he told me he'd waited too long for Jennifer to say yes to put up with any more delay."

"You said he was fitting you for a crown?" Michael asked.

"Russell's my dentist."

"I see. Please go on."

"They were still in the ballroom looking things over when the plane flew in and took out the west wall and every window facing the sea. The noise was deafening. My staff lit out the front door like the devil was after them. I probably would have followed if I hadn't seen Jennifer. She was amazing—ran straight into the wreckage to be by his side, despite the danger to herself from the broken glass and fallen rubble."

"By *his* side, you mean…?"

"Russell. Jennifer wasn't hurt. But Russell was knocked unconscious, and Gina got struck by a piece of glass. Paramedics said that the first aid Jennifer administered to her friend saved the woman from bleeding to death. Last thing I ever imagined was *her* losing it."

"How did she lose it?"

"Gina was treated and sent up to a hospital bed. The E.R. doctor who had been working on Russell came out to tell us that he was awake and expected to completely recover. Jennifer was so relieved. I saw her face. I *know* that's how she felt."

Keller flashed Michael a look as though he expected disagreement.

Michael gave Keller a noncommittal smile and a nod, both to show acceptance of the man's message and to urge him to continue his story.

"The treatment room was needed for another emergency, so they rolled Russell into the hallway to wait for an available hospital bed," Keller continued. "That's where I left him and Jennifer while I made the calls."

"Which calls?"

"Jennifer had gotten hold of Gina's parents, but hadn't been able to reach any of Russell's relatives. Russell gave us his father's cell phone number and his sister's. I told Jennifer I'd make the calls so she could remain with her fiancé. I had to let the hotel owners know about Russell's status, anyway. Even though this accident was clearly not the fault of the hotel, one can never assume that someone won't sue. Not that the owners are only concerned about…I mean, they were genuinely happy to know that Russell and Gina were going to be all right."

"I understand, Mr. Keller. Dr. Winslow told me that you were a witness to the assault?" he prodded, hoping to get the man back to the point.

Keller nodded. "After notifying Russell's relations and the hotel owners, I returned to the hallway where Russell still lay on the gurney. That's when I saw Jennifer dump a full pitcher of ice water all over his...crotch."

The hotel manager paused as he made an unconscious, protective movement toward that part of his anatomy.

"What happened then?" Michael asked.

"Russell howled, then started cursing. An orderly rushed over at the same time that the E.R. doctor poked his head out of the trauma room to see what was going on."

Keller paused again, shook his head. "The doctor saw the way Russell was clutching himself, did a quick examination, got some dry towels to, uh...wrap things. But when he asked what had happened, neither Russell nor Jennifer would say a word."

"So you told the doctor what you saw," Michael guessed.

"Wouldn't have if I'd been thinking straight. Wasn't really any of my business. But I was so shocked, and after everything that had happened... Anyway, I could tell by the way Russell glared at me afterward that he was really angry I hadn't kept quiet. Damn."

Keller stared at his hands as though he wanted to wash them again.

"Are you worried about repercussions?" Michael asked.

The man's frown deepened. "Never a good idea to piss off a guy who could be putting a drill in your mouth next week."

"What happened then?"

"A nurse came over to say that a bed in one of the wards upstairs had become available. She rolled Russell away. The E.R. doctor asked the orderly to escort Jennifer to the physician's lounge. I don't know why. Russell's going to be all right. It's not like he's going to press charges or anything."

"It's routine hospital policy," Michael explained.

"I hope you can find out what the hell happened. They seemed like such a perfect couple when they came into the hotel tonight. And she was so gentle with him when he lay unconscious in the wreckage. This definitely isn't like her."

"Have you known her long, Mr. Keller?"

"I only met Jennifer this evening. But after watching her on TV for the past year, I feel like we're old friends. She comes across so...well, honest and down-to-earth. Her weather reports are some of the best stuff on the tube."

Michael stared at Keller through several heartbeats as the man's words registered. "Are you talking about Jennifer *Winn?*"

"Yes, of course. Didn't the E.R. doctor tell you who she was?"

Michael mumbled a quick thank-you to Keller before hurrying back into the hospital. He dove through the mass of humanity toward the doctor's lounge.

A grim-faced orderly guarded the entry, legs apart, arms akimbo. Michael told him to go back to the floor, and yanked open the door.

She was alone, standing at the back of the room, staring at the wall—a slim silhouette in a dark blue sweater and slacks. Her face was a profile of soft, familiar curves. Her golden-brown hair fell in a tangled tumble to the middle of her back.

Michael wouldn't have thought it possible, but she was even lovelier in person than he remembered. For several seconds he simply stood there, trying to steady himself emotionally.

"Hello, Jennifer," he said finally, his tone friendly but carefully circumspect.

Since the moment he'd heard her name, he'd been working to keep a lid on his feelings. With this woman more than any other, maintaining a strict professional detachment was an absolute necessity.

But when she turned toward him and he saw the tears in her eyes, his resolve unraveled.

CHAPTER TWO

JENNIFER RECOGNIZED Michael's voice instantly.

She told herself she was wrong. This had to be a trick of the senses, brought about by the disorienting events of the evening.

But when she turned, his solid frame spanned the doorway. The same rich brown hair she remembered. The same blue eyes, warm as a sunlit sea.

Five years peeled away and she was back in his seminar on grief at the local community college, his deep voice and gentle words spreading over her like a healing balm.

During that six weeks, he'd made the world a good place to be again.

And during the final sixty seconds, she'd made a complete fool of herself.

For five years she'd thought about what she would say if she ever saw him again. She'd rehearsed a dozen lines—all sophisticated and witty, covering every conceivable circumstance. Problem was, she'd never conceived of this one.

"It's you," she heard some mindless idiot say, knowing all too well that mindless idiot was her.

His lips lifted in a half smile. "Right on the first guess."

Closing the door behind him, he started toward her. For one delirious second, she was back in one of those old daydreams in which he suddenly walked into a room, took her in his arms and—

"I understand the evening has been an eventful one," he said.

She saw it then. The clipboard in his hand with a patient chart. *Her* patient chart.

Dear heavens. He was the psychiatrist called in to evaluate her mental state. If she'd had any doubts about this being the most humiliating night of her life, they were gone.

Jennifer lowered herself onto the nearest chair, grabbed a tissue out of her purse and dried her eyes. She was not going to cry in front of him. Not while there was even one shred of her dignity still left.

"So, they sent in the famous Dr. Temple to evaluate the raving lunatic," she said, trying to make her tone light.

He took the chair next to her. "Actually, I came to see the heroine who saved a woman's life."

Seconds passed before Jennifer realized that he meant her.

"Heroine," she repeated in disbelief.

"True, the average man on the street might choose to call you crazy for having rushed into the wreckage of that plane crash, risking life and limb. But as a stroller down the hallowed halls of psychiatric wisdom, I can assure you that the technical term we use for such behavior is *brave.*"

He smiled at her.

Jennifer's heart sighed. No one had ever been able to part the dark clouds of her world and let in the light like he could. God, it was good to see him again.

The door to the lounge burst open and a harried-looking doctor sent Michael a quick nod of recognition as he sprinted to the coffee machine.

"Let's go someplace where we can talk," Michael said to Jennifer, getting to his feet.

She assumed he meant to his office. But when they left the physician's lounge, he headed toward the admissions desk. After making some notes on the chart, he left it with the stack of others and started for the hospital exit.

"Where are we going?" she asked.

"I don't know about you, but I could use a drink about now."

"A...drink?"

"The Courage Bay Bar and Grill is right up the street. That okay with you?"

Jennifer nodded, mute with surprise. This couldn't be the

same Dr. Temple who had turned down every invitation extended by the adult students in his night seminar to socialize outside the classroom.

Get a grip, Jennifer. This isn't socializing. This is his job. You attacked someone tonight. He's with you for one reason and one reason only. To assess whether you're a danger to yourself and others.

That was the depressing truth, despite his kind words to her earlier. He was going to be asking some personal questions soon. What's more, he knew how to ask them. More than once in that grief seminar, she'd found herself telling him things she'd never meant to.

But not tonight. She was going to keep her mouth shut. He was the last soul on earth she wanted to know about her newest romantic disaster.

Better he think her some raving lunatic.

The bar turned out to be packed, the function room overflowing, and there was a long wait for the dining room. A waiter suggested they try the rooftop patio. Even with the fog obliterating the view, it was crowded. They got the last table.

Jennifer excused herself to visit the rest room so she could wash her hands and face, put on fresh makeup and brush her disheveled hair into some order. She might be resigned to the fact that he was going to think her a loony, but she didn't want him to see her looking like one.

You are nuts, she said to her reflection in the mirror.

When she returned to the table, the waitress was delivering their drinks—a concoction that Michael had recommended called Flame. To Jennifer it looked like a mixture of citrus juices. When her first taste told her that there was a bracing amount of alcohol in it as well, she swallowed in welcome surprise.

A stiff drink and a restful atmosphere to relax the lunatic. If this was the new direction psychiatry was taking, she was all for it.

Chinese lanterns hung over the small dance floor in the center of the rooftop patio. The corner table where she and Michael sat was lit by a miniature hurricane lamp. Radiant heat drifted from the walls, taking the chill off the cocooning fog. The piano player's slow songs and the murmur of voices from the other patrons seemed to come from very far away.

She sipped her drink and waited for his first question, trying to prepare herself to deflect it. That would be the best she could do. Telling an outright lie—especially to him—wasn't in her.

"Let's see," Michael said after taking a healthy gulp of his Flame. "Five years ago you had just completed your bachelor's degree in atmospheric science and were trying to decide if you should continue at UCLA and get your master's. Right?"

She didn't know exactly what she'd been expecting him to ask, but that definitely wasn't it.

"I'm surprised you remembered," she said. "I only mentioned that in passing during the seminar."

"It was an important decision facing you. Whether to follow in your parents' footsteps and go to work for the government, or step out on your own. Did you enter the master's program at UCLA?"

No, because that would have meant staying in the area and possibly—just possibly—running into you.

She took another sip of her drink. "I got my master's at an eastern college, then went to work for the National Oceanic and Atmospheric Administration back there."

"What did you do?"

"For a while I was in research. My title was synoptic meteorologist, which is a fancy name to describe my sitting in front of a computer trying to see if I could come up with more sophisticated mathematical models for weather forecasting."

"Which you did."

"I found a few new approaches," she admitted, pleased that he had no doubt. "But I also found interacting with a computer all day somewhat less than rewarding."

"Where did you go from there?"

"I became an operational meteorologist at the National Weather Service's Severe Storms Forecast Center in Kansas City."

"One of the brains behind the country's storm alerts."

"One of the meteorologists who read the instruments and

hoped to hell she got it right," Jennifer corrected. "Even with all the latest in satellite, computer and radar technology, a prediction of cloudy skies can still turn into a tornado."

"I can see how that might be embarrassing for a meteorologist."

"Especially if a professional golf tournament is being played that day—or would have been played if the sudden appearance of the whirling cloud hadn't sent everyone scurrying for cover after the second hole and ended up costing millions in lost advertising revenue."

"Did that happen to you?"

"To one of my colleagues. But it could just as easily have been me. When it comes to reading the weather, we still get it wrong."

"Your prediction rate at KSEA has been perfect so far."

"How do you know?"

"I'm one of your many fans."

His words warmed her even better than the drink.

"Are you folks ready for another?" the waitress interrupted.

Jennifer looked down in some surprise to see her glass was empty. She realized then that she'd been getting carried away. And no wonder. Michael listened as though everything she said was important to him.

After the waitress had left to bring them refills, he asked, "How did you get from the severe storms center in Kansas to doing the weather five nights a week on local TV?"

"About eighteen months ago an opening came up at the NWS operational station in this area. I decided to take it. A couple of months after relocating here, KSEA offered me their meteorologist slot."

"Going to let me in on the secret of your accurate forecasting?"

"I've been using one of the new mathematical models I developed at NWS to predict the effect of the different converging air currents for which Courage Bay is renowned."

The waitress returned, set their refills on the table and left.

"Can this mathematical model predict how long this fog is going to be with us?" Michael asked.

His question was good—the very one she'd been wrestling

with the past week. Reminding herself that he was a psychiatrist and she his patient, Jennifer faced the fact that he might be trying to get her to relax by discussing a safe subject that didn't matter until he could comfortably steer her into the one that did.

Was he?

She stared at her glass, fingered the rim. "Maybe you should ask me the questions for your report so we can get it over with."

"I don't have to ask you any questions," Michael said. "'My report', as you call it, is finished."

"You don't want to know what happened?"

"I know what happened."

She gathered her courage to look at him. "How do you know?"

He returned her gaze evenly. "There's only one reason why a woman would suddenly dump ice water on her fiancé's crotch. You caught him cheating on you."

Jennifer downed a good portion of her second drink. She should have known he'd figure it out.

"Do you want to talk about it?" he asked.

No, I don't.

"It might help."

To make me look and feel like an even bigger idiot? Yeah, that would certainly top off the sterling events of the evening.

"If you'd prefer, we can get back to the weather," he said. "Pretty safe topic for most of us. Of course, as the meteorologist who's had to forecast this incessant fog every night for the past week, you may find it a sensitive issue. I'm conversant on the far sunnier subjects of war, famine and pestilence. Any of those appeal to you?"

He was smiling at her.

She remembered then…all those times she'd found herself telling him things. It wasn't because he'd coerced her. Or manipulated her. Or lulled her into a sense of security so she'd drop her defenses.

It was because he hadn't tried to do any of those things.

Jennifer took a deep breath, then slowly let it out. "For the past six months, my fiancé's been having an affair with my best friend. If she hadn't confessed to me tonight, I never would have known."

She gulped more of her drink.

"You believed he was honest with you because you were honest with him," Michael said gently.

Nice of him to see it that way. She wished she could. But the truth was, she'd made a critical error in judgment. She firmly believed that her choices reflected who she was. Her choice of Russell was so deeply flawed it made her cringe.

"What did he say when you confronted him about the affair?" Michael asked.

"He told me it was no big deal, just sex. Nothing for me to be concerned about."

Jennifer stared at the tablecloth, shaking her head as she relived that unbelievable scene with Russell. His total lack of remorse for having betrayed her. His dismissal of her feelings as though they were unimportant.

"From our first date he's pushed for an exclusive relationship between us," she said. "For a solid year I've been hearing nothing but how I was the only woman for him. How committed he was to me and our future together. How he could never want anyone else."

She downed the rest of her drink, relishing the bracing trail of warmth it left.

"When did you agree to marry him?" Michael asked.

"A week ago. Looking back on it now, I realize that ever since we set the date, I've had this feeling that something wasn't right."

"But not before?"

"Candy, flowers, cards, the daily phone calls. Russell had all the right moves down. I just didn't realize the wrong man was behind them. Look, I know I acted like a two-year-old tonight. I'm sorry I—"

"You have nothing to be sorry for," Michael interrupted. "What you did tonight was what any self-respecting woman would have done. The cheating bastard deserved everything he got and a lot more."

Jennifer stared at Michael, stunned at both the message in his words and the passion with which he'd delivered them.

She'd fully expected him to remind her that maturity meant channeling anger in healthy, nonviolent ways. Certainly, the calm and objective Dr. Temple had suggested that often enough to his seminar students.

But this Dr. Temple was being anything but calm and objective. He was openly incensed and taking her side.

Jennifer had wanted to hug him on numerous occasions in the past, but never more so than at this moment.

MICHAEL FINISHED HIS DRINK as he worked to control the anger that had so rapidly gotten the better of him. And belied every tenet of his training.

For ten years he'd been a psychiatrist, exposed to every heartache and demon that could inhabit the human psyche. And in all that time, no matter what emotions he'd felt, he'd kept them strictly to himself.

Until now.

"Are you always this nice to your patients?" she asked.

"You're not my patient, Jennifer."

She was still staring at him in a kind of wonder. He knew he'd shocked her by his outburst. He'd shocked himself as well.

"Thank you for that," she said. "And for understanding about Russell. And for suggesting we have this drink. Why did you?"

"I thought you could use a friend tonight."

"I've never had a better one."

She meant it. That was one of the first things he'd noticed when he met Jennifer. Everything about her came across as genuine. He knew that was one of the reasons why her TV weather forecasts had become so popular. Viewers saw that quality in her, as well.

Jennifer called to a passing waitress and ordered another round. Michael could have declined his. He should have.

But seeing her again had brought to the surface feelings so strong that they interfered with his normal good sense. And talking face-to-face with her like this was a reminder of those special times they'd shared five years before.

He'd given the seminar on grief at the local community college to try to be of service to others as well as give himself something to do with his empty nights. On a personal level, reviewing the steps toward healing also proved helpful in his own private journey.

Jennifer had been only twenty-three then, in the throes of a deep grief from having lost both of her parents in a boating accident the month before.

He remembered her soft gray eyes gazing up at him as she sat in the front row of the classroom, listening so attentively. How good it had felt to watch her change from a sad, withdrawn woman into a joyful and vibrant one.

When she stayed after a session to discuss a point further, he was happy to indulge her. After all, she was working hard at her recovery. Of course, it didn't hurt that she was also a very beautiful woman.

As they strayed to other topics, he'd discovered her sharp mind and easy humor. And refreshingly positive view of people and life. Talking with her in the deserted classroom after each evening's session soon became the highlight of his day.

Michael carefully kept his growing feelings for Jennifer to himself. He knew how wrong it would be for him to do anything else.

Then on the final night of the seminar, she'd once again lingered. He'd thought it was to thank him and say goodbye. He'd never expected she'd put her arms around him and give him a kiss that said anything but goodbye.

Michael had wanted nothing more than to return that kiss and show her how he felt. But instead he'd gently extricated himself from Jennifer's arms and, calling upon every ounce of his self-restraint, told her that he was married.

She'd mumbled an apology and fled.

He knew he'd done the right thing—the only thing he could do. But when she'd left that night, a light had gone out inside him.

As he looked at her sitting across from him now, Michael faced the fact that being with her like this wasn't wise. He should have taken her up to his office at the hospital and stayed with her until he was sure she was going to be all right.

But in an office setting, she would have felt like his patient. He couldn't do that to her. Or himself. A psychiatrist did not feel about a patient the way he felt about her.

Their refills arrived. Michael took a healthy swig of his. He should not ask her any more questions about Russell. Her relationship with the guy was none of his business. But none of his business or not, he wanted to know.

"You said earlier that Russell had been asking you to marry him for a year, but you only agreed a week ago. Doesn't sound like he swept you off your feet."

"A woman needs her feet firmly planted beneath her when she's facing something as serious as marriage."

"You weren't in the throes of a mad, careless rapture?" he asked, needing the confirmation and yet disappointed in himself for that need.

"I want a family. Russell said he wanted one as well. He presented himself as the kind of man who would be a good husband and father."

So, she wasn't madly in love with the guy. The relief that surged through Michael was both immediate and inappropriate.

"What will you do about the wedding?" he asked.

She stared at the engagement ring on her finger, pulled it off, shoved it into her purse. "There'll be no wedding. I told Russell we were finished."

"What if he acknowledges how wrong he was? Gets on his knees and begs your forgiveness? Gives you his solemn word that it will never happen again?"

"I wouldn't believe him."

And you'd be right not to. Guys like him seldom change.

"Nor will I ever be able to trust Gina again. Losing her friendship is hard. We've shared so much this past year. No one could have convinced me she'd do something like this."

"Because you never would have done it to her," Michael said. "We tend to see the traits in others that we possess."

Jennifer studied him for a moment. "Is that one of the pro-found tenets they taught you while strolling down those hallowed halls of psychiatric medicine?"

"Actually, I got that one from my father."

"Is he a psychiatrist, too?"

"He's a full-time chef and a part-time teacher of parasailing out on the bay. Both of which work out quite well for me from a selfish standpoint. Anytime I'm in need of a meal, I can go see him. And when his parasailing customers screw up and land on their heads, he sends them to me."

Her laugh was low and warm and had the capacity to disarm him as easily as her tears. Michael finished his drink.

"Now that it's over, I think I'm actually more relieved than anything else," she said. "I no longer even want to slit Russell's throat. So, what do you think, Doc? Should I be losing my homicidal tendencies this soon?"

Carefully, he repeated the message he'd given to her earlier. "I'm not here as a therapist."

"That's what makes your company so therapeutic."

Her smile was full. And felt too good.

She was going to be fine. She didn't need him anymore—if indeed she had needed him at all.

One of the things he'd discovered on those nights they'd shared their thoughts and feelings was her surprising strength. Even the strongest of life's blows didn't keep her down for long. It was time to see her home and then be on his way.

"Jennifer Winn! I thought that was you."

Michael twisted toward the guy who had suddenly appeared at their table. Twenty something. Dressed like an Eddie Bauer catalog ad except for the Dodgers baseball cap on his head. And nearly drooling as he stared at Jennifer.

"Hugo Bryson, this is Dr. Michael Temple," Jennifer said, polite but cool.

Hugo exchanged a brief nod with Michael.

"Boy, it's been a lot of years, Jen. Not that I don't see you on the tube. Never would have thought you'd be Courage Bay's weather babe one day. I've called the station several times. Guess you didn't get my message."

He pulled a business card out of his pocket and slapped it down in front of her. "I'm a tax accountant now at Swanson and Munro. Top-notch firm."

She didn't pick up the card.

Drawing closer, he laid his hand on her shoulder. She pulled away.

Hugo still wore his leering smile. Either he was incredibly obtuse or he simply chose to ignore her message.

"I'm sitting over there with a couple of the senior partners at our firm," he said. "Box seat tickets at the game today. Nothing but the best when you travel with these guys. Have a drink with us. We can catch up on old times. Bring your friend here."

The reference to Michael was punctuated with a dismissive wave of Hugo's hand.

Before he could think of all the reasons why he shouldn't, Michael was on his feet, edging Hugo away from the table, holding out his hand to Jennifer.

"Sorry, Hugo, we were just about to dance. You'll have to catch up with Jennifer another time."

She slipped her hand into his without hesitation. As Michael led her onto the dance floor, Hugo yelled after them. "Call me, Jen."

Jennifer neither looked back nor responded.

"Weather babe." She repeated the phrase with distaste when they'd reached the middle of the dance floor. "Hugo was an obnoxious creep when we were freshmen in college and he hasn't changed an iota."

"Sounds like you did get his message."

"A long time ago. I gave him a bloody nose back then when he tried to put his hands on me. As a so-called TV personality, I have to be more circumspect these days. Not that you could tell, given the ice-water incident this evening."

"What I can tell is that you have too much sense to put up with creeps."

She faced him, rested her hand on his shoulder and smiled. "Your shining armor is positively blinding tonight, Dr. Temple."

Michael hadn't danced in seven years and had never been very good at it. But he forgot all that as she came to him, an armful of warmth and softness.

They swayed together to the slow, bittersweet ballad as the piano player sang about a love lost and found.

It's just a dance, he reminded himself. *Don't get carried away.* But with every turn on the floor, he couldn't stop himself from gathering her closer.

JENNIFER HAD BEEN WRONG. She did enjoy dancing. Being in the circle of Michael's strong arm felt wonderful.

He moved with her in an effortless, natural rhythm that eliminated all worries about what the next step would be. She rested her cheek on his chest, closed her eyes, feeling the music and his warmth flow through her.

What a difference the right partner could make.

I thought you could use a friend tonight.

That's what he was being. She had to keep that clearly in mind. Michael was married. Once before she had misinterpreted his kindness and concern for her. She was not going to make that mistake again.

The song ended. They came to a standstill on the floor, but she made no attempt to move away from him, and he didn't take his arm from around her. When the next song started, they danced again.

Jennifer understood Michael was continuing to dance with her in order to keep Hugo at bay. She floated outside of time in a state of bliss. Whether the sensation was the result of a night of shocks, three drinks downed on an empty stomach or simply being held by Michael, she didn't know. She didn't much care. All she wanted was for it to go on.

"Time I saw you home," Michael said.

She lifted her cheek from his chest and opened her eyes. The music had stopped and the dance floor was deserted but for them.

"It's okay," Michael said. "Hugo and his pals left awhile ago."

"What happened to the music?"

"The piano player is taking a thirty-minute break," Michael said. "As of about five minutes ago."

Which meant she'd been standing in his arms for five minutes.

Jennifer quickly stepped back. "I'm so sorry. I was off in another world."

"Seemed to be a nice one."

"How could you tell?"

"By the sounds accompanying it."

"Please don't tell me I was snoring in your ear."

He smiled. "You were sighing."

Just as bad.

She headed for the table. "You should have said something sooner."

"I might have, if I hadn't been off in a world of my own. The drinks hit me about the fifth song."

They'd danced to five songs? At least he'd kept some track of time.

She'd collected her handbag and was reaching inside for her billfold when he placed the money on the table to cover their tab.

"I ordered the last drink," she protested. "We should at least split—"

"We're not."

Quietly determined, unmistakably emphatic. It reminded her of how Michael had looked and sounded when he rose to take her hand for their dance and effortlessly shoved the obnoxious Hugo out of the way.

This wasn't a side of him she'd seen before tonight. It was a nice surprise.

She closed her handbag. "My car is in the visitor parking lot back at the hospital."

"You can pick it up there tomorrow. Neither of us is in any shape to be driving tonight. We'll get them to call a taxi for us downstairs."

But when they made their request at the bar, they were told

that due to the high demand caused by the fog, the wait for the next available taxi was an estimated two hours.

"We've lost our table upstairs," Michael said, having to raise his voice to be heard over the packed and noisy barroom, which afforded standing room only and barely that. "The dining room has a long line waiting to get in as well. How far away do you live?"

"About a thirty minute drive."

Jennifer knew there was probably a simple solution to the dilemma, but getting her alcohol-soaked brain to focus on finding it wasn't easy. All she really wanted was to be back on the dance floor with Michael.

"It's the TV meteorologist!"

Jennifer angled her head in the direction of the voice to see a middle-aged woman pushing her way through the throng of bodies to reach them. As she came closer, Jennifer got a strong whiff of beer breath.

"Honey, I watch your show every day," the woman said. "You're the best thing on—well, maybe except for the romance movies they run on the women's channel. You know the ones?"

Jennifer smiled. "Watch them all the time."

"Autograph this for me."

The woman held out her damp napkin and dug a pen out of her purse. She then offered her back as a writing surface. Jennifer scribbled her signature and handed the napkin and pen back.

"Thanks, honey," the woman said as she stared at her napkin prize. "I'm going to call my sister in the hospital and tell her you're here. Wait until she hears that I got your autograph. She's just had her gall bladder removed. No way she can get out of bed and come over to see you. Ha! She's going to be so pissed. Here, hold this."

The woman shoved her empty beer glass in Jennifer's hand and twisted around, pushing her way through the crowd, apparently in search of a phone.

Jennifer couldn't stifle a chuckle.

"Are you up for a walk?" Michael asked.

"To where?"

"My place is a few blocks from here."

His place?

He extracted the woman's beer glass from Jennifer's hand and set it on the counter. "At least there you won't be pissing off sick sisters or getting a cramped hand signing autographs for the next two hours."

Several people had turned to stare at her, and whispers were being exchanged. Jennifer had the uncomfortable feeling that they would be having more visitors soon.

"I can also offer you a chair," Michael said, so close to her ear that his breath sent a tingle down her neck.

And a chance to meet the missus? And no doubt the kids? Maybe it would be good for her to have a sobering shot of reality about now.

"Lead the way," Jennifer said.

Michael got them out the door before they could be waylaid by any more autograph seekers.

After the din of the overly warm bar, the cool and silent night was a welcome relief. Jennifer filled her lungs and hoped she was clearheaded enough to pull off the upcoming introductions. At least her walking didn't seem to be too impaired.

Streetlights, barely discernible in the dense fog, glowed overhead like dull, distant candles. Her sense of direction was totally gone by the time they had taken ten steps. Michael pressed on without hesitation.

"How do you know where you're going?" she asked.

"I walk it every day."

"You *walk* to and from work?"

"You sound surprised."

"I'm flabbergasted. Didn't anyone ever tell you this is Southern California, where the mode of transportation known as feet was banned decades ago?"

He chuckled. "I like to be different. It helps my patients to know that they're talking to a kindred spirit."

Yes, she was certain that his patients found him easy to talk to. And that every one of the women fell in love with him. How could they help it?

And how was his wife going to feel about his bringing home a strange woman tonight?

A few minutes later, Michael stepped onto a side path that led to the iron entry gate of a well-lit condo complex. With a swipe of his card key, the gate opened and they entered the inner courtyard of the U-shaped building, fashioned after the style of an early California mission with thick adobe walls and a red tiled roof.

He led the way up the stairs to the second floor. Once he'd unlocked the corner unit, he flipped on the light behind the open door and beckoned her to precede him inside.

No one to greet him?

Jennifer stepped in and was treated to a spacious expanse of beige—floors, walls and arched ceilings. The furniture was heavy wood, covered with thick brown cushions. Black, wrought-iron tables matched the chandelier. No pictures adorned the walls. No knickknacks cluttered the tabletops.

Spare and monklike, not at all what she expected.

"I'll call the taxi," he said, closing the massive wooden door behind them.

He walked into the kitchen that opened to the right of the living room, separated by a bar and three black, wrought-iron bar stools. It, too, was clean, uncluttered and devoid of a feminine touch.

"May I use your bathroom?" she asked.

"Down the hall on the right."

Pulling a telephone directory out of a drawer, he began to flip through the pages.

Jennifer made her way down the hallway, passing a good-size study filled with books and a computer on a heavy desk. The guest bath was the next room, the one that Michael had directed her to.

Before entering it, she looked at the partially open door at the end of the hall, fighting an overwhelming curiosity. She realized she'd lost the battle when her hand pushed the door all the way open. Slipping inside, she found herself in the master bedroom suite. Its king-size mattress was covered with a brown comforter. A single nightstand—in that same black wrought iron—sat beside it. Nothing adorned the walls.

Acknowledging that she was officially snooping now, she decided she might as well do a thorough job, and made her way to the connecting closet. Nothing but men's clothes and shoes. The adjoining bath was beige with brown towels. The drawer held a man's hairbrush and comb. The entire contents of the medicine cabinet were a razor, extra blades, saving cream, toothpaste and a toothbrush.

After peering into the hallway to make sure the coast was clear, she let herself out of the master bedroom suite and entered the guest bathroom. More beige with brown towels. The drawer had an extra washcloth. The medicine cabinet contained a box of Band-Aids and a bottle of aspirin. Nothing else.

Jennifer knew with a certainty that no woman lived here. Nor was one even a regular visitor.

What had happened to Michael's wife?

CHAPTER THREE

MICHAEL DROPPED THE PHONE on its base. Five tries and five busy signals. Even getting through to the taxi company was going to be a challenge.

If he'd stopped at one drink, he could be driving her home now. And he never would have danced with her so long. Or held her so close. Or still be able to smell her perfume on him.

His hand was less than steady as he reached for the coffee-pot. Inviting her here to wait for a taxi had seemed to be the logical thing to do at the time. Now he wondered whether he'd made a mistake.

Once he had the coffee brewing, he started opening cup-boards. After his Saturday night workout at the gym, he always ate out. Tomorrow was his day to shop. The shelves were pretty bare. He'd just checked the refrigerator when he heard her light footsteps on the tile floor behind him.

"I haven't been able to get through to the taxi company," he said, looking over his shoulder at her. "You may be stuck here awhile."

"I can think of worse fates."

He caught himself staring at her smile and turned back to the refrigerator.

"Hungry?" he asked.

"As a matter of fact, I am."

"All I can offer you is steak and eggs with a fresh orange for dessert."

She moved beside him—close enough that he felt her warmth. "Sounds good. What can I do to help?"

"Nothing. The menu is minimum effort."

"How about I set the table?"

"No table. I use the bar counter. Silverware is in that drawer."

When she followed his pointing finger, he got busy pulling two steaks out of the freezer and putting them into the microwave to defrost. Then he turned on the broiler.

"How long have you lived here?" she asked, brushing up against his arm as she opened a cabinet and lifted out the plates.

"Bought it a couple of years ago to be closer to work," he said, retreating to the phone. "I'm going to try the taxi number again."

All he got was another busy signal in his ear.

"No luck?" she asked.

Shaking his head, he put down the receiver.

His eyes went to the counter. Their plates lay side by side. She'd put the silverware on paper towels, folded into neat napkin squares. A woman's touch. He'd forgotten the difference it could make.

The microwave timer went off. He retrieved the defrosted steaks and placed them under the broiler. When he straightened, he found her beside him, holding out a cup of the freshly brewed coffee.

"Black, right?" she said.

That's how he'd always drunk it from the coffee machine at the college on those nights when they'd talked for hours.

"You'll need some milk for yours," he said. "Unfortunately, I'm all out."

"What about ice cream?"

"There's a pint of vanilla in the freezer."

"A little of that should work."

Retrieving the ice cream, he told himself to relax. Enjoying her company wasn't a crime. They'd eat, he'd sober up and then he'd drive her home. What was the worst that could happen?

It wasn't as though she was going to kiss him again. And he certainly had more sense than to do something dumb like kiss her.

"ARE YOU STILL GIVING seminars at the community college?" Jennifer asked.

"Not since…it's been awhile," Michael said.

Having finished their meal, they'd retired to the living room. Jennifer turned on the stereo in the corner. A station she recognized filled the room with a favorite song.

"I do the weather forecasts for this radio station," she said as she sat on the couch next to Michael, holding her after-dinner coffee, laced with another dab of ice cream.

"I've heard you banter back and forth with the DJ."

So, he'd listened to her on the radio as well as watched her on TV?

They're local stations, Jennifer. Most of Courage Bay tunes in to them. Don't go reading stuff into this that isn't there.

He sipped his coffee. "Doing the weather reports for the radio is not a problem with the TV station?"

"Anytime I'm seen or heard elsewhere, they consider it good advertising. And since I have to prepare the forecast for my TV spot anyway, doing the radio one requires no extra work, simply a call to the DJ after the six o'clock KSEA broadcast."

"A call? I thought you were in the radio station."

"The magic of technology," she explained. "I'm on a phone line that's fed into a separate microphone from that of the DJ. When the techno wizards get through with their tweaking, they make it sound like the DJ and I are in the same room."

He was watching her again. Now that she had some food in her stomach, she didn't feel quite so spaced out from the alcohol. And she was noticing that he was looking at her a lot.

Wishful thinking? He'd made it clear up front that he was only being a friend to her tonight.

But they were alone together. And his place told her that there was no woman in his life. And he hadn't picked up the phone to call a taxi since before dinner.

"Have the police talked to you yet about the plane crash?" he asked.

"A patrol officer at the scene took my name and number. When I told her I wanted to follow the paramedics to the hospital, she said that someone would be in touch."

"You'll probably be getting a visit from the National Transportation and Safety Board. They're the ones who will have to determine the official cause of the crash. Would you like to talk about it?"

"I'd rather talk about you," she said.

"Me." The word came out with a slight hesitation.

"All those times we discussed music, books, how clouds form, why birds sing and those other seemingly inconsequential topics we got off on, I came away with the sense that I knew you. But I really know very little."

He regarded her silently for a moment. "What do you want to know?"

"You've heard about all the changes in my life over the past five years. Tell me about the changes in yours."

He slowly sipped his coffee, not once taking his eyes from hers. "Nothing has changed in my life, Jennifer."

Maybe it was hard for him to talk to her about his marriage breakup. In all those conversations they'd had in which he'd freely shared his views on so many things, not once had he brought up anything related to his personal life.

Just because she found him easy to talk to didn't mean he felt the same way about her.

"You don't consider writing a book that ended up on every bestseller list this past year worth mentioning?" she asked.

"All that means is that the stodgy academics of this world suddenly decided they needed another boring text gathering dust on their shelves."

"Your book wasn't boring. It was deeply caring and wise."

He leaned forward. "You read it?"

"Me and a few million others. I think one of the reviewers quoted on the dust jacket said it best. 'Finally, an approach to psychiatry that treats human beings, not symptoms.'"

A tension she hadn't noticed before seemed to ease from his shoulders as he rested back on the couch cushions.

"You dedicated it to Tom and Alice Temple, as I recall," she said.

He nodded. "My parents. It was the least I could do after making them read through the chapters to find all the grammatical errors."

"Do they have a background in editing?"

He smiled. "Simply a strong family loyalty when it comes to keeping their son from looking like a total illiterate to his editor."

She chuckled, then took a sip of her coffee, hoping he'd volunteer more. He didn't. Was it modesty that prevented him from mentioning his several interviews on TV morning shows? His election to president of the California Psychiatric Association?

And how was she going to mention them without sounding like some groupie?

"Are you going to be entering the Courage Bay Charity Run again this year?" she asked instead.

"How did you know I ran in that?"

"KSEA covered the event last year. I was the station's last-minute emcee when our sportscaster took ill. I saw your name on the entry list."

"I'm surprised you found my name among the twenty-five hundred entrants."

"I looked for it after I recognized you running past our broadcasting booth," she said. "You came in fifth. That was something. A lot of the guys who run in that race are pros. Do you compete in any others?"

He finished his coffee, set it on the table. "Just the local one."

"Because it's for charity or because a local one is all you have time to train for?"

"Both."

She put her coffee cup next to his. "I couldn't help noticing that you had your own private cheering section at the race."

"My parents always insist on coming. And my sister drags her husband and their kids along. It's one of the few times they get encouraged to yell and scream."

Still not one word about a wife. Or kids of his own.

Jennifer relaxed back on the couch. "This is comfortable. Do you have one like it in your office?"

"If you mean a psychoanalyst's couch, no. I'm not a believer in long analysis. Focusing on current behavior problems and finding a solution to them is what I find helpful. For that, most people prefer a regular chair and face-to-face communication."

"People, not simply patients. That's how they came across in your book. Their case histories were really life stories. You emphasized the experiences that connected them with others—not simply the ones that set them apart. That made them so much more human and understandable."

"If I ever need a publicist," he said, "I'm calling you."

She read everything she wanted to in his smile.

"When did you know you were going to be a psychiatrist?" she asked.

"I was in the fifth grade and a classmate, Ben Thayer, punched me for no apparent reason. It was either punch him back or try to find out what was going on."

"What did you find out?"

"Ben's brother, Devon, had told him that I'd stolen his bike. After some persuasion, I got Devon to admit to Ben that he'd actually sold the bike to another kid. Ben and I became friends, and I haven't stopped looking for the answers since."

"So your career was mapped out by the time you were in the fifth grade. Were you as quick to mature in the social graces?"

"By social graces you mean…?"

"When did you learn to dance?"

He chuckled. "I never did. Couldn't you tell?"

"Matter of fact, I couldn't. Maybe we should try it again."

Standing, she held out her hand to him—just as he had done earlier to her. For what seemed like a very long moment, he remained motionless. Then he slipped his hand into hers and rose to stand before her.

The tune coming out of the stereo speakers was slow and sweet. He held her lightly, slightly away from him. But when she moved closer and rested her cheek on his chest, he drew her to him, and she could feel the pounding of his heart.

For several exciting seconds, she was lost in the aching sweetness flowing through her as they moved as one to the music. Then he stopped.

"I have to get you home," he said.

She eased back, looked into his face. He didn't like what they were doing. He couldn't have made that any clearer than if he'd said the words.

Once again she'd read him wrong.

"Are you going to try the taxi company?" she asked, doing everything she could to keep the disappointment out of her voice.

He didn't respond, simply looked at her as the seconds ticked by and her heart grew heavier in her chest.

She tried for a light tone. "You're right. Probably a waste of time. Get me some sheets and a pillow, and I'll sleep on your couch. You have my solemn word that I will not sneak into your bed tonight, providing you keep the door to your bedroom locked, of course."

She was going for one of those perky smiles that her producer was always asking her to wear, when Michael's mouth suddenly lowered to hers.

Full and deep, his kiss absorbed her. Her heart went wild as she wrapped her arms around him and returned the kiss with joyful abandon.

When he finally pulled back, he held her from him, his hands firm on her shoulders, his breathing fast. "Jenny, forgive me. I had no right."

"Michael, I wanted you to kiss me. And if you couldn't feel that, then you definitely need to see a doctor."

"I've taken unfair advantage of you. When I think of all you've been through tonight—"

"You were there for me tonight. And I'm grateful. But make no mistake. Gratitude had nothing to do with my kissing you just now."

He sucked in a very deep breath. "I have to get you home."

"Do you, Michael?"

"Yes. You deserve so much better."

"What could be better than you?"

"God, Jenny…" He swallowed hard as his grip tightened. "No, I can't do this. I don't even have anything to protect you."

"I don't need protection from you, Michael."

His eyes locked with hers. "Do you know what you're saying?"

"I know what I want. What do you want?"

His answer came out in an exhalation against her lips. "You."

He pulled her to him, and she went with all the need and longing that had been buried inside her for five long years.

THE ILLUMINATED DIGITS on the nightstand clock read three-thirty. Michael lay awake with Jennifer nestled beside him. She had drifted off into dreams. But he was enjoying consciousness too much to sleep.

Her back was to him, her head on his pillow. Kissing her hair, he inhaled the sweet scent that was her. The feel of her bare flesh against his was dizzying.

Why this woman and no other, he didn't know. What he did know was that he couldn't fight it anymore.

Long before the drinks had hit him tonight, he'd wanted her. And he'd been clearheaded enough even before the dinner they'd shared to keep his hands off her.

He had no excuse for his behavior. He wasn't looking for one. Regretting a moment of this night with her wasn't possible. She'd given herself to him without hesitation and with an energy that still left him breathless.

As he nuzzled her neck in fond remembrance, only one question remained in his mind. How would she feel about this in the bright light of day?

Jenny, please don't regret this in the morning.

He heard the change in her breathing, felt her stir. She rolled over to face him.

"Hi." Her voice was husky with sleep.

He pulled her to him. "Hi."

And that was the last breath he wasted on words.

JENNIFER OPENED HER EYES to the bright sunlight pouring into Michael's bedroom. Sounds of the shower came from behind his bathroom door. The clock on the table beside her read nine-fifteen.

The night that had started out to be one of the worst in her life had turned out to be the best. Making love with Michael had been everything she'd hoped for, dreamed about. She knew now that marrying Russell—even if he hadn't proved to be faithless— would have been a colossal mistake.

After one long, lovely stretch, she got herself out of bed and padded down the hall to the guest bathroom. The woman staring back at her in the mirror was a sight. But her smile was happy. She turned on the shower and stepped in, humming.

Michael was waiting for her in the kitchen when she came out a few minutes later. He wore a black T-shirt and jeans, his hair still damp from his shower.

She openly admired the muscled arms and board-flat stomach normally hidden beneath his suits as she took a cup of freshly brewed coffee from his hand.

"Good morning," she said.

His sudden smile was a dazzling gleam of white. "Yes, it's a very good morning."

Picking up the container of ice cream, he asked, "One teaspoon or two?"

"Two. I'm feeling reckless today."

They stood side by side, leaning against the kitchen counter, silently drinking their coffee. A gentle breeze drifted in the open window. Looking out, she could see the top floors of Courage Bay Hospital.

It felt good to get her bearings again. The deadly fog was gone, and she knew instinctively that it wouldn't be returning. *This feels so right.*

"I don't have anything to offer you for breakfast," he said after a moment.

"My refrigerator and pantry are full. How about you drive me to my car, follow me home and I feed you?"

He set his cup down, circled his arm around her waist and brushed a kiss against her hair. "I won't be able to stay for breakfast."

"Previous appointment?" she asked, enjoying the scent of his freshly shaved chin, the warmth of him, the limitless possibilities of the day.

"Yes."

"You can't postpone?"

"I'm going to see my wife."

His words dropped into her wide-open heart and exploded.

Jennifer jerked away, her coffee cup rattling on its saucer like machine gun fire as she shoved it onto the counter. "You're still married?"

He stared at her as though he were the one in shock. "Jenny, you asked me if there had been any changes in my life. I told you there hadn't been. You said you'd read my book. I thought—"

"That I would sleep with a married man? Is that what you thought? For God's sake, Michael, I haven't even slept with Russell!"

She gestured wildly at the empty walls around them as the pain seared through her. "What is this place you brought me to with no sign of a woman anywhere? Is this your bachelor pad in town where you entertain your women while your wife stays at the country home with the kiddies?"

He stared at her, his eyes unblinking blue stones.

Jennifer whirled away from him and ran out of the kitchen, grabbing her purse. She yanked open the front door, then slammed it behind her.

Half a block later, the tears began.

THE SUNDAY NIGHT TV NEWS was full of footage of the emergency teams responding to the plane crash at the Courage Bay Grand Hotel on Saturday.

Sitting alone in the darkness of his living room, Michael watched KSEA's top news reporter, Don Hardrick, on camera at the scene of the crash. The flashing red lights of police, fire and paramedic vehicles lit the night around him.

In his deep tone and with a deadpan countenance, Hardrick told of the pilot being pronounced dead at the scene and the fact that two injured people in the hotel had been rushed to the hospital. As he spoke, the steady wail of sirens could be heard in the background.

"Emergency teams have established an inner and outer perimeter around the wreckage site in anticipation of the arrival of the NTSB accident investigation team," Hardrick said. "Neither the name of the pilot nor the injured have been released pending notification of family."

The weekend news anchor next appeared on the screen. "We go live now to city hall and Police Chief Max Zirinsky for an update."

"The pilot of the private airplane has been identified as Carlos Esposito," Zirinsky said into the camera. "Mr. Esposito was a prime suspect in an illegal alien smuggling ring. The case against him was dropped when a chief witness was murdered."

"Is there a connection between the murdered witness and this plane crash?" an off-camera reporter asked.

Zirinsky's mouth drew into a hard line. "If there is, rest assured we'll find it."

Michael muted the set through the rest of the press conference coverage. When the KSEA weekend anchor came back on camera, he waited to see if Jennifer's image would appear on the screen. But whatever additional information was being given didn't include a mention of the station's meteorologist being at the scene of the plane crash.

He flipped off the set, knowing it was foolish to have turned it on, promising himself he wouldn't do it again. What had he hoped for? To catch a glimpse of her? A quick interview?

Mere scraps. Yet he was hungry for them. After their one incredible night together, that was all that was left to him.

For God's sake, Michael, I haven't even slept with Russell!

Her words continued to tear at his heart. For they told him more than anything else could what that night had meant to her.

No wonder she hated him now.

DON HARDRICK STEPPED INTO Jennifer's path Monday afternoon, bringing her to an unceremonious halt in the hallway leading into the KSEA newsroom.

Hardrick was the station's number one newsman, a tough, streetwise journalist who wrote the stories that made the news anchors sound so well informed. But there was something about the broody, cynical guy that bothered Jennifer.

It might have been the fact that he never smiled. Or the way he stared at her sometimes when he didn't think she was looking.

"I never expected you'd be in today," he said.

"I won't be doing the live broadcast at the school until Wednesday," Jennifer said.

"I know your schedule. That's not what I meant."

No, of course not. Hardrick had to have heard all about the plane crash and Russell's injuries. Jennifer felt a little guilty about not calling in the story. But with Hardrick's many contacts among Courage Bay emergency teams, she was sure that plenty of sources had filled him in.

"The worst is over," she said.

He seemed surprised. "Is it?"

Jennifer felt a tap on her shoulder and turned to find herself face-to-face with the news director.

Liz Otley was a Pulitzer Prize winning newswoman turned broadcaster. When Timeright Communications bought out KSEA from independent ownership two years before, they'd brought in Liz from their New Jersey affiliate to take the position as news director. Ratings had steadily climbed from the moment she took the helm.

Liz had an infallible eye for picking stories and people. Of course, on the latter item, Jennifer acknowledged that she might be prejudiced. It was Liz who had hired her.

"You shouldn't have come in," Liz said. "Go home."

Her boss's admonition surprised Jennifer. "If you're not dying, drag it in here" was Liz's normal mantra to station employees.

"I'll take her home," Hardrick said.

"No you won't," Liz told him. "You're going to get your news copy to the TelePrompTer operator right now, or there isn't going to be any show or the need for someone with your considerable expertise."

Hardrick muttered something unintelligible as he gave Jennifer one last glance before walking away.

The news director shook her head. "He's still got that thing for you."

"He's the least of my concerns at the moment," Jennifer said as her eyes darted to her watch. "I've got to run computer models, satellite pictures, and check the numerical data that's feeding into my computer workstation via the satellite downlink as we speak. Plus which I'm going to need at least ten minutes in the makeup chair."

Liz stepped forward, lifted the dark glasses off Jennifer's face. "You look like hell."

"Okay, fifteen minutes in the makeup chair."

"Forget it, Jen. I called in Wally to cover for you the moment I heard about Russell. Now, you go home and—"

"Don't worry about me. I'm fine."

Liz's strong features softened. "No one whose fiancé has just died could possibly be fine."

Died?

Jennifer felt the floor swaying. Except it wasn't the floor.

Liz grabbed her arm and pulled her into her office, sat her down in a chair. "Geez, Jen. You're white as a sheet."

"Died. You said died."

Liz's jaw dropped. "My God, you didn't know Russell's dead?"

Jennifer shook her head, stiff with shock. How could Russell be dead?

The news director let out a soft curse. "I had no idea you... I'm so sorry."

"What happened?" Jennifer asked when she could.

"He died in the hospital Saturday night."

"But his concussion was mild. He was expected to fully recover."

"Don told me the pathologist is doing an autopsy to determine cause of death. What did the hospital tell you when you went to see him?"

"I didn't go to see him. I stayed home all day yesterday and today with my phones turned off. I didn't even answer the door."

Liz circled her desk, plopped onto the chair. "No wonder all I've gotten is your voice mail. But how could you not have heard? It's been all over the news."

"I haven't watched the news."

As blasphemous as such an admission was, Liz made no comment.

"I didn't even turn on the TV or radio," Jennifer admitted, still numb with shock. This couldn't be real.

"You spent yesterday and most of today holed up, incognito," Liz said. "You didn't go to see Russell in the hospital and you're not wearing his ring. You broke up with him, didn't you?"

Before Jennifer could answer, the news anchors, Andrew and Ursula, popped through the open office door.

Andrew walked over to Jennifer's chair and rested his hand on her shoulder. "We came as soon as Hardrick told us you were here, Jennifer. What a difficult time this must be for you. Is there anything we can do?"

The impeccably dressed news anchor wore the same stoic expression and his voice was at precisely the same pitch as when he stared into the TV camera five nights a week, reading stories off the TelePrompTer to the viewing public.

But his formal appearance and bearing didn't fool Jennifer. She'd seen him in shorts at the station's picnic the summer before. Whimsical tattoos covered every inch of his arms and chest—one of the cutest of which had been a sleeping black-and-white cat with the word Fluffy beneath it.

"I'm okay, Andrew," she assured him. "Thanks."

Ursula remained in the doorway, stick thin but beautiful, fiddling nervously with her belt buckle. "I'm…sorry," she said in a hesitant voice.

On camera, Ursula was all poise and confidence. But the moment she was out of the spotlight, she became curiously shy, even tongue-tied, like now. That always fascinated Jennifer. For most people, it would be the other way around.

"Thank you," Jennifer said, not knowing how else to respond. She and Ursula clicked on the set, but off the job, they rarely talked. Hard to carry on a conversation with someone when it was mostly one-way.

"Don't you two have a show to do?" Liz asked as she sent a meaningful glance toward the wall clock.

"Quite right," Andrew said. "Take care, Jennifer. Come, darling."

Ursula followed him out the door and they scurried toward the set.

"Their new coziness is proving profitable," Liz said. "Love between two news anchors. Who would have thought that would turn out to be such a draw for watchers? I've been thinking of moving their chairs closer together on the set. What do you think?"

"I think I should call Russell's parents," Jennifer said as she slowly got to her feet.

It was the right thing to do, but she was reluctant to do it. When in the throes of such a personal tragedy, words of condolence—no matter how well-meaning—seemed so empty. The only thing that had helped her through her dark days when her parents had died was Michael.

Michael. The pain—momentarily smothered by the shock of Russell's death—opened like a new sore. Until Liz shoved the box of tissues toward her, Jennifer didn't realize there were tears on her cheeks. How many were for Russell and how many for Michael, she didn't know.

Pulling tissues out of the box, she wiped her eyes and fought for control.

"Are they aware that you split?" Liz asked.

It took a moment before Jennifer realized Liz was talking about Russell's parents. "I don't know."

"Before you call them, you may want to—" Liz began.

"Jennifer Winn?" a sharp male voice interrupted.

Coming through Liz's open office door were two solemn-looking men in suits.

Liz shot out of her chair. "What are you doing here, Batton?"

"My duty as one of Courage Bay's finest," the older, hard-eyed one answered. He approached Jennifer and flashed his badge. "Detective Batton, Ms. Winn. And this is Detective Chaska. We'd like to talk to you."

"Why?" Liz demanded.

"It's okay, Liz," Jennifer said. "The officer I spoke with on Saturday mentioned someone would be by."

"Is there a place where we can speak privately?" Batton asked.

"My office is—" Jennifer began.

"Wally's in the weather center," Liz reminded her. "Look, Batton, Jennifer has just lost her fiancé. Do you have to do this now?"

"Right now," Batton said. "If there's no place here, we'll be escorting her downtown."

Liz exhaled. "You can use my office. I'm due in the studio, anyway. Got a news show to watch."

She snatched a binder off her desk and gave Jennifer's arm a reassuring squeeze on her way to the door. Her backward glance at Batton contained a curious mixture of emotions that had Jennifer wondering. Detective Chaska closed the door behind her.

Gesturing toward the two guest chairs, Jennifer took a seat behind Liz's desk. "I really can't tell you very much about the crash," she said. "The fog obliterated the plane from view. One minute it wasn't there, the next it was coming through the windows."

"We're not interested in the crash," Detective Batton said.

Jennifer frowned. "Then why are you here?"

"Tell us about your relationship with Russell Sprague."

"Russell…has died, Detective. Why would you care about my relationship with him?"

"Because he didn't just die, Ms. Winn. He was murdered."

CHAPTER FOUR

MICHAEL'S TUESDAY MORNING rounds were going well. His primary concern had been Darren, a forty-one-year-old manager of a large retail store who had suddenly gone berserk and begun smashing his own merchandise with a baseball bat. It had taken three cops and a broken collarbone before he'd finally given up the fight.

After the E.R. had tended to his injury, they'd called Michael in to evaluate his mental state.

Prior to today, the guy hadn't gotten so much as a parking ticket. He was a loving husband and father, a volunteer at his church. Everyone who knew him said that he'd become withdrawn recently, but all were baffled by his violent behavior.

Which made Michael suspect that it had a biological origin.

When he got the results of Darren's blood workup, his suspicion turned into fact. His patient's cholesterol was dangerously low—only 55 milligrams per 100 milliliters of blood. Normal was between 180 and 240 milligrams.

Everyone talked about high cholesterol being bad. But few knew that low cholesterol was just as risky because it was linked to clinical depression. And unlike women, who became sad and tearful, men often manifested their depression in anger and hostility. Like suddenly taking a baseball bat to the furniture.

Sifting through the often puzzling pieces and finding an answer for unusual human behavior was one of the things that made psychiatry so rewarding for Michael.

As he passed by the door to Gary and Leon's room, he smiled

as he listened to their heated argument about who was the best pitcher in the National League.

He did not go inside to talk to the two young men. It wasn't necessary. The nurses had all noted the lessening of their anger, their renewed interest in food, the signs of their growing friendship. A large part of connecting with another human being was a shared experience. And no one could understand a devastating physical injury like a person who had one.

As Michael approached his office, he found two plainclothes officers waiting for him, their badges out.

"Dr. Temple?" the older one asked.

Michael's name tag was prominently displayed on his hospital jacket and he was unlocking an office with his name on the door. He nodded anyway.

"Detective Batton," the man said. "This is Detective Chaska."

"Come inside."

He swung open the door, gestured them to seats. Setting the notes from his rounds on his desk, he took the chair behind it. The only case he currently had that involved the police was Darren. He waited for them to ask their questions.

"We're here about the patient who was murdered in this hospital Saturday night."

Murdered? "What patient?"

"Dr. Sprague."

Detective Batton was looking at Michael as though the name should mean something to him.

"Doesn't ring a bell," Michael said.

The detective's eyebrows lifted. "You're saying you didn't know Dr. Sprague?"

"No one by that name has been a patient of mine. Admissions will be able to give you the name of his doctor."

"I know who his doctor was. I need you to tell me about the people in Dr. Sprague's life."

"I don't know them."

"Well, now, that's curious. Because according to this hospital's records, you evaluated his fiancée, Jennifer Winn, when she was detained for assaulting Dr. Sprague Saturday night in the E.R."

Michael shot forward. "His name was *Russell* Sprague?"

"I see you remember him now."

Michael's mind raced as all the implications began to sink in. Since he'd purposely avoided watching the news since Sunday night, he'd had no idea that Jennifer's fiancé had died, much less been murdered.

"I don't remember him," Michael said. "I never met him. I didn't even know his last name until now. Ms. Winn only referred to him as Russell. How was he murdered?"

"With cunning and guile. Now, let's get back to my questions. What did Ms. Winn tell you about Russell Sprague?"

Michael was used to far more courtesy from members of the Courage Bay Police Department. This detective's manner was bordering on hostile.

"If you want to know what she said, I suggest you ask her," Michael answered, careful to keep his voice even and nonconfrontational.

"I'm asking you."

"It would be unethical for me to discuss our conversation."

"Any more unethical than a doctor taking his patient out for a drink after a psychiatric examination?"

So, Detective Batton knew he'd been at the Courage Bay Bar and Grill with Jennifer. Michael wondered what else he knew.

"Ms. Winn was not my patient, Detective."

"Then why would it be unethical for you to discuss your conversation with her concerning Russell Sprague?"

"Because what she said to me was in confidence, knowing that I am a psychiatrist. Breaking that confidence would be unethical."

"Splitting hairs a bit, aren't you, Doctor?"

"The guidelines I follow are no less precise than the laws you adhere to."

"Why did you take her out for a drink?" the detective demanded.

"I will answer any questions that relate to the murder of Russell Sprague," Michael said, maintaining his even tone. "But I don't intend to answer any others."

"Questions regarding the whereabouts of a suspect at the time the crime was committed could hardly be called unrelated."

Michael's stomach constricted. "You consider Ms. Winn a suspect?"

"She dumped ice water all over the guy while he lay helpless on an E.R. gurney, and four hours later he's found murdered. Doesn't take too big a leap of the imagination. So, you got anything you want to tell us?"

Batton leaned back in his chair, folded his hands over his stomach and stared at Michael. Even the quiet Detective Chaska had stopped taking notes and was looking up expectantly.

Michael knew he had no choice. But the ramifications of what he was about to do sent a chill through him.

"Ms. Winn could not have murdered Dr. Sprague," he said. "She was with me."

Batton eyed him quietly for a long moment. "Let's start from the top," he said. "What happened after you evaluated Jennifer Winn?"

"We left the hospital and went to have a drink at the Courage Bay Bar and Grill."

"What time was this?"

"Around eight."

"Have you ever taken a patient out for a drink before?"

"As I said before, Ms. Winn was not my patient."

"What is she to you?"

Michael took a careful breath. "I met Ms. Winn when she attended a grief seminar I gave five years ago."

"So you've had a relationship with her for five years."

"No. Saturday night was the first time I'd seen her since the seminar ended."

"Your affair ended with the seminar five years ago?"

"We didn't have an affair," Michael said. "She was an attendee at my seminar."

"Were you drinking buddies during the seminar?"

"No."

"Then why take her out for a drink all of a sudden?" Batton asked.

"After the upsetting events of Saturday evening, I thought she could use one."

"What upsetting events?"

"A private plane had crashed into the ballroom where she, her fiancé and best friend were, injuring them. Perhaps you heard about it."

Michael had been careful to keep his tone even and devoid of sarcasm. Allowing his irritation toward this suspicious detective to show was not going to help Jennifer.

"How long were you at the bar?" Batton asked.

"A couple of hours."

"Did she leave you at any time?"

"For a few minutes to visit the rest room when we first arrived. That was all."

"Where did you go after the bar?"

"I took Ms. Winn to my place. She spent the night there."

"You live pretty close to the hospital?"

Michael had no doubt that Detective Batton already knew exactly where he lived.

"My condo is about a fifteen minute walk from here."

"So Ms. Winn could have left your home sometime during the night, returned to the hospital, murdered Russell Sprague and sneaked back into your place without your knowing it."

"No. She was with me the entire time."

"Same room, same bed?"

Michael did not like the look on Batton's face. "Yes."

"Are you a sound sleeper, Dr. Temple?"

"I didn't sleep at all that night."

Had Michael been another kind of man, he would have gotten up and punched Batton for the expression the man now wore.

"At what point did you and Ms. Winn part...company?" Batton asked.

"A little after ten Sunday morning, when she left my house."

"You didn't drive her home?"

"No."

"Why not?"

"For reasons unrelated to your investigation. I have given you all you need to clear Ms. Winn as a suspect in the murder of Russell Sprague."

Batton locked eyes with Michael for several seconds before the man suddenly shot to his feet. Detective Chaska took his cue and also rose.

"We'll be in touch, Doctor," Batton said.

They let themselves out. Michael stared at the closed door a long time.

Despite the disheartening events of the following morning, his night with Jennifer would remain one of the sweetest memories of his life. Telling that detective about his time with her had been difficult and damn distasteful.

And it hadn't helped. Detective Batton didn't want to believe him.

"YOU SURE YOU WANT TO DO this?" Liz asked over the phone.

"I'm sure," Jennifer answered as she tucked her feet beneath her on the couch. She was watching the sixty-five-year-old, white-haired Wally on the TV screen. Wearing his trademark goofy grin and iridescent bow tie, he was putting happy faces on a national weather map where the sunshine would be in the morning, and saying nothing about Courage Bay's temperatures or the wind that was already kicking up outside.

"I need to work, Liz. Tomorrow I'll go live at the grade school at six as we originally planned, and then be back in the studio to do the ten o'clock spot."

"I can't pretend I'm not relieved, Jen. Two nights without you around here and it's already a mess. Oh, no. Now he's giving the temperatures in Montana."

Jennifer had muted the set but could see the closed-captioned strip of Wally's report. After Montana, he gave temperatures in New Mexico, then Honolulu. And as yet, not one from Southern California, much less Courage Bay.

In her ear, she could hear Liz calling to the floor producer to tell Wally to throw it back to one of the news anchors or she was going to personally tighten that bow tie around his neck like a noose.

The only stipulation that the previous television station owner had made when he'd sold out to Timeright Communications was that his nephew, Wally, would be kept on. Wally had been the weathercaster for KSEA for more than thirty years, despite the fact that he'd never had any education in even the rudiments of meteorology.

For every broadcast, he'd relied on reports from the National Weather Service, reading off the temperatures predicted for the nation. Even when Southern California was included, local Courage Bay conditions were never addressed.

Liz let Wally read Jennifer's previously prepared scripts when he did the weather on Saturdays and Sundays, with the strict stipulation that he not improvise. But for the past two evenings, he'd had no script to read. And he was back to the kind of weather reporting that had made KSEA one of the least watched stations prior to the Timeright takeover.

Liz returned to the phone line a few seconds later, right in sync with the reappearance on the TV screen of Andrew, the newsanchor.

"Remind me to give you a big raise when your contract comes up for negotiation in a few weeks," she said in Jennifer's ear. "Did the NTSB ever talk to you?"

"Yes, but there wasn't much I could tell them."

"What do you think about the pilot of the airplane being a smuggler who was suspected of shooting the informant who ratted on him to the police?" Liz asked.

"I think you and Don are fanning the flames of an already hot news story."

"The pilot's sordid past. An injured victim of the plane crash later turning up murdered. Yeah, it just keeps getting better and better." The news director's voice dropped. "Oh, hell, I'm sorry. I can't believe I just said that to you. I'm an insensitive lout."

"No," Jennifer corrected, "just an award-winning newswoman."

"You must have some suspicion as to who would do this to Russell?" Liz asked.

"None," Jennifer said. "I'm still having a hard time believing it's true. Russell was well liked. Detective Batton wouldn't tell me how he was killed. Do you know?"

"Not even Don has been able to get a line on it. Word of Russell's death wasn't released to the press until Monday. We wouldn't have known then that he was murdered if it hadn't been for your telling us what Batton said. How did the family react when they learned someone killed Russell?"

"Are you asking this as news director or as a friend?"

"They wouldn't talk to Don."

"I can't use my position with Russell's family to feed you information, Liz."

"Jen, you know the business we're in. Exclusive is everything with TV news. You're our inside source on this story."

"Only because I was questioned as a suspect in his murder. If I hadn't had an alibi, I have a feeling Detective Batton would have carted me off to jail. Then you'd really have a scoop. Straight from the prisoner's cell."

"Don't even joke about such stuff, Jen. Batton's no one to fool around with. The police department's giving him the Investigator of the Year award in a couple of weeks. That's about as high a decoration as a detective can get."

"You seemed to have a history with him."

"We were involved in a case about eighteen months ago," Liz said.

"What kind of case?"

"He and his partner were after a guy who'd written threatening letters to a bunch of women in a local beauty pageant. Batton was certain that the guy had some part in the pageant. He wanted my help to catch him."

"And you told him that as a member of the press, it was your job to report the news, not bring in the bad guys," Jennifer said confidently.

"At first."

"At first?" Jennifer repeated in surprise.

Dozens of times she'd heard Liz caution her news reporters against having opinions on the stories they were writing. Liz was a stickler for journalistic ethics. *You do not take sides,* she pounded into their heads. *Objectivity means you find and report the facts. Nothing more, nothing less.*

"What happened?" Jennifer asked.

"We became...involved."

Now Jennifer understood the look that Liz had given Batton Monday afternoon when she was leaving her office.

"He convinced me that if I didn't help him, one or more of the women in the pageant could be hurt, maybe killed," Liz said. "So I told the cameraman to film close-ups of the male employees and get signatures of release from them so Batton would have an example of their handwriting. I turned the footage and signatures over to Batton. He found the guy he was looking for."

"I don't remember hearing about the case," Jennifer said.

"It happened before you came back to Courage Bay...never went to trial. The guy took a nosedive off a five-story building before Batton and his partner could arrest him. And Batton never returned another one of my calls."

"He used you," Jennifer said.

"Cops, politicians and car salesmen. They all hand you a line. I sure as hell swallowed Batton's."

"Maybe you saved the life of one or more of those women."

"With all the resources at the department's disposal, Batton could have found another way to get the information he wanted. He chose instead to sleep with me a few times and whisper lies in my ears so I'd do it for him. No mystery why the bastard's been divorced three times."

"No, I guess not," Jennifer agreed.

"He's a good cop, though. Put some real bad-asses away. Batton's also very determined. Are you sure your alibi is airtight?"

"Yes."

"Who is he?" Liz asked.

"Now that's a big assumption."

"But I'm right, aren't I? I'm not finding fault here, Jen. Wouldn't be the first time a wronged woman found solace in the arms of an understanding man. And Russell sure as hell wronged you."

"What makes you say that?"

"You're forgetting Don's a first-rate reporter. He knows about Gina and the ice-water incident at the hospital. But don't worry. It's not getting on the air."

"Thanks."

"You're welcome. Still, it's not simply my affection for you that's keeping those particulars quiet. Unless they can be tied to Russell's murder or you volunteer to talk about them, they're your private business. But watch out. Don said that woman crime reporter from the paper is nosing around."

Jennifer had already received several calls from the newspaper reporter in question. She hadn't returned them.

"All that stuff you gave us on Russell about his being a high school soccer star and how highly he was regarded in the chamber of commerce made him so much more than merely another victim when we ran the story about his murder," Liz said. "But what we really need now is an interview with someone who knew him intimately."

"Please don't say you mean me."

"You'd be first choice, but if you don't want to, I understand. Do Russell's family know he was cheating on you?"

"I certainly don't intend to tell them. They're going through enough as it is."

"Can you steer me to one of them who would be willing to go on air and talk about what a good guy Russell was?"

Jennifer had spent most of the day with the Sprague family at their home. Their reaction to the horror of Russell's murder had been a stiff, silent rage. And although they had not openly chastised her for not getting in touch with them sooner, she'd felt their silent censure. Only one of them had greeted her with warmth.

"Try Russell's sister, Caroline," Jennifer said. "She owns a beauty salon on Fifth."

"Caroline's Coiffures?"

"That's the one. Caroline's a bit more forthcoming than the others. And between you and me, I think she really wants to talk about him. But send one of your female soft news reporters to do the interview."

"Why?" Liz asked.

"Caroline needs to be approached at her salon and treated gently. That will be the way to get her to open up. Once she's in the family bosom, she circles the wagons like the rest of them."

"Thanks, Jen. Oh, hell. Wally's got himself tied up in the camera cord again. Got to go. See you tomorrow."

Jennifer dropped the telephone receiver on its cradle and sank against the couch cushions.

The police had no doubt talked to Michael by now. She'd pleaded with Batton to be discreet. The hard-eyed cop had given her no guarantees.

It would shame her deeply to be publicly labeled the lover of a married man. But she could weather the stigma. What she feared most were the professional and personal hits Michael would take.

Jenny, you asked me if there had been any changes in my life. I told you there hadn't been.

He had told her that. And he had told her other things as well—things that hadn't made much sense to her at the time.

Jenny, forgive me. I had no right.

He'd just kissed her with a fervor that had made her blood sing. And she'd been with him all the way. Yet he'd pulled back, tried to stop what was happening between them with those words. Now she knew what he'd meant by them. He had no right to kiss her because he was married.

You deserve so much better.

Better than an affair with a married man. Why hadn't she asked him what he meant by those words at the time? Because she didn't want to know? Had she heard only what she'd wanted to hear Saturday night?

And Sunday morning, there was something in their conversation that had also struck her as odd, something that she'd been too upset to think much about.

You said you'd read my book.

Jennifer got up and went over to the shelf, pulled out *The Human Touch* by Dr. Michael Temple and took it back to the couch.

Flipping to the index, she scanned through the chapter headings. Each one was a separate case history. There were nineteen in all. She'd read the first ten when the book came out the year before, and had marveled at their wisdom.

But life had gotten very busy for her then, what with the new job at KSEA and meeting Russell. She'd put Michael's book on her shelf without completing it. She hadn't wanted thoughts of him coming between what she and Russell might have together.

Settling back on the couch now, she began at the beginning.

A renowned and scholarly researcher in the field of clinical psychiatry who was also a professor emeritus at the nearby university had written the foreword. She'd initially skipped it because Michael wasn't the author.

Examining it now, she found his comments on Michael's work were glowing. But it was the fifth paragraph that caught her attention.

> The wisdom of this book comes from the life experiences of real people in pain and the compassion of the man who left no stone unturned to help them, even when all others had given up. But it isn't what they learned from this man that is so remarkable. It's what he learned from them and has passed on to us. These are not simply case histories to Michael Temple. These are flesh and blood people— one of them his own wife. Chapter nineteen is her story.

His wife's story? Jennifer quickly flipped to chapter nineteen. Its title was simply "Lucy."

MICHAEL FOUND Brad Winslow in the E.R. doctor's lounge, working on patient charts. He got himself a cup of coffee from the machine and went to join him.

Brad looked up, smiled. "Still drinking that sludge, I see."

Michael could smell the richness of the home-brew coming out of the thermos cup in his friend's hand. Brad's marriage to the curator of the Courage Bay Botanical Gardens the year before and the subsequent birth of their son surrounded him with a happiness that damn near reached the aura stage.

"How are Emily and the baby?" Michael asked as he sat across from him.

"Perfect," his friend said with a deep smile. "But you didn't come down here to ask about the family. What's up?"

"I need you to tell me what you know about the murder of Dr. Russell Sprague."

Brad frowned. "That Detective Batton grill you, too?"

"Yes. When did you talk to him?"

"He was waiting for me when I came on shift a couple of hours ago. Emily and I were in San Diego Monday and Tuesday, visiting her folks. Batton acted real annoyed, as though I had deliberately left town to avoid talking with him. Guy isn't exactly Mr. Personality."

"I know what you mean. Got my dose of him yesterday. Was he the one who told you about Russell Sprague?"

"No, Dr. Field called me early Sunday morning. Sprague's death surprised us both. When I saw him in the trauma room, Sprague was fully conscious. No loss of memory or confusion. No visual disturbance, nausea or dizziness."

"What about his CT?"

"Mild concussion consistent with having hit his head in a fall. Chest X ray was clear. When he left the E.R., his vital signs were normal."

"What did Dr. Field say?" Michael asked.

"Sprague's chart showed he'd been checked every hour. He seemed to be doing fine. Then around midnight, the nurse discovered he wasn't breathing. The doctor tried to revive him, couldn't. His death made no sense."

"Is that why you asked for an autopsy to be done?"

Brad nodded. "Pathologist said he'd have the body held and get right to it."

"Did he tell you the results?"

"He left a message on my voice mail early Monday saying he needed to talk to me right away. Before I could get back to him this morning, Batton had come calling. I gave him the medical facts regarding my treatment of Dr. Sprague."

"And the incident involving Jennifer Winn?"

"Batton had already learned about it from the orderly who'd been on the floor Saturday night," Brad said. "I relayed the little I had personally observed and referred him to the manager at the Grand Hotel for the rest."

"Have you talked to the pathologist since your meeting with Batton?" Michael asked.

"I called and left word on his voice mail, but he hasn't called back. His name is Nealy. He's new to the staff and we're not that well acquainted, but I understand he's good—was a leading medical examiner for a police department in Washington State before joining the staff at Courage Bay. You know what he found?"

"He says that Batton warned him not to talk to anyone about his findings, especially me," Michael said.

"I'm not surprised. Batton kept asking me questions about you and Jennifer Winn. Really annoying ones."

"Annoying?"

"Yeah, like how long had you two been dating. Did your wife know. Crap like that. The guy obviously knows nothing about you. What's his problem?"

"He thinks Jennifer did it," Michael said.

"Killed Russell Sprague? No, I don't buy that. Sure, she was mad at him about something that night. But not like that."

This was one of the reasons why Michael liked working with Brad so much. His people instincts were as sharply honed as his medical skills.

"I tried to tell Batton she didn't do it," Michael said, "but he wouldn't listen to me. I think he's going to try to pin it on her."

Brad eyed him closely. "You sound like you're taking this very personally."

"I am."

Brad sipped his coffee, then put it down. "Have you thought about talking to Ed?"

Ed Corbin was Emily's brother and a detective in the Courage Bay Police Department. In addition to being Brad's brother-in-law, Ed was also Michael's good friend.

"Ed's next on my list. I'm hoping he can tell me why Batton's fixated on Jennifer." Michael got up to leave.

"Emily knows her."

He stopped, turned back to Brad. "Your wife knows Jennifer?"

"They met as volunteers during literacy awareness week last year. Emily really liked her. Said she was real. You met her before last Saturday, didn't you?"

"Yes."

"And?"

"Emily's right. She's real."

Michael quickly left before his friend could ask any more questions.

DETECTIVE ED CORBIN slipped onto the bar stool next to Chaska at the Courage Bay Bar and Grill. "Buy you a refill?" he offered.

"Yeah," Chaska said, a little surprised. "Thanks."

Ed signaled to the bartender, pointed to Chaska's beer and held up two fingers. The bartender nodded.

Chaska had joined the detective squad six weeks before. Batton had twenty years in. Word around the department was that Batton was giving his new partner a hard time. Ed knew if he was going to get the information he was after on the Russell Sprague murder case, it would be from the rookie.

Ed had no problem doing this for Michael. Their friendship had grown out of a difficult case he'd been called out on three years before. An enraged man had taken his ex-wife and their two-year-old daughter hostage in the wife's apartment and was holding a knife on them.

The windows had been boarded up, the doors barricaded. There was no way to get into the apartment without risking the hostages' lives.

When Ed discovered the man had a history of psychological problems, he called the psychiatric ward at the hospital, hoping someone could suggest something. Ten minutes later, Michael arrived at the scene.

For nearly four hours, Michael stood beneath the boiling midday sun, outside one of the boarded-up windows, talking to the man inside. At the end of their conversation, the man opened the door, walked out and gave himself up. His ex-wife and daughter were unharmed.

Ed had shaken Michael's hand and told him he owed him. Michael had denied he owed him anything and told Ed to call him anytime. Then for the next two hours, Ed had watched Michael take care of the ex-wife and child down at the police station, helping them to deal with the trauma they'd been through. Ed had learned a lot about the kind of man Michael was on that long, hot day.

In the intervening years, the two men had worked on other cases together and gotten to be good friends. All of which was why Ed was sitting on this bar stool, ready to poke his nose into another detective's case, not something one cop did to another in the closed circle of the police family.

"I understand Batton's a real joy to work with," Ed said after the beers had been delivered.

Chaska snickered. "Oh, yeah. A real joy. I'm twenty-nine with an advanced degree in criminology and he keeps calling me kid. 'I'll do the talking, kid.' 'Take the notes, kid.' 'Type up the report, kid.'"

Chaska did a very good imitation of Batton's condescending tone.

Ed nodded. "Some of these old-timers are real pains in the butt. At least you've got an interesting case with that murdered dentist. All I'm on these days are street shootings. How's it going?"

"All the good suspects are coming up with alibis."

"I hate it when that happens. Didn't I hear somewhere that KSEA's TV meteorologist is involved?"

Chaska chugged some beer, nodded. "The vic's fiancée."

"She one of the ones with an alibi?"

"Sort of. We interviewed the psychiatrist she said she was with that night, a Dr. Temple. His account matched hers and he coughed it up right away. Took us three hours to drag it out of her. You would have thought she was the married one."

"So, the meteorologist is off the hook?"

"Batton still thinks she did it. Says all her hesitation, evasion, begging us to be discreet wasn't to protect her married lover from a scandal. He says she was simply trying to get us to buy into her alibi."

"What do you say?" Ed asked.

"I watch her on the tube all the time. She's believable. But I tell that to Batton and he says, 'Wise up, kid. She's an actress.'"

"How does Batton explain Dr. Temple backing up her story?"

"Says he was acting, too."

Chaska paused to throw out his somewhat less than bulky chest as he mimicked his more muscularly endowed partner. "'The whole world's a stage, kid. Just remember that when you interview suspects.'"

"Since when did Dr. Temple become a suspect?" Ed asked, careful not to show his growing concern.

"Since the moment he told us he slept with her. Batton thinks that either Jennifer asked Temple to lie for her and he's doing it, or they killed Sprague together."

"Why?" Ed asked.

Chaska's chest pushed out again. "'Love. Lust. Call it what you will, kid. When it gets hold of a man, he's capable of doing anything.'"

Some men, maybe. But not Michael Temple. Ed knew him better than that.

"What about you?" Ed asked. "You think Dr. Temple would do that for her?"

Chaska finished his beer. "I'm not comfortable with him as a suspect any more than I am her. But I have to admit Batton's right when he says they have a lot of motive. And then there's that thing we found at the scene."

THE WESTERN SUN SKIDDED across the parking lot asphalt into Jennifer's eyes. She repositioned herself so the glare wouldn't blind her while still letting the cameraman get a good shot of Courage Bay Grade School behind her.

On the front steps sat the fourth grade class, hair combed, smiles from ear to ear, ready for the moment when the camera would scan their eager faces.

Giving an hour's talk on meteorology at the local schools, followed by a live shoot, had become a regular monthly event for Jennifer. The kids loved being on TV. Their parents loved seeing them. And Jennifer loved turning on young minds to meteorology.

Today her co-star would be eight-year-old Penelope with the frizzy hair, thick glasses and chipped front tooth.

The director kept telling her to pick photogenic children with good articulation. But Jennifer always selected the ones who she knew could use the self-esteem boost.

Penelope stood next to the weather station that Jennifer had set up at the school. When the time came, the girl would have the fun of giving the barometric pressure to the viewing audience and explaining what it meant.

And tomorrow Jennifer would see that a tape of tonight's program was sent to Penelope, a keepsake for her and her family.

The TV station was firmly behind these live segments, which Jennifer had begun the year before when she'd started installing individual weather stations at the schools. Fan mail about them clogged the post office box and the station's e-mail.

Jennifer appreciated the upbeat letters. The high ratings. And it was fun to be a positive role model for the kids who watched the program.

Still, she didn't let the attention go to her head. That wasn't the reason she'd gone to school for so long and studied so hard. Three-fourths of those who gave weather forecasts on local TV stations had no training in meteorology. Like news anchors, they were chosen because they looked and sounded good.

Being a meteorologist was serious business to Jennifer. Ninety-five percent of viewers tuned in to their local news station to find out about the weather. They were counting on her to get it right.

All the instruments had been read, the computer work done ahead of time. Jennifer needed no script. Everything was in her head. This was the easy part for her. Just relax and talk to her viewers, let them know what to expect.

The engineer and cameraman were set up, ready to go. Through her earpiece she could hear the producer back in the studio saying that she was up in ten seconds. She rested her hand on Penelope's shoulder.

"Ready to wow them, Penny?"

The girl nodded eagerly, her glasses slipping down her nose. Jennifer smiled as she set them straight again.

Three…two…one. And they were on.

MICHAEL WATCHED JENNIFER as she stood in front of the camera, talking about the day's high temperatures and letting her viewers know that if they were going to be out tonight, they'd need sweaters because of the brisk ocean breeze.

She had a relaxed, conversational style, as though she were sitting across from her audience in their living room. And a natural warmth that people were happy to invite into their homes.

When she introduced the young girl beside her, Penelope read the barometric gauge and explained in a squeaky voice that the number had dropped over the past hour, creating a low pressure. That was the reason the southern breeze off the sea was being drawn toward Courage Bay.

Michael knew why Jennifer selected the children she did. It was one of the many things that attracted him to her.

When she'd run out of his house Sunday morning, he'd understood that she never wanted to see him again. He'd fully intended to honor her wishes. But he couldn't now. And a selfish part of him was glad. For despite the reason that brought him here today, just being able to see her again made him feel like smiling.

After letting the viewers know there would be some light

morning fog that would clear the beaches by noon and leave the next day full of sun, Jennifer threw it back to the news anchors. A second later, the engineer told her they were clear.

She bent down and gave her beaming co-star a warm hug. Then she headed toward her car at the far corner of the lot.

Michael was leaning against the driver's door.

Jennifer stopped short, freezing at the sight of him. After that brief moment of hesitation, she came steadily forward.

Michael had prepared himself for her anger. Tears. Being told to go away. Even being ignored. But when she finally stood in front of him, the expression on her face was calm.

"Hello, Michael."

Relief flooded through him. "You've forgiven me."

"Nothing to forgive. I was the one who…pushed things last Saturday. What happened was my fault."

He eased closer. "Does there have to be a fault?"

She retreated a step. "I didn't read chapter nineteen of your book until yesterday. I realize now that your situation is not typical. Whatever you do to…cope with the circumstances is understandable."

"Cope with the circumstances," he repeated. "Is that what you think Saturday night was for me?"

"It doesn't matter, Michael. It's over. Please let's leave it in the past. I have to be going."

She circled him, put her key in the car door.

"Jen, I need to talk to you."

"There's nothing more to say."

"It's about Russell's murder."

Her body stiffened as she faced him.

"I didn't want to tell that detective where I was Saturday night, but he gave me no choice," she said. "I'm sorry you were dragged into this."

"It's not a problem. What is a problem is the fact that Detective Batton didn't believe us."

"How do you know?"

"A friend of mine, another detective in the Courage Bay Police Department, spoke with Batton's partner."

"Am I understanding you correctly? Detective Batton doesn't think we were together Saturday night?"

"Oh, he thinks we were together. He also thinks that we murdered Russell. And he's doing his damnedest to build a case against both of us right now."

CHAPTER FIVE

"WHY IS BATTON FOCUSING on us?" Jennifer asked.

They'd driven to a restaurant on the outskirts of Courage Bay to have dinner and discuss what they should do. Michael had asked for a table in the back, as secluded from the rest as possible. Jennifer didn't consider the gesture a romantic one. For this conversation, they simply needed privacy.

"According to the case he's trying to build, Batton believes our motives are twofold for killing Russell," Michael said after the waiter had taken their order and left.

"*Our* motives. He really thinks someone like *you* could be a party to murder?"

"That's not any stupider than thinking that someone like *you* could be."

Jennifer's eyes slid away from the open affection on Michael's face. She had no doubt of his attraction for her. Not after Saturday night.

The knowledge was intensely bittersweet. She'd already made a serious error in her selection of Russell as a mate. She was not going to commit another folly by falling for an unattainable man.

"Batton has statements from the hospital orderly, the E.R. doctor and the hotel manager about the ice-water incident," Michael said.

"I explained that Russell and I had quarreled because I'd learned he'd been unfaithful. When Batton pressed me for the other woman's name, I gave him Gina's."

"Have you talked with her since the accident?" Michael asked.

"No, but she's left several messages on my voice mail saying she was sorry."

Jennifer fought the sadness those words brought. Gina's betrayal had been as disheartening as Russell's. Mere days before they had been the two people closest to her. Now both of them were out of her life forever.

Michael reached across the table, covered her hand with his. No inane and insulting platitudes about how hard things must be for her as she grieved her losses. No fancy psychological advice about how to move on. Just the warmth of his touch.

"You're KSEA's meteorologist," an older man said as he and his wife approached the table. "Jennifer Winn, right?"

Jennifer turned toward them and put a smile on her face as Michael withdrew his hand.

"Is this your husband?" the woman asked, gesturing toward Michael.

One of the problems with appearing in viewers' homes every night was that after a while her audience began to think of her as extended family and felt free to ask personal questions.

Jennifer kept her expression pleasant as she answered, "A friend."

She listened politely while the couple talked about how much they enjoyed her weather reports. And then the man had an amusing story he wanted to share about a trip he and his wife had taken to the Colorado mountains and how an inaccurate weather forecast there had ended up with them being stranded in snow.

By the time they left, Jennifer's jaw ached from so much smiling.

"Something tells me you try to avoid eating out," Michael said.

"I know they don't mean to intrude on my privacy," she said. "They're probably not even aware they're doing it. Where were we?"

"You told Batton about Gina and Russell."

She nodded. "What I don't understand is that even if Batton thought I would kill Russell because he was unfaithful, what possible motive could you have for harming him? You didn't even know him."

"Batton believes that I...didn't want to share you with Russell. And then, of course, there is the assumption that I would receive some of the money."

"Money?" Jennifer repeated.

"My friend in the police department says Russell's parents told Batton about a new will that Russell filed with his attorney this past week."

Jennifer slumped back against her chair. "I forgot about the will."

"But you knew about it?"

She nodded. "Russell suggested we both have new wills drawn up. It was one of the things on his long list that had to be accomplished before the wedding."

"Did you prepare a new will?"

"I was supposed to, but it totally slipped my mind until now," she said.

"Do you know that his parents estimate his estate in excess of five million?"

"That can't be right," Jennifer said. "Russell has...*had* a thriving dental practice, it's true, but it couldn't be worth so much. Besides, he was in a partnership that included a right of survivorship. His interest in the practice will go to his surviving partner."

"Apparently the five million isn't from his business. Russell's grandfather died this year and left him a million in cash and land worth over four million. According to the notes Batton made from his meeting with Russell's attorney, the new will Russell signed last week designated you as the main beneficiary of the estate."

She was the beneficiary of a five million dollar estate? Jennifer sat straight up in her chair. "I can't believe it. We went to his grandfather's funeral together several months ago. Russell said nothing about having received anything from him."

"Was Russell generally a secretive person?"

"I never thought so. He was always volunteering information

about his family and business affairs. Asking for my opinion. Sharing his feelings with me. All of which made me think…"

"Yes?"

"That he had a desire for intimacy." Jennifer shook her head. "What a joke. I can't believe how close I came to marrying him."

"I doubt that you would have gone through with the wedding, even if Gina hadn't confessed what was going on," Michael said. "Something didn't feel right with him, remember?"

"That was only in the past week. Unless the feeling was there all along, waiting for me to acknowledge it—the real reason why I hesitated to marry him despite all the logical reasons that told me I should. How's that for self-analysis?"

"Impresses the hell out of me," Michael said. "We like to think of ourselves as intelligent beings led by logic. But the truth is, the bigger part of us is made up of feelings."

"Nice to know there's a basis for my irrationality," Jennifer said.

"Never underestimate the importance of feelings, Jen. When we don't listen to our logic, we betray our intellect. But when we don't listen to our feelings, we betray our hearts. Logic may be the words to life's song, but feelings are its melody."

"Where did that one come from?" she asked. "Hallowed halls of psychiatric medicine or your father?"

"That one comes straight from my mom."

She liked his boyish smile when he said that. Even though he was in a tailored suit, freshly shaved, his thick hair neatly trimmed, there was nothing about Michael that came across as scholarly or the least bit formal. He was so tolerant of others' foibles, so wonderfully human.

And so devoted to his wife.

Their food was delivered. Jennifer was silent as she ate. She kept remembering what she had read in chapter nineteen of his book. The love that had poured out onto the pages when he described Lucy.

"Jen, are you okay?"

She'd been lost in her thoughts. Looking up, she found him eyeing the barely touched food on her plate. "I'm not very hungry," she said.

"If I'd just learned I was going to inherit five million dollars, I suppose I might lose my appetite, too."

"I don't want Russell's money. I don't want anything from him."

Michael's expression was warm. "May I talk to you about Saturday night?"

"No." The answer came out quick, sharp. And until it did, she wasn't aware of how much pain still remained.

Jennifer looked around the room, at the people passing by, everywhere but at him. He was not at fault. But their night together had been a dream come true for her. And now the dream was dust.

A woman and her son, no more than seven, came over to the table to tell Jennifer how much they enjoyed watching her weather reports. The boy asked for her autograph and for her to pick his class the next time she came to his school.

After giving him her autograph, Jennifer promised she'd seriously consider his request.

"Ever think about wearing a disguise when you go out in public?" Michael asked after the mother and son had left. "Dark glasses. Wig. Beard?"

She smiled, relieved he'd let go of the previous subject. "It's a thought. Batton wouldn't tell me how Russell was killed. Do you know?"

Michael shook his head. "The pathologist has been told not to talk to me. Did Russell have any enemies?"

"No one comes to mind. Russell was personable, well liked. I keep thinking there must be some mistake."

"We need to try to figure out what could have motivated someone to kill him."

"Are you suggesting we attempt to find his killer?" she asked.

"It's a sure bet Batton isn't going to. He's focused on us."

"But, Michael, we know we weren't involved in Russell's death, so there can't be any evidence to prove that we were. Should we really be concerned about this detective?"

"I'm your alibi and you're mine. By saying we did it together, he dismisses both of our explanations as to where we were."

"Still, that's only his opinion that we've lied. We know we haven't. Without proof that we have, what can he do?"

"Batton's already made a call to the ethics committee at the hospital and told them I had sexual relations with a patient."

The message in his words bit keenly. "Michael, I'm so sorry."

"There's nothing for you to be sorry about."

"But I was the one who pushed—"

"You didn't push me into anything. I don't regret a second of Saturday night. I never will."

The warmth of his words and the look that accompanied them slid past all of her defenses. She reached for her water glass and took a long drink, trying to dampen the dangerous yearnings inside her.

Jennifer, don't be a fool.

"What are you going to do about the ethics committee?" she asked, when she could.

"There'll be a hearing. I'll have to appear, explain my actions."

"And then?"

"They'll either consider you my patient because I filled out a psychiatric evaluation chart, or determine you weren't, based on what I wrote."

"What did you write?"

"That the incident did not qualify as a psychiatric one since you dumped ice water on Russell in response to extreme emotional provocation, causing him momentary discomfort but not injury."

"You wrote that even before we talked?"

"I know you."

He said that with such calm certainty. No one had ever made her feel so special for simply being who she was.

"What happens if they decide I was your patient?"

"I don't think they will. And at the moment, I'm more concerned about what Batton plans to do in regards to you."

"What can he do?" Jennifer asked.

"I'd say it's a fair assumption that he's already implying your guilt to Russell's family through the questions he's asked them. He'll do the same thing with your co-workers at KSEA.

According to my source, this is an approach that Batton often uses to try to make his suspects' friends and even family begin to doubt them."

"But even if he were to convince people around me that I'm guilty, how can that develop a case against me?"

"When someone begins to think you're guilty of something, they're no longer objective. People see what they look for, Jen. Even the most innocent comments you've made about Russell may now be viewed in a sinister light."

"KSEA's news director warned me about Batton."

Jennifer told Michael how Batton had used Liz to get the identity of the man who worked at the beauty pageant.

"Sounds like Batton isn't above personal manipulation to get what he wants," Michael commented. "When is Russell's funeral?"

"Services are tomorrow at two in the chapel at the cemetery."

"I'd like to attend with you."

"To look for suspects?"

"Among other things. It's important we work together on this."

Jennifer studied the uneaten food on her plate. He was right. But for her sake—her survival—she needed something to be clear between them before this went any further.

"Michael, there is one final thing I need to say about Saturday night before we put it in the past."

"Yes?"

"I can't ever let it happen again."

He was quiet a long moment. Jennifer continued to stare at her plate, didn't trust herself to look at him.

"I understand," he said softly.

When she finally raised her eyes to his, she saw that he did. All evidence of his attraction for her had vanished.

"May I accompany you to the funeral tomorrow?" he asked. She nodded.

"Give me your address, and I'll pick you up."

She hesitated. He'd agreed to let Saturday night remain in the past. She trusted him to do that. But her feelings for him made establishing boundaries essential. Having him at her place, riding with him in his car—such things would be inviting more personal closeness than was necessary or wise.

"I think we should meet at the chapel," she said.

"I'd feel more comfortable if we arrived together and left together."

The subtle change in his tone had her eyes seeking his. "Are you worried that something might happen?"

"I'm certain Batton will be there, possibly agitating things. Do you have an attorney?"

She shook her head, a little startled at the question.

He pulled a card out of his suit pocket and handed it to her. "This is mine."

She read the name off the card. "Ben Thayer. He's the childhood friend you told me about."

"He's also straightforward and highly competent. I've filled him in on the situation. If you want him to represent you, he will."

The implication made her draw in an unsteady breath. "You think we're going to be charged."

"I think we should be prepared for anything. And I don't think either of us should be talking to Batton again without an attorney present."

Jennifer could think of only one reason for Michael to say these things. "There's something else, isn't there. Something you haven't told me."

He returned her gaze squarely. "When a member of the maintenance staff was cleaning up the hospital room in which Russell died, she found an earring next to the bed. Batton showed the earring to Russell's mother. She identified it as one of a pair he bought for you. With it, Batton puts you at the scene of the murder."

IT WAS OVERCAST AND COOL at the cemetery. The chapel's large parking lot was filled with cars. Michael wondered how many of the mourners were people who actually knew Russell. The morbidly curious always showed up when word of a murder got out.

Batton had been quoted on the news as pursuing leads on the

case, but nothing more. At least for the record. Jennifer had been identified as Russell's fiancée in the paper, but the local TV news had not mentioned her association with the deceased.

What KSEA had run was a tearful interview with Caroline Sprague in which she had described her brother in a way that only a loving sister could.

Michael was relieved Jennifer had let him accompany her today. From the moment they stepped inside the chapel, nearly all heads turned in her direction. And from the expression on the faces of many and the whispering back and forth, he knew that Batton had been busy sowing the seeds of mistrust.

They stood against the wall, since there were no seats available. Michael selected a spot that would give him a good view of people in the pews. As the chaplain called family members to speak about the deceased, Michael studied them carefully.

Russell's brother, Kevin, was the first to rise. He looked about thirty and wore an air of entitlement that Michael had often seen in the children of well-to-do parents.

Before picking Jennifer up today, Michael had made a concerted effort to learn more about the Sprague family.

Lloyd Sprague had inherited his father's prosperous real estate business and had gone on to make even more money. His wife, Harriet, had come from a prominent family as well.

Russell had been an up-and-coming member of the chamber of commerce and mixed in the same social circles as his parents. His sister, a successful businesswoman in her own right, also attended chamber of commerce meetings.

But there was no information about his brother.

"Russ and I had a bet about which of us would buy it first," Kevin said, his expression and tone about as emotional as tap water. He turned toward the closed casket. "Never thought I'd win that bet." And with that, he sat down.

Russell's mother was next to speak. From the pictures the TV news had run, Michael could tell that Russell had her dark coloring and fine features.

In a tearful voice, she told of what a bright and handsome son he'd been. She described in detail several recent Christmas and birthday presents Russell had given her. How carefully he had picked them out and how much meaning each held for her.

When her voice broke and she dissolved into tears, Russell's sister took her place.

Caroline repeated a lot of what she had said in her TV interview. How she had always looked up to Russell. How he had counseled her in business and her personal relationships—a dear friend as well as a beloved brother. She, too, was weeping when she finally sat down.

Russell's father, Lloyd Russell Sprague, was the last to rise, physically big, emotionally stoic. He grasped the podium as he surveyed the crowd, and the quiet seconds slowly ticked by.

Then his eyes found Jennifer's face and stayed there.

Michael tensed at the change in the man's expression. Lloyd suddenly pushed away from the podium and stomped down the aisle. He stormed out of the chapel, slamming the door behind him.

The murmur that went through the crowd was quieted by the chaplain's raised hands. "It's often difficult for a grieving father to express himself at such a time," the minister said. "Our prayers go with Mr. Sprague."

The second the services ended, Michael ushered Jennifer to the door of the chapel.

"Are we rushing for some reason?" she asked as he led the way to the car.

He'd forgotten she was in high heels, and slowed his step. "Sorry. Was Gina there?"

She stopped and turned back toward the entrance. "That's her coming down the stairs now. She's the one on the right."

Michael followed Jennifer's gesture to see a tall, shapely woman with short black hair and an even shorter dress. Her face was averted as she headed toward the opposite end of the parking lot.

Harriet, Caroline and Kevin Sprague emerged from the chapel. When they spied Gina, they all came to a halt. There was contempt on Harriet's face. Pain on Caroline's. Kevin was checking out Gina's legs.

"I'd like to speak with them," Jennifer said.

"Now might not be the best time," Michael cautioned.

"Leaving without saying anything doesn't feel right."

As much as he wanted to, Michael didn't argue. They retraced their steps to the chapel entrance.

Jennifer smiled and said hello.

Harriet stiffened, turned her back and walked away.

"She thinks you did it," Caroline said. "Dad does, too."

"What do you think, Caroline?"

"I…oh, Jen, I loved him so much. But I'm glad he was a brother and not a boyfriend."

"When did you learn about Gina?" Jennifer asked.

Caroline dabbed at the tears on her cheek. "That detective told us about her and what you did with the ice water. He showed Mom the earring, the one from the set Russell bought for you."

Caroline's tears started to flow in earnest.

Jennifer stepped forward, gently resting her hand on Caroline's forearm. "Russell didn't—"

"We don't need to hear about our brother from you," Kevin interrupted as he grasped his sister's shoulder and pulled her back. "Are you going to be at the grave site?"

"No," Jennifer said.

"Smart choice. See you at the will reading. Come on, Caroline. Mom and Dad are waiting."

After Kevin and his sister had walked away, Jennifer turned to Michael. "Even if I told them that Russell never gave me any earrings, they probably wouldn't believe it."

"Have you thought about who he might have bought them for?"

"I suppose it could have been Gina."

Michael caught a glimpse of Detective Batton on the other side of the parking lot. A woman Michael recognized as the newspaper reporter who'd been trying to see him was with the detective. Michael urged Jennifer toward the car.

"It's happening just like you said," she commented when they were a few miles down the road. "Batton's turning them against me."

"I don't think Caroline wants to believe it. Tell me about her."

"She has a good heart and she's a real go-getter, like Russell. Her beauty salon, Caroline's Coiffures, is very upscale and quite successful. Their parents gave Russell, Caroline and Kevin each a hundred thousand dollars as a college graduation present. Both Russell and Caroline put it into their business and made a success."

"And Kevin?"

"He bought a new car."

"How does he make his living?"

"He doesn't. From what I can tell, his parents provide for his every need."

"Not exactly an overachiever."

"What's always irked me is that Caroline's sweet and works hard, but it doesn't make a bit of difference. That reprehensible mindset that tends to value daughters less than sons is a strong undercurrent in the Sprague household."

"Even with her mother?"

"Especially with Harriet. She's always lavished her attention and accolades on Russell and Kevin."

Michael was familiar with that type of mother. She'd probably been the devalued daughter when she was growing up. Kids learned so much from how they were treated. In many cases, far too much.

"Harriet's very capable," Jennifer said. "I'm certain Russell got his organizing skills from her. But when she's around her husband, she takes on this persona of deference and humbleness that resembles a damn doormat."

"Did she ever seem concerned when you didn't show such behavior around Russell?"

"Russell always made a concerted effort to try to please me. The only thing we disagreed about was having a big wedding."

"Who didn't want one?"

"I'd always visualized my wedding as an intimate affair. Besides, the only family I have left are a couple of distant cousins in Canada that I haven't seen in years. My parents' work required us to move around so much when I was growing up that maintaining relationships was difficult. I have a few friends from college, some from work, but not a whole lot more to fill my guest list."

"But Russell did."

She nodded. "In addition to his immediate family, he has a slew of uncles, aunts and cousins, not to mention all the people he wanted to invite that he considered important business contacts. Right from the start, he envisioned a first-class-wedding with all the trimmings. Said it was what I deserved. What he really meant was that it was what he wanted. I can see that now. But I wasn't smart enough to understand it then."

She still couldn't say the words without disillusionment darkening her eyes. Michael knew that she was still haunted by her choice of Russell.

"What did Harriet think about your marrying her son?" he asked.

"No woman would have been good enough for Russell as far as Harriet was concerned. But she was gracious to me."

"And Lloyd Sprague? How did he react to Russell choosing you?"

"Greeted me with a big smile from the first moment Russell introduced us some ten months ago. After our engagement was announced, he seemed proud to show me off to his friends and business associates as his future daughter-in-law. Although clearly that has changed."

"And Kevin?"

"I didn't see much of Kevin until three months ago, when I attended Russell's thirty-fourth birthday party at his parents' home. Kevin told me I should dump Russell for a real man. The way he said it sounded like a joke, and that's how I took it. Only, he got a little too free with his hands, and I told him to back off. He responded by acting all shocked and innocent, like I was the one out of line."

"Did you tell Russell about the incident?"

She shook her head. "I didn't want to cause problems between them. Russell always called Kevin the family screwup. He didn't have much respect for him."

"Did Kevin get out of line again with you?" Michael asked.

"No, he kept his distance. Are you asking me these questions about the Spragues because you think one of them might have killed Russell?"

"The sad truth is that people are generally murdered by those closest to them."

"His parents and sister showed a lot of affection for him. And although he and Kevin weren't close, I never sensed anything like anger between them."

"Did you get a call from Russell's attorney about the reading of the will?" Michael asked.

"It's Friday at ten."

"Be interesting to hear what it says."

"I thought you said Batton's meeting with Russell's attorney indicated the disposition of the property was to me?" Jennifer asked.

"The main distribution goes to you. There may be other bequests. Remember Kevin's comment about seeing you at the will reading? That tells me he's been mentioned in it as well."

"The whole Sprague family probably is. And considering the way they feel about me, I wish I didn't have to attend."

"I'll be with you, Jen. If you want me to."

He'd made the offer without taking his eyes off the road. When he saw her nod in his peripheral vision, his hands relaxed on the wheel.

"If you're thinking that the motive for his murder could be financial, his family would certainly have to be crossed off the list of suspects," she said after a minute. "None of the Spragues need money. Where are we going?"

"There's a café at the beach that serves a great sherbet made with real strawberries. My favorite meteorologist said it's going to be beautifully sunny along the coast today, in the low seventies with a light breeze."

"Is it a very popular place?"

He knew she was concerned about being approached by fans. "Yes, the café is quite busy, but I know the owners and they'll let us use their private balcony."

She nodded and he made the turn onto the Pacific Coast Highway.

They arrived at the Seacrest Café a few minutes later. The air was fresh and warm, the sky a clear, bleached blue. Michael collected their sherbets and led Jennifer to chairs under a canopy on the private balcony.

In the distance the ocean stretched as smooth as an ironed sheet. A gentle breeze lifted the ends of Jennifer's long hair as she stared out at the horizon. Her sad look was one he'd noticed inside the chapel, and it told Michael she was thinking about the man who was being buried today, trying to sort through her conflicting feelings.

Sometimes the best way to get to the end of something was to start at the beginning.

"Where did you meet Russell?" Michael asked.

"At a black-tie dinner party I attended a couple of months after joining the staff at KSEA. In addition to business leaders, there were local politicians and the TV news team. After thirty minutes of deflecting the typical come-on lines, I was ready to forgo dinner and get out of there. Then Russell walked up to me, told me I had great teeth and asked me who my dentist was." Her lips curved at the memory. "At least he had an original line."

"Not to mention the ability to recognize beautiful teeth when he saw them," Michael said.

This time her smile was for him. Michael basked in its light for as long as it lasted. She'd laid the ground rules for their working together. He would abide by them. But he couldn't shut off his feelings.

That he had to hide them was hard enough.

"You mentioned Russell's business partner will now own all of what was a shared dental practice," Michael said.

"And you think that implies he had a motive for killing Russell?"

"Could be. Was he at the funeral today?"

"You remember the tall, skinny guy with the slightly bald head who sat in the row behind the Spragues?"

"All Adam's apple and legs?" he asked.

"That was Harvey Thompson, fellow dentist, Russell's longtime friend and business partner. The short, blond woman with him was Dorie, Russell and Harvey's office manager."

"From the way they were nudging each other in the pew it looked to me like Dorie and Harvey are an item."

"They started dating several months ago," she confirmed.

"So it was one big happy family at the dentist's office?"

"Every time I was there."

"You were a patient?"

"No. Russell tried to persuade me to become one, but I couldn't handle the idea."

"I doubt I could have, either. Not exactly romantic to be kissing the person who's on an intimate basis with your cavities and tartar."

Her chuckle was soft. The sadness that had darkened her features earlier was no longer in evidence.

"So how do we go about this sleuthing stuff?" she asked.

"I'll start by questioning the hospital staff. Nurses know nearly everything that happens on their floors. If I had pictures of Russell, as well as his family and friends, it would help."

"I have some at home. I'll get them for you when you drop me off. Or better yet, why don't I come with you when you ask your questions?"

He got to his feet and threw their empty sherbet cups into the trash. Word about him and Jennifer had already swept through the staff, thanks to Batton. If Michael appeared with her at the hospital, it would no doubt generate more talk.

Still, she was the one who knew about Russell's background. Something could trigger a question for her that wouldn't for him.

Besides, she'd asked. And refusing her wasn't in him. "I'll pick you up after your six o'clock spot tonight."

She glanced at her wristwatch. "Time I got changed and headed for the station. On the way out, I want to stop and thank your friend who made our sherbets. Best I've ever had. How are you managing to maintain your schedule at the hospital?"

"I've handed off quite a few of my patients to other doctors."

"Because you're worried about Batton's case against us?"

"Because the hospital administration suggested I not treat any more female patients until after the findings of the ethics committee."

CHAPTER SIX

JENNIFER FOUND MICHAEL waiting for her in the KSEA station parking lot after her six o'clock spot. He held the passenger door of his car open for her, a smile of welcome on his face. "Hi."

"Hi," she repeated.

The simple exchange brought a flood of vivid memories. Waking up in his arms. Rolling over to face him. Saying hi to each other before making love again.

He'd told her he had no regrets.

She had regrets. Serious ones. That night had cost him dearly. Because of it, he was a suspect in a murder case and under review for a breach of ethics, his reputation compromised.

If she'd let him back away as he'd tried to, none of this would be happening to him.

"Are you okay?" he asked.

She realized then that she'd been frozen in place in front of the passenger door, frowning at his shoulder.

"Sorry," she said, slipping onto the seat. "My mind went off the air there for a moment."

He circled the car, got in, started the engine. "How are things at the station?"

"Batton has talked to everyone. Liz said his questions were full of implications regarding my guilt, which is probably why the news anchors and nearly everyone else avoided me this evening. Fortunately, she didn't."

"Liz sounds like a friend."

"Tell me you have a few like her."

"The hospital administration is simply following procedure

based on what Batton has reported. Those on the staff who know me aren't taking the man's insinuations regarding my role in Russell's murder seriously."

"So, he's trying to turn them against you the same way he's been doing with the people around me. Michael, I'm so sorry I—"

"Don't, Jennifer."

His tone had taken on that emphatic quality that she'd first noticed on the rooftop of the Courage Bay Bar and Grill. He didn't want her apologizing for their night together.

"The nurse we'll be talking to tonight is in Oncology," he said after a moment. "That's where Russell was taken after the E.R."

"Why did they give him a bed in that ward?"

"The hospital was overflowing Saturday night, due in part to the injuries caused by the fog. It was the only free bed available at the time he was admitted. The ward is not a very pleasant place to be. Are you sure you want to come with me?"

"Someone left that earring in Russell's room. If the nurse can give us a description of that person, I want to hear it."

VIVIAN, THE HEAD NURSE for the night shift in Oncology, was in her late forties and had a reputation for being tough. Where she worked, a nurse had to be.

Michael had spoken with her a few times but didn't really know her. Except for emergency call-ins and some long shifts, he worked days.

They found her coming out of a patient's room, shaking her head. Michael introduced Jennifer.

"You featured my nephew John on your show a few months ago," Vivian said. "Sheldon Elementary."

"I remember—John Middleton," Jennifer said. "Very smart and a lot of fun. How is he?"

"Hell-bent on becoming a meteorologist, thanks to you. He loved the tape of the show you sent him. He still plays it every time I stop by."

Vivian's tone was cordial, but the inquisitive way she looked at Jennifer told Michael that she'd spoken to Batton. Whether she'd believed the detective, Michael couldn't tell. Experienced nurses made very good poker players.

He gestured to the room Vivian had just come out of. "Hard one?" he asked.

"He pickled his liver with liquor," she told him. "He's on enough meds to mellow out an elephant and still keeps begging me to sneak him in a drink. It's not like he could even taste the damn stuff, much less get a buzz off it anymore."

"Clarence Castle," Michael guessed.

"You know him?"

"An oncologist on day shift asked me to look in on him a few days ago. She was concerned that Castle might be entertaining self-destructive thoughts."

"His self-destructive thoughts began when he opened his first bottle of booze," Vivian said. "The guy knows he doesn't have much time left. Says he can't sleep without his 'nightcap' and doesn't, despite medication that should knock him out."

"I have some nonalcoholic beer in a refrigerator in my office," Michael said. "I'll send some down to you."

"Power of suggestion," she said, catching on. "Thanks. So what brings you to the ward tonight?"

"Ms. Winn and I would like to know about the death of Russell Sprague."

Vivian eyed Michael. "Detective Batton told me I wasn't to talk about it to anyone, especially you and Ms. Winn."

Michael returned the nurse's steady gaze. "I'm not surprised."

She studied Michael a moment more before glancing around to see who might be in the hall. When she found it empty, she hurried them into a nearby closet, full of cleaning supplies, and closed the door.

"If anyone asks, I'm going to deny I told you anything," Vivian said.

Michael nodded in understanding.

"That night was a madhouse, Dr. Temple. Moment I arrived I had a guy code on me. We no sooner stabilized him and got him to the ICU when my most experienced nurse called in sick. Another got stuck in a pileup because of the fog. Every bed was occupied and I couldn't borrow from anywhere. Selma, one of my newer nurses, was the only help I had to cover the entire floor. We were at a full run for twelve hours straight."

"Do you remember Russell Sprague?"

"Very well. He took the bed of the guy we rushed to the ICU. Sprague was a good-looking man. We don't get many of those in this ward." Vivian paused to glance at Jennifer. "Your fiancé, I understand."

"Yes, he was," she said.

"I'm sorry." Vivian sounded like she meant it.

She turned back to Michael before continuing. "Sprague was an overflow from the regular wards. Our care of him was minimal. I checked him every hour."

"Who was the other patient in his room that night?"

"George Unger. Brain cancer. He didn't even know who he was, much less anyone else. We lost him Monday night. Seem to be losing a lot of patients lately. For many it's a blessing."

"Who visited Sprague?"

"The older man and woman who arrived first identified themselves to me as his parents," Vivian told him. "I believe the other four I saw traipsing in later were also relations."

"Four?" Michael repeated.

"Two couples. Thirtyish. Came in at different times."

Jennifer took some snapshots out of her purse and showed them to Vivian. "Any of them look familiar?"

Vivian shook her head. "Sorry. I didn't get a good look at their faces except to assure Batton that you and Dr. Temple weren't among them."

"Did you see anyone else go into his room?" Michael asked.

"No, but truthfully, I wasn't watching. I took the male patients, on the north end. Selma handled the female patients, on the south. Only way we could cover the floor that night. There were no breaks, no time for dinner."

"When did you realize that something was wrong with Sprague?" he asked.

"At midnight I found him lying on top of the sheet. I thought he was asleep. When I started to take his vitals, I realized he wasn't breathing and yelled for Dr. Field."

"Where was Dr. Field?"

"Looking in on another patient down the hall. He came right away and we set to work on him. Sprague's heart had stopped. We tried to get it going again, but it was no use." Vivian paused, glancing over at Jennifer. "He was gone."

"Any indication of what brought on his sudden death?" Michael asked.

"Dr. Field found nothing lodged in his breathing pathways. He wasn't on an IV drip or any meds, so he couldn't have had a reaction to anything we'd given him. The E.R. doctor had done a chest X ray as well as a head CT. Everything looked fine."

"Were there any unusual marks, bruises on his body?"

"Some developing back bruises from his earlier accident is all."

"You and Dr. Field were the only ones with him when he was pronounced?"

She nodded. "Of all the patients we had that night, he was the one I wasn't worrying about. A healthy guy in his thirties with nothing but a mild concussion and he buys it. I've got patients in these rooms in their eighties, down to ninety pounds and half a lung, and they're still hanging on."

"Do you remember when his callers left that night?" Michael asked.

"I shooed his parents out at ten, when visiting hours ended. The others were already gone by then."

"Vivian, I know you had a difficult night," Michael said. "Could Sprague's eleven o'clock check have been missed?"

"Could have but wasn't. He was returning to his bed from a bathroom break. His balance and coordination were perfect. I asked him how he felt and he said fine, except for a slight headache. Mind you, I didn't have time to do a blood pressure reading or anything else, but his color was good and he gave no evidence of physical distress. All of which I noted on his chart. The one Batton took."

"Did he take anything else?"

"All of Sprague's personal effects. His parents came to me asking for them on Monday, so I called down to the morgue. Batton had already had them shipped with the body to the medical examiner's office."

"Did you hear anything about an earring?"

"The infamous earring," Vivian said, and stole a quick look at Jennifer. "Yeah, housekeeping found it early the next morning when they were cleaning out his room. I was going off shift at the time and stuck it in an envelope. I'd planned to mail it to his family. Figured one of them must have lost it when they were visiting him."

"What did it look like?" Jennifer asked.

"Gorgeous. Star-shaped agate with rubies in gold. I could tell right away it wasn't costume. The workmanship was excellent."

"Clip or pierced?" Jennifer asked.

"Clip, I think. When Batton heard about the damn thing, he cornered me at the nurse's station, angry with me and housekeeping for having touched it. Said we'd ruined any chance for lifting fingerprints. Then he grilled me like I'd been deliberately hiding it from him."

"He treated you like a suspect?" Michael asked.

"Oh yeah. First time he questioned me he came to my home, leaned on the bell and pounded on the door until he woke me up. Asked me if Dr. Sprague had been my dentist, like I might have a motive for killing him."

"You said the *first* time he questioned you," Michael said. "When was that?"

"Monday."

"And he questioned you a second time?"

"Here at the hospital when I arrived for my Tuesday night shift. That's when all his innuendos were directed at you and Ms. Winn. He said he knew she'd been in Sprague's room because the earring was hers, and I'd better get my memory back."

"How did you respond to that?" Michael asked.

"I told him my memory's perfect the way it is."

Jennifer sent Vivian a smile, which she returned.

"You said you assumed one of Russell's family had lost the earring when they came to see him," Michael said. "Do you have any idea who it might have been?"

"I can't even tell you if his mother had on earrings, much less the two other women visitors. I barely got a glance at them. Noticing earrings was not something I had a lot of time to do."

"Is there anything else you remember about that night, anything that might have struck you as out of the ordinary?" Michael asked.

She shook her head. "Sprague's sudden death was it. Everything else was hectic but routine."

Michael was getting ready to thank Vivian for her help when she added, "You could ask Nettie if she saw anything."

"Nettie?" Michael repeated.

"She's a volunteer," Vivian explained. "Reads to the patients, gives them massages, even brings them home-baked cookies. There are dozens of volunteers in the children's ward and every other ward in this hospital. But she's the only one who volunteers here. Wish we had a thousand more like her."

"And she was here Saturday night?"

"She's here most every night. Matter of fact, she's such a fixture that I didn't think to mention her to that detective. Not that he would have listened, anyway. He wants to believe you and Ms. Winn did it."

"Do you have Nettie's phone number and address?"

Vivian was being paged. "I'll get them off the computer later when we have a lull," she promised.

Michael pulled out a card and jotted some notes on the back. "This is my home e-mail address. And my telephone number, if you prefer to call. If I'm not there, you can leave the information on my answering machine."

She grabbed the card, stuffed it in her pocket, then drew open the door to the storage room. "Remember, we never talked."

Michael called a thank-you before she disappeared into the hall. He and Jennifer waited a couple of minutes, then let themselves out of the closet.

"We're trying to keep a low profile for Vivian's sake, I assume," Jennifer said as Michael led the way to the stairs and they climbed them to his office on the next floor.

He nodded. "Batton's already tried to make trouble for me at the hospital. If he learns she's spoken to us, I've no doubt he'll make trouble for her as well."

When they arrived at his office, Michael fetched the fake beer from his small refrigerator in the corner. He was in the process of wrapping it when he heard Jennifer read aloud the plaque on the wall behind his desk.

"'We would never learn to be brave and patient if there were only joy in the world.'"

He looked up.

"That's a quote by Helen Keller," she said.

"You sound surprised."

"I am. Considering the hallowed halls of psychiatry you frequent, I expected some erudite saying by a prestigious colleague. Why did you pick one by her?"

"She knew what she was talking about."

After writing Vivian's name on the front of the wrapped package, Michael left it at the nurse's station in the psychiatric ward with instructions that the orderly on duty take it down to the head nurse in Oncology right away.

"Have you talked to the doctor who treated Russell that night?" Jennifer asked as they headed in the direction of the hospital parking lot.

"I spoke to Dr. Field on the phone. He was apologetic but explained he was under instructions not to talk to me or anyone about the case."

"Nettie may not talk to us, either."

"Since Vivian didn't tell Batton about her, she might not have been warned away. I'll try to set up a meeting with her tomorrow after the will reading. Why did you ask Vivian if the earring was clip or pierced?"

"I don't have pierced ears. I always wear clips. Gina always wears pierced."

"Vivian said she *thought* it was a clip. She didn't sound certain. Was Russell in the habit of buying you jewelry?"

"I refused a gold bracelet at the beginning of our relationship. The only other thing he offered and I accepted was the engagement ring."

Michael checked his watch. "You must be hungry. I know a good seafood place not far from here."

"Thanks, but I have to get back to the station to prepare for my ten o'clock spot."

He said nothing more. From the moment she'd agreed to work with him, he'd made up his mind to enjoy whatever time he had with her. It wasn't going to be enough, but he would take what he could get.

JENNIFER AND MICHAEL WERE the first to arrive at the law offices for the will reading Friday morning. A receptionist asked them to wait in the conference room. Five minutes later, the members of the Sprague family entered.

Jennifer greeted them but didn't get a response. Not even from Caroline. They sat at the other end of the long table, their eyes averted. These people had welcomed her into their family a few weeks ago.

Now they were having trouble sitting in the same room with her.

She wanted to tell them that she had no intention of keeping the money. But Michael had cautioned her not to say anything about knowing what the distribution of Russell's estate would be. To do so would compromise his source at the Courage Bay Police Department.

The clock ticked to fifteen minutes past the hour before the door finally opened and the lawyer representing the estate stepped inside and introduced himself.

"Sorry, folks, but we've been waiting for the last beneficiary," he said as he took a chair in the middle of the table and dropped a folder in front of him. "Doesn't look like he's going to show."

The lawyer turned on a tape recorder and identified the document he was about to read as the last will and testament of Russell Sprague. Russell left a small houseboat to his sister, a speed-boat to his brother and his dental practice to his parents.

That struck Jennifer as odd. Russell's interest in the dental practice should be reverting to Harvey Thompson, his partner. Shouldn't it?

When the Sprague family heard that Russell's current home, in addition to his stock portfolio and any proceeds remaining from the sale of the land left to him by his grandfather, were being bequeathed to Jennifer, the looks they sent her were icy.

"And lastly, I leave a quarter million dollars cash to my son, Jamie Weslan."

"So he had to die before he'd finally do something for his kid," a female voice snarled. "Hell, if I'd known that was what it was going to take, I would have put the bastard in his grave long ago."

Jennifer whirled around to see an attractive woman in her late twenties standing in the open doorway, holding the hand of a small boy. The child's dark coloring and facial features were so like Russell's, Jennifer would have recognized him anywhere.

Except, until this moment, she never knew Russell had a son.

MICHAEL THANKED HIS ATTORNEY and friend, Ben Thayer, flipped his cell phone closed, and went over to sit beside Jennifer on the stone steps outside the law offices where they'd heard the will reading.

"The boy lives with his mother, Elissa Weslan," Michael said. "She was a dental hygienist who worked for Russell. According to Ben, Russell's been paying child support ever since the boy was born four years ago. By order of the court."

Jennifer shook her head. "Why am I surprised? He kept an affair with my best friend and a five-million-dollar inheritance from me. What's an illegitimate son?"

Her attempt at sophisticated sarcasm merely sounded sad.

"I'd like to tell you a story," Michael said.

"Is this going to be full of psychological meaning?"

"Chock-full. The day I reported to my psychiatric residency, I was greeted by a charismatic psychiatric attending who proceeded to take me on rounds of the ward. He treated every patient with warmth and respect. His diagnosis of them was so brilliant I was in awe. I wanted to be this guy. Only then the real psychiatrist attending walked in the door and introduced himself. And I learned that the man I'd been with was a psychopath who had escaped from Admissions an hour before. Jen, anyone can be taken in."

"At least you weren't ready to marry the psychopath."

"If he'd asked, I might have considered it. I tell you, the guy was charming."

She looked over at the small smile teasing Michael's lips and chuckled. In the midst of this madness, he could still make her laugh.

He took her hand and brought her to her feet. "Come on. Let's get out of here."

MICHAEL DROVE THEM to a nearby park and turned off the engine. He lowered the windows and a sweet breeze filled the car with the scent of spring flowers. As Jennifer had predicted the night before, morning clouds filtered the sun. They sat together in silence, staring out at the trees and bushes, green walls blocking out the noise of the street and the exhaust of cars.

"You relinquished your rights to Russell's inheritance?" he asked after a moment.

"You didn't hear?"

"Hard to hear anything over the Spragues' screaming match with Elissa Weslan."

"What an unbelievable name-calling fray," Jennifer said, shaking her head. "And I used to think that Harriet and Lloyd had such class. Even Caroline and Kevin looked embarrassed to hear the language coming out of their parents' mouths."

Michael's mind replayed the ugly scene that had ensued in the law office conference room after Elissa's arrival. What disturbed him most was that the enraged participants had conducted their dispute in front of the child, and that the Spragues had obviously known about Elissa and the boy all along, yet none of them had said a word to Jennifer.

"What did I miss in your conversation with the lawyer?" he asked.

"He's going to draw up the papers and courier them to me Monday," she said. "I sign them in front of a notary, send them back and it's done."

"Who will get what Russell left you?"

"I didn't ask."

And clearly, she didn't care.

"What did you think about Russell leaving his dental practice to his parents?" Michael asked.

"That's a puzzler. I could have sworn he told me that the business was a partnership with a right-of-survivorship clause."

"How long ago did he tell you that?"

"Maybe five, six months."

"Between then and when he had the will drawn up, Russell and his partner could have had a falling out."

"But wouldn't he have told me?" Jennifer let out a self-deprecating snicker. "I can't believe I just said that. I'm still acting as if I knew Russell. I have no idea who he was."

Michael was getting a very good idea, but it wasn't one he felt comfortable sharing with her.

"You'll feel better after we have something to eat," he said. "Any preferences?"

"I'd really rather not hassle with a restaurant right now."

"Then how about a picnic right here?"

He gestured toward the back seat, where a large cooler sat.

"You planned for us to have a picnic?" she said, clearly surprised.

"I didn't take your choice for granted. I also have a wig, dark glasses and a beard in the trunk."

She sent him a small smile and the day got brighter.

"Would you like to eat at one of the picnic tables?" he asked.

Jennifer followed his pointing finger to the tables on the far side of the park, accessible by way of a grassy area where a dozen people marched around in a circle with leashed dogs in what was obviously an obedience class. Her eyes returned to the car, parked under the swaying branches of a shade tree.

"The car would be better," she said.

He nodded, fetched two lap trays from the back seat along with linen napkins, and handed one each to Jennifer.

"You really thought this out," she said with appreciation.

He didn't volunteer the fact that the trays and napkins had been his mother's idea.

Opening the cooler, he brought out blini topped with smoked salmon and cream cheese. The main course was delicate finger sandwiches made with fresh greens and tender chicken. Dessert was a cup of fresh strawberries, grapes and blueberries.

"Where did you find this food?" Jennifer asked after consuming her portions with obvious relish.

"My parents own that café we went to at the beach."

"That was your *father* who made those sherbets for us? Michael, you should have told me. I thanked him so casually, like he was simply a…"

"Great sherbet maker?" Michael suggested when she faltered. "That's what impressed him most. You went out of your way to thank him *without* knowing. I dropped by their place this morning before picking you up to see what they had on hand."

"And they had this on hand," she said in wonder. "It's incredible."

The depth of his pleasure at her enjoyment of the meal was far in excess of what it should be.

"The station is always putting together affairs of one kind or another," she said. "This is so much better than what gets served. Would your parents consider sending over a sample menu?"

"Consider?" Michael said. "They'll probably offer me a commission for having mentioned their business to you. Here's the number of their café."

He pulled out one of his cards and wrote down the information for her.

The female trainer of the dog obedience class was advising the owners in a crisp, clear voice that gentle words and reward— not screams and punishment—were the secret to a loving and happy relationship with a pet.

"Too bad that trainer doesn't run a class for parents," Michael commented as he handed Jennifer his card.

"I feel terrible for Russell's son," she said, following his train of thought exactly. "What his mother and the Spragues did in front of him today was unforgivable. I've heard that who we become as adults is closely tied to what we're exposed to as children."

"You heard right," Michael said. "We emulate our parents' view of us and the world around us more deeply than we realize."

"I was so lucky to have the parents I did."

They must have been great to have produced you.

"Are you ready to meet with the hospital volunteer?" he asked.

"When is the appointment?"

"Fifteen minutes from now. Which is about the time it will take to drive to her place."

NETTIE QUINT LIVED IN a small clapboard home in an older residential section on the outskirts of town. The hospital volunteer was a cuddly woman, somewhere in her sixties, with eyes that glistened with goodwill.

"You're even prettier in person," she said, taking Jennifer's hand. "And you must be Dr. Temple. What a great-looking couple you make. Come in."

She led them to a small living room with blue and white walls and urged Jennifer onto its blue gingham couch with all the preemptory right of a favorite grandmother.

"Please tell me we're not going to have any more of that nasty night fog."

Jennifer shook her head. "Only a little light fog along the coast for the next few mornings."

"Thank heavens," Nettie said. "You'll have some iced tea?" she asked, looking hopefully at Jennifer and then Michael.

"We'd love some," Jennifer said.

Nettie scooted out of the room to get it.

"Next time I apply for a research grant, I'm definitely taking you with me," Michael said as he sat across from Jennifer on one of the two matching chairs.

"Because you need an example of a woman in desperate need of having her head examined?" she asked.

"Because I want to be accompanied by the woman whose famous and lovely face establishes an instant rapport."

His expression was playful, removing any serious compliment inherent in his words. From the moment she'd told him she wasn't interested in a repeat of their night together, whatever he felt—if he felt anything anymore—was carefully kept in check.

But his words still had the power to move her. And make her want things she couldn't have.

Nettie returned to the room carrying a tray that held a pitcher of iced tea and three glasses. After filling the glasses, she handed them out and sat next to Jennifer on the couch.

"Very good," Michael said after taking a sip.

"Would you like some cookies with it?" Nettie asked.

"No, we've had lunch, but this iced tea hits the spot," he assured her. "How long have you been a volunteer at the hospital?"

"More than a year now. Jim and I were together thirty-three years. Could have easily been fifty-three if he hadn't smoked. I begged him to quit. But he wouldn't, not even after he was diagnosed."

"Lung cancer?" Jennifer asked.

Nettie nodded. "His last month in that ward was awful. He was on a respirator and fed intravenously. Got so he couldn't even lift his hand."

She paused and shook her head, as though trying to shake away the bad memories.

"I read to him, gave him massages…anything to try to ease his suffering. I even brought in my freshly baked cookies so he could smell them. He couldn't eat them anymore, but he still loved their smell."

"When did you decide to help other patients?" Michael asked.

"It just kind of happened one night maybe a week before Jim died. He had finally fallen asleep when the man in the next bed asked me if he could have one of the cookies I'd brought. I gave him the whole plate, sat by his bed, talked to him while he ate.

The next night I gave him a back massage to help him sleep. Soon word got around and I was getting a lot of requests."

"And when your husband passed, you kept going back to help the others," Jennifer surmised.

"At first it was for those I'd gotten to know during Jim's final days. But every time I went to see them, I'd meet someone else who'd been admitted and felt lonely and scared. Many are there for surgery and chemo. A lot get better and are eventually released. But the others…the others are there to die."

Nettie's face grew sad again.

"The night is generally the worst for them," she continued after a moment. "Especially for those who can't sleep. For many, all I can do is sit beside them, be there. For others, I fulfill special requests they or their families make."

"Special requests?" Jennifer echoed.

"Back rubs or foot rubs or reading to them from a particular book. Massages are really popular. I mix up the lotions for them myself."

"Why is that?"

"The ones you buy over the counter have all these dyes and perfumes in them. Many of the patients are very sensitive to both. My lotions contain no dyes and are naturally scented. And then there are the cookies. Of course, many of the patients are so ill they can't eat. But some still can, and they really love my cookies."

"Do you keep track of what you do for the patients?" Michael asked.

Nettie nodded. "The hospital asked me to. When I arrive each night, the nurses give me the special request slips the patients have made. I record them in my schedule book. If I have time, I check with other patients to see what they might like."

"You go to a lot of trouble for them," Jennifer said.

"It's no trouble. My son lives in Sacramento and he's so busy with his job and my grandkids that I hardly see any of them. Those people in the hospital need me."

"Nettie, do you mind talking to us about last Saturday night?" Michael asked.

"Not at all," she assured him. "You said on the phone that you wanted to ask me about a patient who died?"

"Russell Sprague," Michael said. "His death made the news."

"I don't watch the news," Nettie admitted. "Too much anger in the world. Jennifer's weather reports are what I tune in to. Do you have a picture of Mr. Sprague? I never forget their faces."

Jennifer pulled a recent photo of Russell out of her purse and showed it to Nettie. After picking up a pair of prescription glasses and putting them on, Nettie gazed at the photo and nodded.

"Ah, yes," she said. "I remember him. The nurses were talking about him last night. Is it true he was murdered?"

"We believe so," Michael said. "What can you tell us about him?"

"He was new to the ward, and quite young compared to most who end up there. I felt very bad for him. I gave him a massage. What room was he in?"

"Four twenty-three," Michael said.

"Just a minute."

Nettie left the room to return with a large monthly planner. "Last Saturday," she muttered. "Room 423." She flipped the pages. "Yes, here it is. A back massage with my special peppermint lotion was requested by his brother."

"What time did you give him the massage?" Michael asked.

"I don't make a note of the times."

"Can you take a guess?"

Nettie closed the planner, set it on an end table. "Let me see if I can refresh my memory. That was the last night of our terrible fog and the bus was a half-hour late. I don't drive anymore. Too many crazy people on the roads. It was also the night the storeroom key got misplaced by the day staff, which caused a very annoying delay."

"Why is that?" Michael asked.

"The nurses let me keep my cart with all my lotions in the storeroom so I don't have to lug them back and forth on the bus. That way I can also get my night's supply of surgical gloves."

"You use surgical gloves?" Jennifer asked.

"Hospital policy. Giving my own husband a massage bare handed was one thing. But when I started to give other patients massages and hand out cookies, I was asked to wear gloves so as to avoid passing germs. What might be a simple infection for us could end up being deadly for them. I change gloves after each patient."

"So there was a delay because the key to the storeroom door had been misplaced?" Michael prodded.

"Yes. I had several books I was reading to patients locked up in there, as well as my massage supplies. All I could do for a while was hand out the cookies I'd brought and talk with the patients. Then Vivian finally had the time to hunt down the key."

"What time did she open the storeroom door?"

"Around ten-thirty."

"Did you give Russell Sprague his massage then?" he asked.

"Not right away. I first gave a foot rub to a postal clerk on the women's side of the floor. She was so excited because she was getting a bone-marrow transplant. After days of despair, she was suddenly full of hope for her recovery. When I left her room, I went to his to begin his back rub."

"Was anyone in the room with him?" Michael asked.

"The man in the other bed wasn't cognizant. Soon as I told Mr. Sprague I was there for his massage, he turned off the TV and rolled onto his stomach. No IV in his vein. No oxygen being fed into his nose. No heart monitor. What kind of cancer did he have?"

"None," Michael said. "Only a mild concussion from an accident."

"Oh." Nettie was clearly surprised. "I just assumed he was one of those cancer patients who declined invasive medical intervention. Some do, you realize. They sign DNR—Do Not Resuscitate—orders so they can simply go when it's time."

"He said nothing to you during the massage?" Jennifer asked.

"No, but after rubbing his shoulders, I felt him wince when I touched his back, so I stopped. He thanked me and I left. Afterward, I went down the hall to read a book by Henry James to this grumpy old guy who kept accusing me of mumbling because his hearing aid batteries were failing."

"Nettie, when you were with Russell Sprague, did he have any visitors?"

"Not while I was giving him his massage. But initially, when I went to his room, I saw this woman going in, which is why I gave the foot massage to the postal worker first. Later, when I went back, he was alone."

"He had a visitor in his room after hours?" Michael asked.

"She was a patient. She wore a hospital robe and was hooked up to a rolling IV stand, but she didn't come from the women's side. If she had, I would have recognized her."

"What did she look like?" Jennifer asked.

"Hmm, let's see. A tall gal with short black hair. Around your age. Oh, and she had what in my day we politely called a Rubenesque figure."

CHAPTER SEVEN

"GINA WENT TO SEE RUSSELL that night," Jennifer said to Michael after they had left Nettie's.

"Description certainly fits," Michael agreed. "Tell me about her."

"If you're asking me if I think she could have killed him, my answer is no. Of course, if you'd asked me last week if she was sleeping with him behind my back, my answer would also have been no."

"You haven't spoken to her since that night?"

Jennifer shook her head.

"But she's still calling," he guessed.

"She left a message on my voice mail this morning—said she really had to talk to me."

"Might be helpful to hear what she was doing in Russell's room that night. Feel up to it?"

Jennifer pulled the cell phone out of her purse and stared at it for a full minute before punching in a number.

Her end of the conversation was brief. She said hello, after which there was a considerable pause, an "okay," a "yes" and finally an "all right."

Ending the call, she rotated toward him. "Gina wants me to come over now. I told her I would."

"You didn't tell her I'd be with you."

"She's handed me quite a few surprises lately. Let's see how she handles you."

GINA WASN'T DISPLEASED to find Michael on her doorstep with Jennifer. And from the perfectly timed, come-hither glances she kept giving him whenever Jennifer looked away, it was not hard for him to understand why.

Michael had met women like Gina before. She was addicted to male attention, the female equivalent of the guy who had to make a play for every woman he met. By the time she'd led the way into her living room of overstuffed furniture and campy red walls, the top two buttons on her blouse had come undone.

Some women had a built-in antenna that warned them about the Ginas of this world. Jennifer clearly did not.

"Thanks for coming, Jen. I know you may never forgive me, but it's important that you know I told Russell it was over."

"It wasn't over when we were together in the ballroom that night," Jennifer said, her tone even. "Is that why you went to visit him in his hospital room later?"

Gina rubbed her right arm as a frown puckered her brow. Michael suspected it was Jennifer's question that was making her uneasy, not the discomfort from her healing wound.

"How did you know that I—"

"You were seen," Jennifer interrupted, her voice calm, not accusing.

Gina let out a curse. "Should have known he wouldn't keep his damn mouth shut," she muttered as she sank back on the couch.

Her comment confused Michael. Did Gina think that Russell had talked with Jennifer after he'd seen her?

"Tell us about that night," Michael suggested.

"Not much to tell. They pumped blood into me and something to kill the pain, and told me they were going to remove the glass stuck in my arm. Next thing I knew I was waking up in a hospital bed hours later."

"How did you get to Russell's room?"

"When I asked the nurse how he was doing, she checked and learned he was in a bed on the floor above, in good condition. I told her I wanted to see him, but she said it was too late. I'd have to wait until morning."

Gina uncrossed her legs, resting her elbows on her knees as she leaned toward Jennifer. "I couldn't wait. You saved my life that night. The paramedics told me. I knew I needed to break it off with Russell right then. I owed you that. So when nobody was looking, I took the elevator up to his floor."

"What time was that?" Michael asked.

Gina waved her hand. "I didn't look at a clock."

"How did Russell react?" he asked.

"When I walked in he grinned, made some lame joke about how we'd have to do it some other night 'cause he had a headache." Gina turned back to Jennifer. "Then he started railing at me for telling you about us. Said I'd screwed everything up and we were going to have to cool it until he won you back."

She rubbed her arm again. "When I finally got through to him that I was there to end it, he told me he didn't give a damn. Plenty more like me around. But you—hell, you were his pure virgin queen."

Irritation laced Gina's voice. Michael knew she hadn't really wanted Russell. But she had wanted him to want her.

"What do you mean 'virgin queen'?" Jennifer asked.

"He loved the fact that you wouldn't sleep with him before you two married."

"He told you about that?"

"Bragged about it. Said every other woman he'd pursued had given in within days, as though saying no to him had been some kind of important test the rest of us had failed. Boy, did he want you."

"Whatever for?" Jennifer asked, and there was a real question in her words.

"His pure little wife, of course. The woman worthy enough to share his name and have his kids and reflect the proper image to his family and friends."

"The proper image," Jennifer repeated with distaste.

"That's what it was all about for him," Gina said. "Image. You had the right one. Lily pure. Too bad he didn't live long enough to find out who you spent that night with." Her eyes strayed over to Michael. "Man, what I would have given to see the look on Russell's face when he learned about you."

"What gives you the idea that Jennifer and I spent the night together?" Michael asked.

"One of the first questions Batton asked me was about you and your relationship to Jen. How often you'd stayed over at her place. If Jen had told me you were together that Saturday night." Gina twisted toward Jennifer. "You could have filled me in on the doc here. I wouldn't have spilled it to Russell. But that detective's a real bastard. You shouldn't have told him anything you didn't want spread around."

Jennifer looked a little sick.

"Gina, did Russell ever give you any gifts?" Michael asked.

"Gifts?" Gina repeated, then laughed. "Russell thought *he* was the gift. No, I take that back. I got a gift from Russell once. I became his patient, because as Jen's friend, he assured me I was entitled to ten percent off all procedures. First time I went in, he filled a cavity, locked the door and we did it in the chair. Afterward, his office manager sent me a bill with fifteen percent off. That was my gift. An extra five percent discount. Ha."

Michael could see Jennifer shaking her head. He understood why. Russell and Gina had views on life so far removed from her own that it was impossible for her to comprehend their behavior.

"Gina, did you tell Detective Batton that you visited Russell in his hospital room that night?" Michael asked.

"Hell, no. Is Don Hardrick going to? Damn that TV reporter. He swore he'd treat me like a confidential source."

Gina's question told Michael something important. If Gina thought Hardrick might tell, it had to be because he'd seen her there. Was Hardrick the person Gina had been silently cursing before? Did she think he and Jennifer had learned about her being in Russell's room from him?

"I don't think Hardrick has volunteered that information," Michael said.

"Good, 'cause if he opens his mouth about my being there, I'm going to tell Batton that Hardrick saw Russell after I did. And when I left, Russell was still alive."

So Hardrick had been there.

"Look, Jen, I don't think you killed him, no matter what that detective implied," Gina said. "But Russell could be an insensitive bastard. So if I'm wrong, and you did it, I don't blame you. You hear me? It's okay."

"IT'S OKAY WITH HER IF I murdered him," Jennifer said after they had left Gina's. "What a friend."

Michael knew the revelations of the interview had left her newly disheartened.

"I wonder if it's possible to ever really know anyone," she said sadly.

"Maybe the important thing is that we try."

"What do you look for?"

"The way someone views the world, their style of relating to others, what their goals are, how they pursue them," Michael answered.

"And if you're still not sure?"

"Then I fall back on that surefire psychological standby and flip a coin."

She chuckled.

"Tell me about the time you and Gina met," he said.

"I was driving home after my ten o'clock broadcast when one of my rear tires went flat. As I pulled onto the shoulder, my front tire got stuck in a storm drain. It was a rainy, miserable night and nobody was stopping. My cell phone wouldn't pick up a signal in the car, so after a few minutes, I got out and walked up and down the shoulder, desperately trying to get one. All to no avail. By the time I returned to the car, I was soaking wet and freezing."

Michael wished fervently that he had been there.

"A few minutes later, I saw headlights pulling in behind me," Jennifer continued. "The next thing I knew, Gina was knocking on my car window, asking if she could help. When I lowered the window, she somehow recognized my soaked face and laughed. Said if I was going to forecast crappy weather, the least I could do was pack an umbrella. She drove me home, and I called the tow truck from there. We ended up drinking too much wine, laughing too hard and talking all night."

He remained quiet as she savored the memory.

"You're doing the same thing with Gina that you did with Russell," she said after a few quiet miles down the road. "The same thing you used to do in the seminar."

"What's that?"

"Getting me to focus on the good things. 'You never really lose anything you've been given that was good. It's always there at the touch of a memory.'"

Five years and she could quote verbatim things he'd said in that seminar.

"Do you mind if I ask you a personal question?" he said.

"How personal?"

"Why didn't you sleep with Russell?"

She was quiet for so long, he wasn't sure if she was going to tell him.

"My parents had the obligatory sex talk with me when I was a teenager," she said finally. "Each took me aside separately. My father was first. He told me that I should wait to have sex until I had met a man who cared for the real me. He said that I wouldn't fully appreciate the experience unless my partner had those feelings."

She stopped, stared out the window, reliving some memory. Michael gave her a moment before asking, "And your mother?"

"My mother told me that I should wait to have sex until *I* cared for the real me. She said that I wouldn't fully appreciate the experience unless I felt that way about myself."

"You had very wise parents," he said.

"I should have listened to them. Instead, I had my first experience in undergraduate school before I even knew who I was, with a guy who cared only about himself. Needless to say, the experience wasn't fully appreciated."

"So you decided to wait until the right feelings were in place before you tried it again."

She nodded. What she didn't say—what she didn't have to say—was that the next time, when she thought everything was right, had been with him.

God, Jenny, I wish you'd let me talk to you about Saturday night.

"I'm not surprised that Don Hardrick was in Russell's room that night," she said with an abrupt change of subject. "He's been known to sneak in to see hospital patients after visiting hours. Don was probably trying to get Russell to give him an interview."

"Without a cameraman?"

"Don has a small camera he hides in his jacket when he conducts sensitive interviews. The quality isn't great, but when it shows on the news, that just adds to the feeling the viewer gets of being in on an exclusive conversation."

"He was one of the last people to see Russell alive," Michael said.

Jennifer nodded, and from her expression, he knew that she'd been thinking the same thing.

"Tell me about him," he said.

"Dedicated. Highly competent."

When Jennifer had spoken of the news director, Liz, her voice had conveyed the warmth of their relationship. When she spoke of this newsman, her tone was cool and professional.

Michael had a feeling he knew why. "Married?"

"Divorced."

"How many times has he asked you out?"

Her head swung in his direction. "A few. How did you know?"

Jennifer, you are incredibly beautiful, smart and sweet, and any single man who didn't ask you out would have to be a fool or gay.

"Did he still pursue you after he knew you were seeing Russell and that it was serious?" Michael asked, sidestepping her question.

"When I agreed to marry Russell, Don backed off. You can't be thinking that he killed Russell."

"Hardrick might have reasoned that with Russell out of the way, he'd have a better chance with you."

Jennifer's eyes clouded. "He should be in for the six o'clock show. Most of his interviews are taped beforehand. He likes to be on the set when the anchors preview his stories in case they have questions. I'll talk to him then."

"I'd like to be there."

"You want to come to the station tonight?"

"Would that be a problem?"

She shook her head. "I should be reporting in soon."

"We're heading in that direction now."

DON WASN'T AT HIS DESK when Jennifer and Michael arrived. With a couple of hours to air time, Jennifer found that unusual. After taping a note on his phone, she led Michael to the weather center.

When she'd joined KSEA the year before, she'd personally seen to the building of the center and the installation of the essential equipment. Around the bright white walls, red fluorescent numbers glowed out of the polished chrome instruments. Three computer monitors circled her workstation. Above it was a skylight.

"To tell you if it's raining outside?" Michael asked as he nodded toward it, a grin on his face.

"When all else fails," she answered with a smile.

"What's this computer for?" he asked, pointing to one.

"Graphics. We use a technology called Chroma Key to change the maps behind me while I stand in front of the camera giving the forecast. See that odd shade of green on the blank wall out there?"

Michael nodded and glanced at the newsroom set on the other side of the weather center's thick glass panels.

"In Chroma Key, that particular color forms a hole in the background so that the maps and photos I put together on this computer can be superimposed on the hole. The viewers see the changing weather maps transmitted from the computer while the wall remains blank."

"If the wall remains blank, how do you know where to point?"

"There are monitors on both sides of the green wall. When I look at them, I can see my image on the screen and the televised weather graphics behind me."

"No wonder you always look so relaxed. You're talking to yourself."

She chuckled.

"What do you use this computer for?" he asked, gesturing toward the one directly in front of her chair.

"To download the raw figures that help me create a forecast."

"And those monitors on the wall are radar," Michael guessed.

She nodded. "That data is coming from the National Weather Service, which tracks storms and their strengths. And thanks to a nineteenth century Austrian scientist who taught us that sound waves shift to a higher frequency when they approach and to a lower frequency when they recede, the radar can also detect wind speeds and directions."

"The Doppler principle," Michael said.

"You obviously took more than psychiatry in school."

"Actually, my interest in weather only developed over the past few years. So you assemble all the data and out comes the forecast."

"Feeding the raw data into computer models and consulting the charts and radar reports are all part of the process. But when it comes right down to it, any prediction of the future involves some intuition."

"What's your intuition telling you now?" he asked.

"That if I don't get to work, I won't have much to say when the camera rolls my way in a couple of hours."

MICHAEL STEPPED OUT OF the weather center and helped himself to one of the cups of coffee sitting on the table for the staff.

Station members scurried back and forth with preparations for the upcoming broadcast. He tuned out their frantic activity and ever-increasing noise as he watched Jennifer behind the glass of her workstation.

She was something to watch. There was a hushed quality to her concentration, as though she were in tune with another world. Her lovely gray eyes shone with the intensity of her focus as they went from one computer screen to another. The afternoon sun spilled through the skylight, tumbled in her hair.

"Few men don't stare," a female voice said from behind him.

He turned and found himself looking at a quietly attractive woman in her forties wearing a dark suit and a guarded expression.

"The ratings shot up within two weeks of my putting her on," the woman told him as she pointed toward Jennifer. "But the outside consultant we hired said it wasn't only because of her beautiful face. She's believable and she gets it right. And that's what it's really all about around here. I'm Liz Otley, the news director, Dr. Temple."

Michael was wearing a Visitor tag on his jacket, but Jennifer had not given out his name to anyone. He sent Liz a questioning look.

"Detective Batton has made sure that you are well known to Jennifer's friends and associates," she responded. "I've just come out of a meeting with the station manager about the two of you. Let's talk in my office."

Michael followed her down the hall. She closed the door after them and sat in a guest chair across from him, instead of behind her desk.

He understood that she'd done so because she wanted to keep this friendly. That she made the gesture also told him that what she was about to say wasn't going to be especially friendly.

"I've been holding back on reporting Jennifer's relationship to Russell. I've been told I can't do that any longer."

"By the station manager?" Michael guessed.

"He's right. The newspapers have already printed it. And as much as we'd like to think that the people of Courage Bay get their news from us exclusively, the e-mails and telephone calls that have been coming in over the past couple of days tell us otherwise. If we don't get something on the air right away, viewers are going to wonder what we're hiding. What Jennifer's hiding."

"Is there some reason you're telling me this and not her?" Michael asked.

"She'll be hearing it from me as soon as she gets her forecast together. Don Hardrick will be doing a live interview with her as part of tonight's news update on the story. I'm telling you because I don't think you should be seen with her anymore."

"Where exactly have we been seen?"

"A bar. A restaurant. The beach. The funeral. The will read-ing. A park."

"You have someone following Jennifer?"

"Hardrick is on the story and he takes his assignments seri-ously. He's not the only one. Batton is doing everything he can to find evidence against you two. And every time Jennifer is seen anywhere, someone ends up calling us to ask who she was with and why. Most people in Courage Bay know her face on sight. And they've been seeing it with yours a lot."

"What bothers you about her being seen with me?" he asked.

"Tonight we're going public with the fact that she's grieving a dead fiancé. She's not going to come across as too credible if she's being romanced by a good-looking doctor."

As much as Liz's message disturbed Michael, there was a blunt honesty about this woman that he begrudgingly admired.

"Just for the record," he said, "I'm not romancing Jennifer. We're trying to find out who murdered her fiancé."

"Aren't you in enough hot water with the hospital adminis-tration for spending the night with her?" Liz asked.

"You seem to possess a lot of information that hasn't made it onto the air."

"That part won't. At least not at this station. Look, if Hardrick can find out all this stuff, you can bet the newspaper reporter who's been sniffing around will as well."

"Are you aware that Hardrick was at the hospital that night?" Michael asked. "In Sprague's room just before he died?"

"Of course. We couldn't get ahold of Jennifer. After he inter-viewed the orderly and found out about the ice-water incident, he went to see Russell. Don't go imagining that there's some-thing sinister about his having been there. He's a newsman."

"What did Russell tell him?"

"To get out, that he wasn't feeling well. Hardrick got him on tape, all thirty seconds. It was a nothing footage."

"I'd like to see it," Michael said.

"Well, you're not going to. I have no intention of encourag-ing you to play private eye with my meteorologist. You may not care about your career, but I care about hers. She's going to need to keep a very low profile outside of this studio until this damn thing blows over."

"And if it doesn't blow over?" he asked.

"Batton's no dummy. Sooner or later he's going to realize that Jen isn't a killer. When he does, I'd like her to still be our meteorologist. Please, if you care about her, back off."

MICHAEL WATCHED behind the cameras as Hardrick interviewed Jennifer. She sat between the newsman and Frank Keller, the manager of the Grand Hotel.

Liz had put them on the morning show set, with softer lighting, cushioned chairs—a more informal space than that of the nightly news.

"She ran to be by his side through the rubble, falling plaster, the live wires, heedless of the danger to herself," Keller told Hardrick in a voice full of admiration.

Bringing the hotel manager in as part of the interview had been smart. While Keller told Hardrick of Jennifer's heroism, the camera focused on her embarrassed face.

When Hardrick asked her why she hadn't allowed herself to be interviewed before this, she answered that sharing the loss of her fiancé was not something she did easily, not even with the viewers of KSEA.

Everything she said came across as straightforward and honest. Because it was. Michael knew Liz had been right to put Jennifer in front of the cameras.

After the six o'clock segment ended, Jennifer got on the telephone, calling in her forecast to the disc jockey at the local radio station. Michael took the opportunity to seek out Hardrick in his office. He stepped inside and closed the door.

Hardrick sat back in his chair and stared at him, not saying a word. He wore the expression of a man who knew he didn't have to. In his profession—as in psychiatry—the trick was to get others to do the talking.

"I know a very good private investigator," Michael said. "He's going to be following you for the next few weeks. He'll have a video camera with him so he'll be getting everything on tape. The sensitive equipment he uses can pick up images and voices from a hundred feet away." Turning, Michael headed toward the door.

"What in the hell is this all about, Temple?"

He faced the newsman. "I want you to know what it feels like."

Hardrick's mouth drew tight. "I'm only doing my job."

"Do you believe Jennifer killed Russell?"

"No."

"Then what part of your job requires you to follow her?"

Hardrick had no answer. Michael once again turned to go.

"Wait," Hardrick said.

Michael waited.

"Call off your P.I. I won't be following her anymore."

"I ASKED DON ABOUT Saturday night when he was prepping me for the interview," Jennifer said as they drove away from the station. "It seemed the right opportunity."

"What did he say?" Michael asked.

"He admitted running into Gina coming out of Russell's room at the hospital. Claimed he hadn't told me because he didn't want to rub a sore wound. Don said Russell seemed upset and they only exchanged a few words."

"Liz mentioned Hardrick's conversation with Russell had been brief," Michael said. "She also told me that she doesn't think it's a good idea for you to be seen with me anymore."

"I know. She informed me."

Michael glanced over at Jennifer. "I can continue investigating things and call you with what I find."

"No, you can't. Liz means well, but she doesn't know me if she thinks I'd stop seeing you simply because some viewers might misunderstand or think it doesn't fit an image I'm supposed to be projecting. We're doing nothing wrong. If who I am isn't good enough for the station, they can get another meteorologist."

Jennifer had always had a mind of her own and a surprising strength.

"Besides, I'm the one who knows the people in Russell's life," she said. "And, as you pointed out, it's the people who are closest to a victim who are the most likely suspects in a murder case."

Michael was relieved she'd decided to keep working with him. Pursuing leads on his own would have been more difficult. But the real reason for his relief was that he could continue to be with her.

He had no expectations. He couldn't afford to have them. But every hour they spent together made him feel more alive than he had in years.

"So, who do we look at next?" she asked.

"How about Russell's partner at the dental practice?" Michael said. "Will he see you?"

"Harvey's always been friendly. Of course, that might have changed. I'll give him a call when I get home. Are you free tomorrow?"

"I have a few patients to look in on in the morning. Afternoon would be best."

"When are you supposed to appear in front of the ethics committee?"

"Next week."

"Michael, if your being seen with me is causing problems for you, then maybe we should—"

"I'm not going to stop seeing you simply because some review board might misunderstand or think it doesn't fit an image I'm supposed to be projecting. We're doing nothing wrong. If who I am isn't good enough for the hospital, they can get another psychiatrist."

Her smile was wide. "You used my words."

"They were great words."

"Thanks," she said.

"For what?"

"For being you."

Out of all of the compliments she could have given him, that was the best.

SATURDAY MORNING Jennifer made a trip to the café owned by Michael's parents. She told herself she was doing it because she wanted to collect a sample menu to show Liz.

But she knew that she could have called and asked them to send one to the station.

Every table at Seacrest was filled with people enjoying breakfast and a view of a huge white passenger ship gliding by the bay. She walked up to the cash register and asked the clerk if the owners were around.

"He's cooking but she's upstairs, Ms. Winn. I'll call to let her know you're here."

Jennifer hadn't given the clerk her name. But being recognized on sight was something that no longer surprised her.

Less than a minute after the clerk had hung up the phone, a nice looking middle-aged woman emerged from a side door to greet her.

"Jennifer Winn," the woman said, a welcoming smile on her face. "I'm Alice Temple. What a pleasure it is to meet you."

She had Michael's rich brown hair and blue eyes. But whereas he was several inches over six feet and broad shouldered, Alice was slender and only a couple of inches taller than Jennifer's five foot five.

"Do you like Jennifer or Jen?"

"My friends call me Jen."

"Then Jen it is," Alice said warmly. "Let's get you upstairs to the office before the customers recognize you. Michael made me promise that if you were ever to come by, I was not to flaunt you."

Alice whisked her through the side door and up the stairs to an airy room with floor-to-ceiling windows facing the sea.

"Coffee?" she asked as Jennifer sat on a chair covered in mint-green cotton.

Jennifer had been inhaling the heavenly smell of a freshly brewed pot since the moment she'd stepped into the room.

"Love some with a little milk if you have it."

"Coming right up."

Alice filled two cups, poured in some milk she got from a

small refrigerator in a half-moon kitchen adjacent to the office area. She handed Jennifer one of the cups.

"This is wonderful," Jennifer said after taking a sip.

Alice took the chair across from her. "Tom, Michael's father, is our cook. But the coffee is my specialty. I grind the beans fresh and put in a pinch of chocolate and raspberry. I'll send you a bag from the next batch I make."

"I couldn't ask you to do that."

"Jen, I want to do it. When Michael called the other day and told me he needed something special for a picnic, I admit I was pretty surprised. He's never done anything like that before."

So, he hadn't just dropped by to see what his parents had on hand?

"When he called back afterward to tell me you were the one who had shared the food with him, I nearly fainted. Then Tom tells me he made strawberry sherbets for you and Michael the other day that you ate up on our balcony. Like it was nothing! Men!"

"There's no explaining them," Jennifer agreed with a smile.

"Was the picnic the other day okay?" Alice asked.

"The picnic the other day was so okay it's why I'm here. Do you have a menu that I could show the people back at the station?"

Alice set her coffee down, then went to her desk and drew out several sheets of paper from the middle drawer. She handed them to Jennifer and sat down again.

"Those are sample menus of parties that we've catered, and a regular menu of what we serve downstairs. Plus which, we're happy to follow any favorite recipe we're given for a special occasion. Or I should say Tom is. Coffee is the extent of my culinary talents."

Jennifer glanced at the dishes listed on the first page. Just reading their descriptions made her mouth water. "Thank you so much for these," she said as she opened her shoulder bag and folded them inside.

"Pick out a few that look good to you, give me a call and I'll send over samples for you and your co-workers to taste."

"You're a smart businesswoman," Jennifer said. "One taste was all I needed."

"Tom and I would be happy to add KSEA to our list of clients. But whether we do or not doesn't really matter. What's important is that you're here. Ever since that detective came to see us, I've been—"

"Detective Batton came here?" Jennifer interrupted, unable to hold back her distress. "What did he want?"

"His stated purpose was to ask us about Michael's wife. What he really wanted was to make crude insinuations about you and Michael."

Jennifer suddenly found herself staring at her coffee.

Alice's hand covered hers. "It's that fool of a detective who should be embarrassed, Jen. Please, you've no reason to feel uneasy with me."

She met Alice's eyes. "You're very nice."

"That's how Michael described you when I called to tell him about the detective," Alice said as she drew her hand away and leaned back in her chair.

"Michael didn't say a word about Batton having come to see you."

"Probably didn't want to worry you. Don't let it, Jen. Tom and I know our son. Do you mind if I ask when it was that you two met?"

"I was a student at a seminar he gave five years ago."

She nodded as she picked up her cup, took a sip of coffee. "The ones he used to do at the local college, then stopped so abruptly. But you haven't been in touch all this time?"

"No, we only ran into each other again a week ago at the hospital."

"Yes, I thought it must be something like that. He's been different this past week. Even his voice sounds different, especially when he talks about you."

Surprised, Jennifer asked, "Different in what way?"

"In the way a man talks about a woman he's interested in," Alice said very matter-of-factly.

Her candor caught Jennifer completely off guard. She took a deep breath, then slowly let it out, trying to regain her equilibrium.

Alice leaned toward her. "Jen, I'm not sure you understand what's happening here. Michael makes friends easily. With men. But he hasn't had any women friends in a very long time. By choice. Until now. Until you."

Everything Jennifer wanted to hear—if Michael had been free. But Michael wasn't free. Michael would never be free.

"I've read chapter nineteen of his book," she made herself say. "I know he's committed to his wife. His love for her is in every word he wrote."

"So it is," Alice agreed. "Have you met her?"

"No."

"I think you should, Jen."

"Why?"

"For the same reason you came to see me today. You want to know more about Michael. Meeting Lucy will tell you a great deal."

Jennifer studied the intelligent eyes before her. She'd been foolish to try to pretend this visit was something other than what it was.

Setting down her coffee cup, she rose. "Thank you for seeing me, Alice. Someone from the station will call about the menu samples."

"I've upset you," Alice said, her face and voice flashing distress.

"No, you mustn't think that," Jennifer said hurriedly. "You've been gracious and very kind. But I shouldn't have come. Please, don't tell Michael I was here."

She made her way to the door and let herself out.

CHAPTER EIGHT

ED WAS WAITING in the parking lot when Michael exited the hospital late Saturday morning. He motioned him into the passenger seat of his unmarked police car.

"I overheard Batton talking to Adam Guthrie, our chief of detectives, about the case," Ed said. "Batton's less than a happy camper ever since Sprague's attorney told him Jennifer is refusing to accept her inheritance from the estate."

"Any chance Batton's rethinking his suspects?" Michael asked.

"Afraid not. He's still got you and Jennifer pegged as the ones who did the deed. In his defense, he's normally not so far off base. He has a solid reputation for closing cases and giving the D.A. what he needs to convict. He's even getting the Investigator of the Year award. Could be personal stuff getting to him."

"What personal stuff?"

"Batton's long-time partner resigned from the force six months ago due to illness. He died this week. The two were tight."

Michael understood what that kind of grief could do. It wasn't unusual for someone's judgment to be less than top-notch at such a time.

"Have you been able to get a lead on anyone who could be responsible for Sprague's murder?" Ed asked.

Michael told him about Gina and Hardrick having been in Russell's room a short time before he was found dead.

"Finding out how he was murdered would be a big help," Michael said. "Is there any way you can get a look at the autopsy report?"

"Doubt it. Batton hadn't even shown it to Chaska when I cornered him in the bar the other night."

"His own partner doesn't know how Sprague was murdered?"

"Yeah, I know it sounds loony. But Batton told Guthrie he didn't want a new partner when he lost his. Chief told him that was too bad because he was getting one. Batton's pushed away two other guys Guthrie tried to team him with before Chaska."

"And now he's continuing the pattern by not treating Chaska like a partner."

"More like an errand boy. Look, Michael, I'll continue to keep my eyes and ears open, but I can't do much else. Stepping uninvited into a case being run by another detective, especially one as well regarded as Batton—it just isn't done."

Michael understood. He thanked Ed for his help and headed for his car to go meet Jennifer.

He had no doubt in his mind that it was up to the two of them to find the party responsible for Russell's death. Even if they weren't arrested, unless the real murderer was unmasked, they'd be living with unrelenting suspicion over their heads for the rest of their lives.

DORIE ANSWERED THE BELL at Harvey's house Saturday afternoon and escorted Michael and Jennifer to the backyard. When Jennifer had called the evening before, Dorie had answered the phone. She'd not only said she and Harvey would be happy to see them, but invited them over for lunch.

Harvey waved at Michael and Jennifer from his position at the barbecue grill. Michael could detect nothing but a friendly hospitality in the couple.

"We saw your interview on TV," Dorie said to Jennifer as she served the hamburgers Harvey had grilled. "I didn't realize you'd put yourself at risk when you went to Russell and Gina's aid after the airplane crash. I don't think Russell knew, either. He never said a word when we went to see him that night. Potato salad?"

As she filled Jennifer's plate, Dorie called in the direction of the grill, "Hurry up with that last burger, hon. We're ready to eat here."

Harvey nodded, expertly flipping the meat onto a bun. He joined them at the picnic table.

They seemed a mismatched pair. Dorie was quite talkative; Harvey had yet to say a word. But when they looked at each other, Michael saw the affection in their eyes.

"We were going to talk to you after the funeral services," Dorie said, "but we got waylaid by some patients inside the chapel, and by the time we came out, you were gone. All this crazy talk about you and Dr. Temple being responsible for Russell's death must be driving you wild."

"Who told you about it?" Jennifer asked.

"Well, that detective didn't actually say the words, but when he questioned us the second time, it was pretty obvious."

"And the first time?" Michael asked.

"The first time he acted like Harv and I had done it. But we'd announced our engagement to my folks that night. They'd called in all my relatives for an impromptu party, so we had lots of people to alibi us."

"You're engaged," Jennifer said. "That's great."

Dorie returned Jennifer's smile. "We're shopping for the ring tomorrow. We would have gotten it sooner, but Russell's death has sort of put a pall on things. As if I have to tell you. How you holding up?"

"Okay," Jennifer said.

"I told Harv you weren't the kind to fall apart. Didn't I, Harv?" Harvey's mouth was full of food. He let a nod suffice.

"So, you went to see Russell that night?" Michael prompted.

"After Caroline called and told us what had happened, we drove to the hospital," Dorie confirmed. "He seemed okay, so we returned to the engagement party, which went on until one in the morning. I still don't know how Russell was supposed to have been murdered. Do you?"

"No," Michael said. "When you and Harvey saw him in the hospital, did you notice anything unusual?"

"He didn't look bad. And other than complaining of a slight headache and a little tenderness in his back, he said he felt fine."

"When did you leave?" Michael asked.

"Around nine-thirty, I guess." Dorie looked over at Harvey. "That right, hon?"

Harvey's response was another nod.

"Kevin had gotten a ride with Caroline and he was antsy to go," Dorie continued. "Said he'd been playing poker and was on a winning streak. They left a few minutes before us."

"Why didn't Kevin drive to the hospital himself?" Michael inquired.

"Kevin doesn't drive anymore. His distance vision or something is out of whack. Anyway, Caroline said an important customer was in for emergency treatment at her salon and she had to be on her way as well."

Dorie turned to Jennifer. "You didn't go up to the hospital room to see Russell that night, did you?"

She shook her head.

"Because of Gina," Dorie said. It wasn't a question.

"Did Russell say something about her?" Jennifer asked.

"No, but the detective asked us if we knew about Russell's affair with Gina and your dumping ice water on him that night, so it wasn't hard to put two and two together."

It sounded to Michael as if Batton disseminated more information than he gathered.

"How long had you known about Russell and Gina?" Jennifer asked.

"Since the first day she came in for an appointment," Dorie said. "She reeked of perfume and her skirt was up to her thighs. She couldn't have been any more obvious if she'd worn a T-shirt with Slut printed on it. I told Harv that Russell was an idiot to be fooling around with her. Didn't I, hon?"

Harvey just nodded.

"I wanted to say something to you," Dorie continued, "but I knew Russell would have killed me if I did. Harv and I have known Russell since we all met in college. He was no choirboy. When a female like Gina offered, he took."

"Like Gina?" Michael repeated.

"A looker. That's not to say he didn't go slumming with some-one like me every so often, but most of the time he stuck to the model class."

"You had a relationship with him?" Michael asked gently.

Dorie nodded. "My Harv knows all about it. We don't have secrets from each other. He tried to warn me about Russell, but I wouldn't listen. Not even seeing Russell with other women de-terred me. I thought he'd eventually fall in love with me and want to get married. Took a couple of years before I finally wised up."

"And you stayed on as his office manager?" Jennifer asked.

"If I'd been working for him alone, I would have left. But I was working for Harv, too. As long as they were in partnership together, I was going to stay."

"About that partnership," Jennifer said. "At the will reading yesterday, Russell left his interest in the dental practice to his par-ents. How can that be?"

"It can't," Dorie said. "The partnership is still in effect, and when his lawyer checks, he's going to find that out. Harv has sur-vivorship rights. It all goes to him."

"But Russell was trying to dissolve the partnership?" Mi-chael asked.

Dorie looked over at Harvey, then back at Michael. "He talked about it."

"Why?" Jennifer asked. "He told me you were doing very well."

"We are. But lately he'd begun complaining that he was bring-ing in all the clients. That Harv was getting a free ride. Which was a laugh. Harv is the real dentist. Russell's skills were medi-ocre at best."

Dorie shifted uncomfortably in her seat. "Sure, he had the contacts, could charm people into making the initial appoint-ment. And he was good at the chitchat when they were in the chair. But it was Harv's skill that kept them coming back. He's the gifted one. Even patients getting a root canal have walked out telling me they didn't feel a thing. Make an appointment with us, Jen, and you'll see. You'll tell your friends."

Michael had a feeling that this might be the reason Dorie had been so welcoming to them today. She was already looking to the future and how to drum up business for the dental practice.

"How did Russell propose ending the partnership?" Michael asked.

"He was going to use an inheritance he'd gotten from his grandfather to buy Harv out. There's a clause in the partnership agreement that allowed either partner to do that."

"But the buyout didn't go through," Jennifer guessed.

"The papers were drawn up, but the appraiser hadn't come back with the value on the practice. As soon as he did and the check was drawn, Harv would have been out the door. Russell tried to talk me into staying. Suggested we could resume our relationship, like that would be some kind of inducement for me. I told him to go to hell."

"Doesn't sound like you're mourning him," Michael said.

"I'm not glad he's dead," Dorie said quickly. "I wish he'd lived to see how well Harv and I are going to do without him. Harv had been his good friend for fifteen years, and Russ was ready to throw him aside. You know what he said? He said don't take it personally, Harv. It's just business."

Dorie's face was full of anger.

"Can you think of anyone who might have wanted to kill him?" Jennifer asked.

"You mean outside of me?" Dorie asked. "Yeah. Elissa Weslan. He tell you about her?"

Jennifer shook her head.

"Doesn't surprise me. Russell could be secretive about stuff that didn't fit the image he wanted to project to the world. You know she had a kid by him?"

"She brought the boy to the will reading," Jennifer said. "How long have you known about her and the child?"

"I've been Russell's office manager for more than ten years. Not a whole lot I didn't know about his affairs. He hired Elissa to be our dental hygienist. Her only real qualifications were her measurements. As soon as Russell found out she was knocked up, he fired her. She had to drag his butt into court to get him to submit to a paternity test, and when it came back positive, to force him to cough up child support."

"I understand that was four years ago," Jennifer said.

"But it was only two weeks ago that she came stomping into the office, ranting and raving at him in front of the clients that he'd been hiding his grandfather's inheritance from her. She told him that he'd better come up with more child support and fast or he'd find himself back in court."

"How did Russell react?" Michael asked.

"He got really upset, told her to get out of his place of business or he'd call the cops. She warned him that if he did, she'd make him sorry. *Really* sorry. Elissa hated his guts. No doubt in my mind that she murdered him."

"YOU THINK DORIE COULD BE right about Elissa?" Jennifer asked Michael after they'd left the house.

"My contact in the Courage Bay Police Department said all the other possible suspects had alibis that checked out. Still, I doubt Batton knows that Gina visited Russell before he died. And Hardrick. Could be the detective's missed a few things about Elissa, as well. Be a good idea to talk to her."

"I can't imagine why she'd want to talk to me."

"You could always tell her that you've spoken to the lawyer about relinquishing your bequests from Russell's estate to his other beneficiaries."

Jennifer nodded. "So she'll want to try to convince me to give it all to her son. You're not bad at this psychology stuff."

He returned her grin. "My lawyer friend, Ben, got her phone number when he looked up the court records. Want to give her a call?"

Jennifer reached for her cell phone. "Let's see if we can talk to her away from her son. She may not care what she says in front of him, but I do."

Talking to Elissa without her son around didn't prove to be a problem. As she explained to Jennifer over the phone, Saturday was bowling night, and her mother would be taking care of her child.

Jennifer agreed they'd meet her at the bowling alley at ten.

"Why don't I pick you up and we can drive there together?" Michael suggested once Jennifer had ended the call.

"My place is out of your way. Besides, after we see her, I want to swing by one of those all-night grocery stores before I head home. Late nights are always the best time to shop. Very few people around."

He didn't like the idea of her shopping alone late at night. It was on the tip of his tongue to say that it wasn't safe, and suggest they do their grocery shopping together after seeing Elissa, when he realized how that was going to sound.

As though she couldn't take care of herself. As though he had a right to. He didn't. But his feelings for her made him wish he did.

WHEN MICHAEL MET JENNIFER in the parking lot at the bowling alley Saturday night, he noted the tournament banner flying over the entrance. Inside, the place was packed.

They located Elissa at lane three. She came over to the railing that separated players from spectators. "My team's in the finals," she said proudly as she waved the drink in her hand.

"Would you prefer we wait to talk to you until after the tournament is over?" Jennifer asked.

"I can talk between bowls. Besides, after it's over, my group's going out to get blasted."

Yells and howls erupted at the lanes as someone scored a strike. Elissa twirled around to see who it was and let out a curse. Obviously it hadn't been someone on her team.

"When did you beat out the competition in the semifinals?" Michael asked.

She took a sip of her drink. "Last Saturday night. You should have been here. We creamed them."

"The same night Russell died?"

"Yeah, thankfully. That damn detective pulled me away from a teeth cleaning on Monday—acted like he was ready to slap the cuffs on my wrists and cart me off to jail for the bastard's murder. He finally backed off after checking with the eight people I'd been partying with until after midnight."

"Hey, you're up!" one of her teammates called.

Elissa left them to take her turn bowling.

"Looks like she has an alibi," Jennifer said to Michael.

"Getting eight people to lie for you when it's a case of murder would be some trick," he agreed.

Out of the corner of his eye, Michael had been watching a man who'd been chugging a drink as he stared at Jennifer. The guy made his way over to them.

"You're the girl who does the TV weather," he said.

The guy had bloodshot eyes and smelled strongly of alcohol. He was leering as he looked Jennifer up and down.

"You have my wife confused with someone else," Michael said, stepping between him and Jennifer.

Michael was substantially taller and broader and made a point of emphasizing both. The guy mumbled something that could have been an apology or a curse and staggered off.

"Since you didn't have any ice water handy," Michael said as he faced Jennifer, "I thought it would be a good idea for me to handle him."

She said nothing, but her smile felt nice.

"Ben tells me there are no Sprague wills on file in the probate court," Michael said.

"Is that significant?"

"It means that Russell's grandfather must have left the money and land to him through a trust. Trusts pass to beneficiaries without having to go through probate. That keeps them out of the public records."

"But if it wasn't in the public record, how did Elissa learn about Russell's legacy from his grandfather?"

"Exactly the question I've been asking myself," Michael said. "I doubt Dorie would have told her. I didn't get the feeling they'd been friends."

"My guess is that she's kept in touch with someone in the Sprague family. Her shouting match with Lloyd and Harriet leaves them out. Considering Caroline's devotion to her brother, I don't think she'd be the one. Which just leaves—"

"Kevin," Jennifer said. "He made a move on me while I was going out with his brother. I wouldn't put it past him to have made a play for Elissa. I wonder how serious it is between them?"

Michael was watching Elissa flirt with one of her co-bowlers.

"She was probably in it for what she could learn about Russell during the pillow talk," he said. "And the way Kevin was checking out Gina on the steps of the chapel, I doubt if it was any more than convenience for him."

Elissa bowled a spare and was in high spirits when she came back to talk to them.

"So, this thing about the land and money Russell left you," she said, addressing Jennifer. "You really going to give it up?"

"Yes," Jennifer replied.

"His son should get it," Elissa said. "What would his parents or siblings do with more money? They're already choking on the stuff."

"You make a good point," she agreed. "Why did Russell give you such a hard time about acknowledging his son and providing for him?"

Elissa's look was sharp. "Were you in love with him?"

Jennifer met her eyes. "No."

"Well, I thought I was. He cured that real quick. We always used protection, but I still got pregnant. He wouldn't believe it was his. When the paternity test came back, he ranted about how I must've poked holes in the condoms to trap him. Said this in court in front of my family and his, like I was some kind of scheming whore."

Elissa paused to knock back the remainder of her drink. She stared at the glass, her voice as cold and hard as the remaining ice cubes. "I promised myself right then that I was going to make the bastard pay. And I did. Just not enough."

"IF SHE DIDN'T HAVE an alibi, she'd be my pick," Jennifer said after they'd exited the bowling alley and were standing by their cars in the parking lot. "What Russell did to her is the kind of stuff women commit murder over."

A group of loud, boisterous men came banging out of the bowling alley doors. As they passed, Michael shifted positions until he was leaning against the bumper of Jennifer's car, blocking their view of her.

It was a protective gesture, like when he had stepped between her and the drunk who had approached her inside. Like when he had asked her to dance to keep the obnoxious Hugo away when they were at the Courage Bay Bar and Grill.

Jennifer told herself that Michael would do the same for any woman he was with. But he had no idea how cherished she felt when he behaved that way toward her—or what it had done to her when he'd called her his wife.

"Were you with Russell when he bought your engagement ring?" Michael asked after the men were gone.

"No, he presented it to me over a candlelit dinner when he first asked me to marry him. And every time he brought up the subject after that until I said yes. Why?"

"I'm curious what jeweler it came from."

"I have the box at home. I'm sure the jeweler's name is on it. Why are you interested?"

"Russell may have bought the earrings and engagement ring from the same jeweler."

"I see. You're thinking that if we ask the jeweler, we might be able to find out who the earrings were for. I'll check the name on the box and give you a call as soon as I get home. On second thought, I'd better not. It'll be late."

"I'll be up."

"Might be as late as one."

"Not a problem. Tomorrow isn't an early day for me."

There was something seductive about the thought of lying in bed talking to him late at night on the telephone. Too seductive. She pushed it out of her mind.

"I don't have your number," she said.

He pulled out a business card, wrote the number on the back. When he handed it to her, their fingers brushed.

"Be better if I called you tomorrow," she said, looking at the card, not at him.

"I'm going to see my wife tomorrow."

His wife. Just the serious dose of reality she needed about now. Her eyes slowly rose to meet his. "You see her every Sunday?"

"Yes."

"May I go with you?"

Jennifer had never seen surprise on Michael's face before. It gave him a different look, an endearingly vulnerable one.

"You want to go with me," he said when he finally found his voice. "Why?"

"You want to know about Michael," his mother had said. *"Meeting Lucy will tell you a great deal."*

"I'd like to meet her," Jennifer said. "May I?"

His calm veneer was back, but she sensed his struggle with some new emotion. "It'll be a long drive. A long day. Are you sure?"

"Yes."

"I'll pick you up at ten-thirty."

THE MENTAL CARE FACILITY where Michael took Jennifer was east of Courage Bay, a two-hour drive that ended in the mountains.

It was not what Jennifer had pictured when she thought of an institution. Instead of walls, it was surrounded by gardens. The building was in the Italian Renaissance style, with upper-story pilasters, and balustrades on the side porches.

As they walked up the front steps, Jennifer spied a man standing on one of the porches. He looked to be in his twenties, wore nothing but a T-shirt and diaper, and stared out at the trees with a blank, lifeless expression.

She wondered if she were really ready for this. Of all the horrors her imagination could devise, losing her mind ranked number one. How was she going to react when she came face-to-face with a woman who had?

The clerk at the front desk greeted Michael by name and told him that Lucy was in her favorite garden. Jennifer silently followed as he led the way.

They found her sitting on a bench, a crayon in one hand, a drawing pad in the other. An older man with that indefinable air of a doctor sat beside her, watching what she drew.

Lucy wore a pink top and black slacks over her petite frame, her hair a golden-blond halo around her head. As they approached, Jennifer caught sight of large eyes as innocent a blue as the spring sky. Michael had written a lot about his wife's emotional beauty in his book, but nothing about her physical features.

Lucy Temple was lovely.

"Michael!" she said in obvious glee as she jumped to her feet.

He wrapped his arms around her waist, picked her up and spun her in a circle. She squealed with delight, just as any four-year-old might.

For mentally, that's all Lucy was—would ever be—despite the fact that she was in the body of a thirty-five-year-old woman.

Jennifer watched the happiness that infused both their faces as the whirling continued. Trust. Love. Even from a distance, she could see that despite Lucy's tragedy, the bond between her and Michael was solid.

So this was what a dose of reality felt like.

"Hello, I'm Preston Zahn," said a voice close by.

Jennifer swerved to see that the man who'd been sitting on the bench next to Lucy had risen.

"Jennifer Winn."

"You don't have to tell me. I watch and enjoy your weather reports all the time."

She thanked him with a smile. "Preston Zahn sounds very familiar. Aren't you the doctor who wrote the foreword in Michael's book?"

"One of the benefits and curses of having an unusual name is to be remembered," he said. A hint of speculation crept into his eyes. "You're rather a surprise. Michael never said a word about knowing you."

"Are you Lucy's doctor?"

"Her primary one, yes. I'm also the director of this long-term-care facility. All of the patients Michael wrote about in his book live in this residence."

"I didn't know he'd worked here."

"When I was still teaching, Michael was one of my brightest students, arguably the brightest. He gathered the data from patients in this residence for his doctoral thesis. After Lucy had her accident, he came back. Have you known each other long?"

"Not very."

"He must really like what he knows to bring you here. You're the only nonfamily member who has visited. He's very particular about who Lucy meets."

Michael approached then, Lucy at his side. She walked with a slight limp and her coordination seemed to require a concentrated effort. But otherwise, she appeared to be physically normal. He introduced Jennifer to her as simply his friend Jen.

Lucy's face lit up with a lovely smile. "Michael's friend Jen," she said, and opened her arms to wrap Jennifer in them.

There were all kinds of hugs. Wimpy hello hugs. Rib-cracking hugs. Tender hugs. And then there was Lucy's hug—full and exuberant and heartfelt. Jennifer returned it because it was impossible not to.

"Come, Jen," Lucy said, taking her hand and leading her toward a centuries-old blue oak tree in the center of the garden.

Jennifer looked around to get Michael's reaction, but he had turned and was in a conversation with Dr. Zahn. She told herself that if they were unconcerned with Lucy kidnapping her, she probably didn't have anything to worry about.

Lucy beckoned Jennifer to sit beside her on a wooden bench beneath the shade of the ancient tree. Thick milkweed plants surrounded them, the fragrant, globe-shaped flower clusters a lovely deep pink.

Leaning her head back, Lucy pointed upward. "See?"

Jennifer tried to locate what Lucy was pointing at, but all she noticed were the sun's rays dancing across the leaves of the magnificent blue oak. Then it dawned on her—that was what Lucy wanted her to see. The beauty of the light.

She recalled one of Michael's descriptions from chapter nineteen.

Lucy takes full joy in the dawn of every new day. She is able to accept and embrace life as it is. And because she does, she lives with an intense awareness of the miracle of each moment. Maybe we could all use a little of this kind of brain damage.

Jennifer sat still and simply let herself enjoy the light.

Something wiggly dropped onto her shoulder. Flinching in revulsion, she raised her hand to flick it off. Before she could, Lucy clasped her wrist.

"Please, don't hurt."

Lucy's hold was steady, but gentle. Jennifer lowered her hand.

Releasing Jennifer's wrist, Lucy put a finger on her shoulder. A striped caterpillar crawled onto it. Slowly, carefully, Lucy swung her finger toward a nearby leaf and eased the caterpillar onto it.

"Baby butterflies," Lucy said as she pointed.

Jennifer saw them then. Caught in the sunlight washing the leaves on the milkweed were at least a dozen striped caterpillars. And hanging from buttons of silk attached to the milkweed stalks, were the hard-case chrysalides—like tiny green-and-gold jewels—in which some of the caterpillars had already encased themselves. Lucy's babies would soon be emerging as glorious monarch butterflies.

As Jennifer watched, one of the caterpillars slipped off its leaf and fell onto Lucy's hair. Unlike Jennifer, Lucy did not flinch in revulsion. She glanced at the wiggling body in her peripheral vision and smiled.

"Hello," she said to it as she held up her finger. But Lucy's depth perception and coordination were slightly off, and the caterpillar couldn't reach the helpful finger Lucy extended.

Jennifer bent forward, put out her finger. The caterpillar crawled on without hesitation. Its black-white-and-yellow-striped body glistened, its many tiny feet warm feathers on her skin. A beautiful, harmless little creature. And she had so nearly, so unthinkingly hurt one.

Holding the caterpillar up to a leaf as Lucy had done, she watched it gain a firm hold on a sturdy stem.

"You saved!" Lucy's arms came around her, hugging as only she knew how. "Thank you, Jen."

Jennifer returned the hug, deeply touched by the gentleness of the spirit she was with. And the magical moment she had almost missed.

"Thank *you*, Lucy."

"THE CAR ACCIDENT happened seven years ago, the week before Michael's twenty-eighth birthday," Zahn said. "Lucy had gone shopping with her parents and sister, intent on buying him a special present. They'd been married only six weeks."

Zahn and Jennifer were sitting on the bench, watching Lucy lead Michael around the garden's blooming flowers, stopping at each one so she could tell him about it.

"A truck hit them head-on," Zahn continued, his voice soft. "Her parents and sister were dead at the scene. Lucy was barely alive. I told Michael she'd never talk or walk again. The brain damage was too great. He saw the CTs, the MRIs. He knew. But he wouldn't let that stop him."

Jennifer had seen that unshakable determination.

"For the next eighteen months he worked with her here," Zahn said. "At the end of that time, she was talking and walking, as well as saving little caterpillars and every other manner of creature that she finds in need of help."

"Did you know her before the accident?" Jennifer asked.

He nodded. "She was another one of my students. Michael met her in class, dated her all through graduate school. I attended their wedding. Lucy was very smart and sweet."

"I think she still is."

Zahn looked approvingly at Jennifer. "The nurses here will tell you that she alerts them when the hummingbird feeders are empty. Her room is on the second floor in the back. The feeders are in the front on the end. There's no way she can see them. Yet she's always right."

"How do they explain it?"

"When they asked her, she said the hummingbirds told her. The nurses didn't take her seriously, of course, until one of them watched what happened when the feeders emptied. The hummingbirds flew up to Lucy's window. There are two hundred windows in this institution, but they only hover outside hers."

An hour ago, Jennifer would have been skeptical of such a story. But that was before she'd met Lucy.

"Let me show you something," Zahn said as he flipped through the pad he held. When he found what he'd been looking for, he swung the page toward Jennifer.

"I asked her to draw me a self-portrait. This is what she did."

The drawing was rough, very much like what a young child would do. Two eyes and a mouth. The slightly oblong skull had blond hair with large holes in between the yellow clumps.

"I asked her what those holes were," Zahn said, pointing at them. "She told me that she'd been hurt there. But I wasn't to be sad. Because that was where the light now came in."

Jennifer looked at the drawing and then at the artist on the other side of the garden; Lucy was bathed in sunlight, holding up a flower for Michael to smell.

"He couldn't bring back who she was," Zahn said, "but he made possible what she is now. Still, he'll insist it was she who helped him find the unexpected meaning in the shattered fragments of their lives."

We would never learn to be brave and patient if there were only joy in the world.

"I think they found it together," Jennifer said as tears filled her eyes.

CHAPTER NINE

A LIGHT RAIN SMEARED the windshield as Michael drove toward Courage Bay. A CD of his favorite songs was playing. He glanced over to see Jennifer's head back, eyes closed, fingers tapping in tune to the music.

"I don't remember rain being in your weekend forecast, Ms. Meteorologist," he teased.

She opened her eyes and slanted him a look. "We are not in Courage Bay, and this is not rain. It's a moderate drizzle."

"Moderate drizzle," he repeated, putting on the windshield wipers and making a show of squinting through the glass. "Looks pretty heavy to me."

She sat up a little straighter. "Heavy drizzle would put visibility at less than five-sixteenths of a mile. This is obviously between five-sixteenths and five-eighths."

"That obvious, huh?" he baited.

"To the trained eye."

"And by the time we descend into Courage Bay, this light rain is going to be gone?"

"This is not light rain. These drops have a diameter of less than point zero two inches. Raindrops are larger than point zero two inches. And, yes, this moderate drizzle will definitely be gone by the time we reach Courage Bay." She paused to send him a smile. "I hope."

She had a great smile.

The day had been full of unexpected gifts. His wife's condition was difficult for most people to see. The normal response was to turn away. But Jennifer had not turned away. She had accepted Lucy, even shown affection for her, just the way she was.

Michael did not have the words to tell Jennifer what that meant to him.

"In Australia, ants build high walls around their nests to prepare for heavy rain," she said. "They know it's coming, long before it does. Yet even with all of our sophisticated instruments and supposedly higher intelligence, we're never sure. Makes me wonder."

"What is it you wonder?" Michael asked.

"You know about Lucy and the hummingbirds, of course?"

"Yes."

"Maybe like the ants with the rain, the hummingbirds connect with the important things in this world that we so often miss. Like the gentle sweetness inside her."

If Michael hadn't been driving, he would have hugged Jennifer for that. He wouldn't have been able to stop himself.

"You understood what everyone in that grief seminar was going through because you'd been through profound loss and grief yourself," she said. "Why didn't you say anything?"

"Others needed to tell their stories and be heard," Michael said. "Often healing has far less to do with the wisdom of some supposed expert's words than it does with simply being listened to."

"Who listened to you about Lucy?"

"I wasn't smart enough to talk to anyone."

Jennifer twisted in her seat to face him. "You're joking."

He shook his head.

"But you're a psychiatrist."

"Which sometimes makes me blinder than everyone else—especially when it comes to myself. In medicine we're taught that competence and expertise are what matter. I thought using mine to bring Lucy back to what she was would save us both. But it was watching Lucy welcome each day with a willingness to embrace whatever life offered that taught me to accept the unacceptable."

"Thank you for letting me meet her. She's…wonderful."

Jennifer rested her head back and closed her eyes again as her fingers resumed tapping to the music.

Michael pulled into the right lane and slowed to just below the speed limit, letting cars whiz past him. There was a pleasant magic to this day. He was not eager for it to come to an end. But all too soon, he was pulling into her driveway, walking her to the door.

He was about to say that he'd call her in the morning when she surprised him speechless for the second time in two days.

"Would you like to come in?"

Every time he'd picked her up the past few days, she'd always answered the bell in less than thirty seconds, ready to go. And when he'd seen her home, she'd made it a point to give him a quick goodbye at the door.

Michael stared at her for several seconds before nodding.

She put her key in the lock.

Her house was secluded, up a private road nestled in the foothills. From the outside, its silvered redwood, stone chimney and profusion of natural shrubbery exuded a feeling of serenity and simplicity.

Michael stepped into a living room of golden wood floors and cream walls. The furniture had simple lines, the fabrics a watercolor mixture of soft pastels. Knickknacks adorned every shiny tabletop. Potted geraniums filled the windowsills. An old grandfather clock ticked quietly in the corner.

It was a warm room that invited one inside. A room where nothing shouted for attention. A room where the people in it would be the focus.

"I'll get the jewelry box," she said.

The name of the jeweler. He'd forgotten he'd asked her for it. So that's why she'd invited him in.

For a moment there he'd thought…but, no, she'd made her position clear.

He moved to the mantel to study the pictures. Jennifer as a young girl with braids. A college graduation picture of her standing beside a smiling older man and woman. From the resemblance, he knew they were her parents. There were other pictures of them, this house in the background. It had been their home.

In the seminar, she'd spoken of her parents often and always with love. He could see that love in the way she smiled at them in the pictures—and the way they smiled back.

When she returned a moment later, she held out the ring box. Opening it, he found not only the jeweler's name but also the diamond engagement ring.

"I'm going to give it to Russell's mother," she said, "along with the key to his house. But I'd rather wait until things are…settled about his death. Since she thinks I'm responsible, receiving anything from me now would probably only bring her pain."

Not many people would respond to unfair suspicion with understanding and kindness. Michael wondered if Jennifer had any idea how special she was.

After making a mental note of the name of the jeweler, he handed the ring box back to her.

She dropped it into her purse. "I'd like to be there when you talk to the jeweler. I'm free most days this coming week. If I'm not at home, you can always get me on my cell." Moving to the table, she jotted down the numbers on a piece of paper and handed it to him.

He slipped the paper into his pocket. Time to leave. But she wasn't urging him toward the door. She seemed to have something more on her mind and was struggling to find the right words. He waited.

"Michael, I need to apologize to you for what I said last Sunday."

"There's nothing to apologize for."

"Yes, there is. Please, let me do this. Even without having completed your book, I should have known that the man you are would never… My comment about your home being a bachelor pad where you met your women was not only unjust, it was…unkind. I'm so very sorry."

She lifted her face to his, her eyes full of sadness.

He took a step forward, wanting so badly to touch her, struggling to restrain himself.

"Jenny, I understand how shocked you must have felt when you found out I was still married, and didn't know the circumstances. I don't blame you for what you said. Believe me."

"Thank you." Her voice was a soft exhalation of relief. She stretched on her tiptoes to kiss him on the cheek.

It was a chaste kiss, the kind that was meant to last no more than a second. Michael knew that. But the brush of her lips, the scent of her filling his senses—that was all it took to knock every thought out of his head.

Suddenly his arms were around her. For several blinding seconds, the only thing that existed in the world was the feel of her fitting every part of him. Then unwelcome sanity returned, ripping him back to reality.

He forced himself to release her. Without a word or backward glance, he hurried toward the door and let himself out.

Three miles down the road, his hands were still shaking on the wheel.

THE COURIER ARRIVED on Jennifer's doorstep Monday morning with the documents from Russell's lawyer, relinquishing her claim to everything that Russell had bequeathed her in his will. After Jennifer had read them over, she took them to her bank and had her signature notarized.

As she was leaving the bank, she glanced across the street and caught a glimpse of Caroline Sprague coming out of a diner with Frank Keller, the manager of the Courage Bay Grand Hotel. Startled, Jennifer halted in her tracks.

Frank kissed Caroline full on the lips before she slipped behind the driver's seat of her car. Once he'd watched her drive away, he headed to his vehicle on the other side of the diner's parking lot.

Jennifer had had no idea that Caroline and Frank even knew each other, much less that they were this friendly. Caroline had turned thirty-two the month before; Frank was somewhere in his fifties. Not that these things didn't happen every day, but it sure made Jennifer curious as to when this one had happened.

She was still puzzling over those questions as she started for home. A few blocks later her cell phone rang. It was Michael.

"Hi," she said, a pleasant warmth heating her blood. Memories of his firm embrace the night before immediately crowded out every other thought in her head. She came to and braked at the last second, aware she'd almost hit the car in front of her, which had stopped for a red light.

And that, Jennifer, is yet another sign of why such thoughts of this guy are so dangerous.

"You okay?" he asked in her ear.

"Fine," she responded, hoping her heart would stop banging her rib cage sometime soon.

"I heard a squeal of brakes."

"I've been meaning to have them checked. Have you learned anything new?"

"I called because the jeweler said he could see us. But it has to be right away. He's heading for the airport in less than an hour and will be out of town for the next two weeks. Any chance you can meet me at his place?"

"What's the address?"

He gave it to her. She knew the cross streets. "I'm only about fifteen minutes away. See you there."

THE JEWELER GREETED Jennifer by name when she and Michael walked into his store.

"I met Russell at a chamber of commerce meeting five years ago," he told them. "He was offering a ten percent discount to all members. I recall the day I was in the chair and he said that he was on the lookout for a unique diamond for a unique lady. Then he told me all about you. Took him several visits before he selected this stone."

The jeweler had been examining the diamond engagement ring that Jennifer had handed to him. He looked up at her. "It's as flawless as I could find. Russell was a good guy. When I heard about his murder, I was stunned. I can't tell you how sorry I am for your loss."

"Thank you."

"Did Dr. Sprague buy any other jewelry from you?" Michael asked.

"A pair of earrings."

"Can you describe the earrings?"

"I can do better than that. I'll show you."

The jeweler brought out a catalog and pointed to a picture at the bottom of the page. "Star ear clips in eighteen karat gold with agate and rubies. He picked them up a week ago Saturday morning."

The morning of his death.

"Did anyone else know about them?" Michael asked, noting that the earrings cost eight thousand dollars.

"Only one I told was the detective who came to see me last week," the jeweler said.

"Did Russell mention who the earrings were for?" Jennifer asked.

"He said he wanted stars for his star. They were your engagement present, Ms. Winn. Didn't you get them?"

"HE TOLD HIS JEWELER and his mother that the earrings were for me," Jennifer said to Michael as they left the store. "But he gave them to someone else. It can't have been Gina. She won't wear clips. Complains her earlobes are too small and they keep falling off. Could it be he was seeing another woman?"

"Even if he were, I very much doubt he would have given the earrings to her."

"Why?"

"His behavior toward Elissa and Gina suggests that he compartmentalized women. He had no respect for the ones he slept with. You, on the other hand, he would have considered worth the eight thousand dollars those earrings cost."

She shrugged, clearly unimpressed by what Russell had paid for them.

"According to the jeweler, he picked them up that morning," Jennifer said. "Who wore them into his room that night? This doesn't make sense."

"No, it doesn't. Might help if we knew how he was murdered."

"Does the headache or the soreness across his back suggest anything to you?" she asked.

"The headache would be natural following a mild concussion. As for the soreness, he probably was hit by something when the plane crashed—no doubt the something that caused him to fall and strike his head."

"Vivian said there were no other marks on him. What could have killed him?"

"I need to get a look at the autopsy report. And since the pathologist has been warned not to talk to me, that leaves only one option."

He paused, wondering whether he should tell her. If she didn't know and something went wrong, she'd be able to honestly profess her innocence.

"We're in this together, " she said, interpreting his hesitation for exactly what it was. "Please. I'd like to know."

"My sister, Becky, works for a security firm that does consulting work for companies who need to protect the proprietary information on their office computers. She'd be able to gain access to the pathologist's files on the hospital's computer records."

"Would she?"

"If I ask, yes."

"What happens if someone discovers you've accessed the files?"

"Let's just say that I won't have to worry about the findings of the ethics committee."

WHEN MICHAEL REACHED his sister at her office, she suggested they meet for lunch at his place. Jennifer offered to pick up some sandwiches, and dropped by a deli on the way. When she arrived, Michael buzzed her through the gate.

Becky answered his door, a tall woman in a dark blue business suit, wearing a smile that reached into her eyes. She introduced herself, whisked Jennifer inside, closed the door and gave her a hug. "I am so happy to meet you."

Jennifer drew back, more than a little startled.

"Sorry, didn't mean to scare you," Becky said. "But you've been the talk of the Temple family for days. Mom and Dad say hi. Come on. Michael's in the study."

They found him at the computer. Jennifer could see the Courage Bay Hospital logo at the top of the open file on the monitor.

"You got in already?" she asked as she passed out the sandwiches and cold drinks.

"All doctors on staff can dial into the hospital computer from their homes to get to patient records," Michael said. "Now that I'm on the hospital network, Becky tells me that she'll be able to go elsewhere within it and find what we're looking for."

"And we can do it right about now," Becky said as she took a quick bite of her sandwich and laid the rest on a napkin. Michael got out of her way.

Pulling a disk out of her pocket, Becky slipped it into the hard drive and sat on the vacated chair.

"What you're about to see is a demo program I wrote to show companies how vulnerable their sensitive files can be to unscrupulous employees with access to their internal network," she said.

A whirring sound was followed by a pop-up menu.

"What's the pathologist's name again?" she asked.

"Nealy," Michael said, and spelled it.

Becky typed it in. "And you're sure he's on duty now?"

"In the middle of a meeting, according to the clerk who answered my call a couple of minutes ago."

"Good," Becky said, and hit the enter key. "We can't be accessing the files at the same time he is."

A log-in screen requested a password. She hit a function key that set the CD drive whirring once again, and eight asterisks appeared where the password should go.

With another touch of the enter key, a list of the pathologist's autopsy records were on the screen.

"Your hospital needs better security on their computer system," she said. "When this is all over, be sure to give them my card."

She paged down and highlighted the name Russell Sprague. The instant the autopsy report appeared, she hit a button. The laser printer in the corner of Michael's office came to life.

A minute later the report had been printed and Becky had signed out of the pathologist's records.

Sliding out of Michael's chair, she retrieved her disk and gave it a pat before slipping it back into her pocket.

"Even if someone checks the computer records, all they'll find is that Nealy accessed his files for a couple of minutes today. And since it was during his shift, I doubt if even he'll remember whether he did or not."

"It won't show which file was accessed or the fact that it was done by an off-site computer?" Michael asked.

"Your sister's a pro, remember?" Becky said, a big smile on her face.

"That she is," he said fondly. "I owe you."

"I'm collecting. Bring Jennifer to dinner tonight. The boys are dying to meet her. And Steve wants to tell you some interesting things he's discovered."

"About what?" Michael asked.

"He hasn't even told me yet, except to say that a few possibilities began to occur to him after our conversation with that police detective."

"Detective Batton came to see you?" Jennifer asked, unable to keep the concern out of her voice.

Becky twisted toward her. "Don't worry, Jen. I told him to his face that he's an imbecile to suspect you and Michael. So, what time can we expect you?"

"We appreciate the offer, Becky," Michael said, "but Jennifer has a lot to do between her six and ten o'clock broadcasts tonight. Fitting in dinner would be very difficult for her."

Jennifer understood he was trying to give her an out so she wouldn't feel compelled to accept his sister's invitation. It was thoughtful of him—the kind of thing that made him the man he was.

"Michael's right," she said. "It will be difficult. But I can work around the difficulties. I'd love to have dinner with you."

Michael smiled at her before turning back to his sister. "Seven-thirty?"

"Perfect," Becky said. "Now, I'm going to take my sandwich and soft drink and get back to the office, where I am indispensable. Great to meet you, Jen. See you both tonight."

AS MICHAEL AND JENNIFER munched their sandwiches on the leather couch in his study, he tried to keep his mind on the autopsy report in front of him and away from the woman beside him.

When Becky had called to tell him about Batton's visit, she'd been more excited about his involvement with Jennifer than their being suspects in a murder case.

That Becky hoped for a relationship between him and Jennifer was certain. Having dinner at her home tonight could prove to be awkward if his sister let her enthusiasm become too obvious in front of Jennifer.

Becky wasn't the only member of his family who was becoming a problem. His mother, too, kept asking about Jennifer. Even his father had suggested he should bring her by the café again.

Batton hadn't sown any seeds of confusion or mistrust in Michael's family about him and Jennifer. He'd sown seeds of hope.

"Russell died of nicotine poisoning," Michael told Jennifer when he got through the report and put it down.

"The addictive stuff in cigarettes?" she said. "That doesn't make sense. Russell didn't smoke."

"His lungs were clear. He didn't inhale the nicotine."

"Are you saying it was in something he ate?"

"If someone ingests enough nicotine, they'll die of a heart attack. But the analysis of Russell's stomach contents didn't reveal any."

"I'm confused."

"The nicotine poisoning was found through a tox screen. When the initial autopsy showed no obvious wounds or organ impairments to account for the fact that Russell's heart had stopped, Dr. Nealy spent a day and night running different tox screens until he got a positive on the one for nicotine."

"You said the nicotine wasn't found in Russell's stomach. Since he didn't inhale it, how did it get in his body?"

"Before Nealy could do a thorough testing of all possible sites to determine the point of entry, Batton served him with a court order that required him to turn Russell's remains over to the medical examiner's office."

"So we know what killed him, but we're still in the dark as to how it was done."

"We might be able to make some educated guesses. Nicotine is deadly in all its forms, but especially lethal when absorbed through the skin."

"Like a nicotine patch?" Jennifer said.

"Patches typically contain seven to twenty-two milligrams of nicotine, less than the nicotine in a cigarette. But putting four patches of the higher dose ones on someone's skin at the same time could be enough to kill."

"Who would have known that many patches would be fatal?"

"Offhand, I'd say the most likely candidate would be a doctor, which is no doubt why Batton likes the idea of you and me committing this murder together. But practically anyone can find out about lethal doses of nicotine, especially a smoker who's tried to quit."

"Wouldn't the person also need access to nicotine?" she asked.

"Squeezing the juice out of enough cigarettes will give it to you. Or walking into a store and buying the patches."

"Except if someone had tried to plaster nicotine patches on Russell," Jennifer said, "he would have objected."

"Did Russell wear contact lenses?"

"Yes. Why do you ask?"

"If the nicotine was slipped into his lens solution, it could have been absorbed into his eyes."

"How long would it take for the nicotine to kill him that way?"

"The poison would have quickly traveled through Russell's central nervous system, causing seizure, paralysis and finally respiratory arrest. From the concentration of nicotine the pathologist found in his body, I'd estimate it to be less than an hour."

"Then if that's what happened, it had to have been done by someone who saw him between eleven and twelve that night. That points to Gina."

"Or Don Hardrick. Very few autopsies are requested by the

hospital. When someone dies, the physician usually determines the cause from the symptoms and signs the death certificate accordingly. That may have been what the killer was hoping for in this case."

"So this murder was committed by someone who knew about hospital procedures?"

"Possibly," Michael agreed. "The killer may have hoped it would be assumed that Russell died of an undetected aneurysm, a result of his injuries from the plane crash. If the E.R. doctor hadn't requested the autopsy and if it hadn't been performed by someone with the expertise and diligence of Dr. Nealy, that might have happened. Not many pathologists would have thought to check for nicotine."

Jennifer took a last sip of her soft drink and discarded the cup in the trash. "We know Gina and Hardrick saw Russell during the critical time. But we can't be sure that someone else didn't go into his room. Vivian was obviously too busy to notice. Anyone who knew he was there could have entered and left without being seen."

"Agreed," Michael said. "The murderer also had to be someone who not only knew about nicotine but had it on hand in the right quantity and in a medium that could be passed to Russell without his becoming suspicious. That suggests that the crime was carefully planned."

"But no one knew that Russell was going to be in the hospital that night."

"Maybe we need to look at this from a different angle. In the last news report, the NTSB spokesman said that the trauma from the crash caused the pilot's death, but that the plane had been tampered with, which means that the pilot was murdered."

"You can't be thinking that the plane crash was premeditated for the sole purpose of injuring Russell sufficiently to have him taken to the hospital and kept overnight?"

Michael chuckled. "No. That would be too big a stretch, even for my active imagination."

"Then I don't understand the connection."

"Let's say someone had a serious beef with Russell and was planning to kill him with the nicotine. That someone might have seized the opportunity when he learned that Russell had been injured and rushed to the hospital."

"I see," she said. "Russell's name wasn't released that night. That leaves his family and the obvious others. Gina. Dorie. Harvey. And Don, because his contacts on the emergency teams always call him when something newsworthy comes along."

"And someone else we haven't talked about—Frank Keller, the hotel manager. He was one of Russell's patients."

"That reminds me. I saw him and Caroline together today." Jennifer filled Michael in on what she'd witnessed when she'd exited the bank.

"I understand you tried to reach Caroline that night to tell her about Russell," Michael said.

"I called her apartment after I phoned his parents at their home. There was no answer at either place. I didn't have their cell numbers. Russell supplied them when he regained consciousness."

"But not his brother's?"

"He said Kevin had bought a new cell phone a few days before and hadn't given him the number. He told Frank and me that Caroline would know what it was."

"And Frank offered to call her as well as Lloyd and Harriet Sprague," Michael said. "Had Russell mentioned knowing Frank before you met him at the hotel that night?"

"No. All he told me was that he'd gotten a line on a reception hall, and he asked me to meet him at the Grand Hotel."

"How was it that Gina came to be there?"

"We were shopping together at the time he called," Jennifer explained. "She was to be my maid of honor. I invited her to come along. Ironic, isn't it? If I hadn't, if they hadn't been dancing together when the plane hit, they wouldn't have been injured and none of this would have happened."

There was a reflective look on her face, as though she were imagining that other future—being married to the man she thought Russell had been.

She shuddered suddenly, and Michael had to stop himself from putting his arms around her. He didn't trust himself to touch her in any way now, for any reason. Rising from the couch, he retreated to his desk and leaned against the edge.

"Dorie mentioned there was some problem with Kevin's vision that keeps him from driving?" he asked after a moment.

"Yes, although I've never been clear on exactly what it is. He takes taxis everywhere when he can't get a ride with someone."

"He was supposed to have been eager to get back to a game of poker that night," Michael said. "Assuming Caroline drove him there, that would mean that if he took a taxi back to the hospital, there will be a record."

"Wouldn't Batton have checked?" she asked.

"His partner said all the good suspects had alibis. Batton may not have considered Kevin to be a good suspect. On the surface, the only thing he got from his brother's death was a speedboat."

"On the surface," Jennifer repeated. "What could be below the surface that would have made Kevin want to kill Russell?"

"The way an expert sees us often becomes the way we see ourselves. Parents, teachers, older siblings—these are the experts when we're maturing. Even without intending to, we fulfill their expectations of us. Kevin's parents value him even more than his hardworking sister. But Russell saw Kevin as a screwup. Perhaps Kevin believed the only way he could escape *being* a screwup was if Russell were dead."

"You've dealt with cases like this before?"

He nodded. "I'm not saying that's what happened here, Jen. Only that it's a possible explanation. There are a dozen others."

"I'm glad all I have to try to figure out is the weather. Speaking of which, I should be going. I have to shower and change before the broadcast."

Michael walked her to the door.

"I'll pick you up at the station parking lot after your six o'clock spot and drive you over to my sister's," he offered. "That way I'll have the perfect excuse to leave with you when you have to return for your ten o'clock broadcast."

"If I had such a great sister, I'd be thinking of reasons to prolong my stay, not to get away."

Intrigued, Michael asked, "How did Becky win you over so quickly?"

"It could have been the smile she greeted me with. Or the hug. But I suspect it was the fact that she was willing to commit a crime for you. Sisterly love doesn't get much better than that. You must have been a great older brother with some wonderful expectations of her when you two were growing up."

Jennifer gave Michael a grin before closing the door behind her.

CHAPTER TEN

MICHAEL SAT BACK and watched Jennifer captivate his two rambunctious nephews, using dramatic gestures and sound effects to describe the treacherous thunderstorms that began on their mother's birthday in April 1974. One hundred twenty-seven devastating tornadoes had grown out of them, some with winds greater than two hundred sixty miles per hour.

"Eleven states were struck in two days," she said, her voice low and fast, like a whipping wind. "In Ohio, one twister lifted the freight cars of a passing train and whirled them off the tracks. Then it grabbed two school buses and flung them through the wall of a school."

Smack!

Jennifer's perfectly timed clap had both boys jumping in their seats.

"Cool," his six-year-old nephew breathed, his eyes balloons, his voice full of awe.

"Wow, Mom, you never told us what a great birthday you have," the eight-year-old exclaimed to Becky.

Michael smiled. Nothing like chaos and mayhem to catch a boy's imagination.

When dinner was over, Steve saw the boys up to their rooms to finish their homework. "What story would you have told them if we'd had girls?" Becky asked when they'd disappeared up the stairs.

"Since Steve was born in Minnesota during the winter in '72, they would have heard how vapor condenses into tiny drops of water, then freezes into ice crystals that miraculously become a intricately beautiful, one-of-a-kind snowflake bringing white magic to the silver skies of winter."

Jennifer's hands had glided through the air as she spoke, painting the picture, her voice reverent, adding wonder to what she described.

"On the other hand," she added with a twinkle in her eye, "most girls love the tornado story, too."

Becky laughed. "Steve and I volunteer at the Courage Bay Center for the Blind. They're always looking for people with good voices to put books on tape, especially the children's stories. You're a natural."

Steve descended the stairs in time to hear his wife's comment. "Becky's right, Jen. They'd be thrilled to get you. Would you consider it?"

"I'll not only consider it, I'll do it," Jennifer assured them, "providing I don't get arrested for murder and sent off to prison first."

Her grin was good-natured. Both Steve and Becky returned it.

"Now that we're on the subject of murder," Steve said as he hunkered down in the chair next to his wife, "I'm going to confess. Ever since that officious detective came pounding on the door the other day, I've been looking into the files at the insurance company where I work, seeing if I could uncover anything suspicious about the Spragues. I've got some good news and some bad news. Which do you want first?"

"Might as well hear the worst," Michael said.

"Russell Sprague had a million dollar life insurance policy with his folks as beneficiaries."

"Why is this bad news?" Michael asked.

"Couple of days before he died, he filled out a new beneficiary form naming Jennifer. He neglected to sign at the bottom, so the change never went through. Before the office could mail it back to him for his signature, he died."

"So Batton might think that I knew about Russell sending in the form to change the beneficiary on his policy," Jennifer said. "Which would give me a million dollar motive."

"You already turned down the five million he bequeathed to you in his will," Michael said. "I doubt Batton could make much of a case based on a million dollar life insurance policy that you might have gotten, but didn't."

"You turned down five million dollars?" Steve asked, his voice ascending with each syllable.

"Russell meant it for his wife," Jennifer explained. "I didn't intend to become that, even if he had lived. Accepting the money wouldn't have been right."

"Five million," Steve repeated, sounding as awed as one of his boys.

Becky rested a hand on her husband's arm, a big grin on her face. "You'll have to excuse him, Jen. He doesn't meet a lot of ethical people in his job as an insurance investigator. Sort of makes him go into shock when he comes face-to-face with one."

"You mentioned there was good news?" Michael asked, hiding his amusement.

Steve nodded. "I couldn't find any dirt on Lloyd, Harriet or Caroline Sprague, but I did discover that Kevin Sprague's car insurance was canceled on him about fourteen months ago. Seems he lost his license after he was convicted of reckless driving and destruction of city property."

"So his lack of driving has nothing to do with impaired eyesight, as everyone in the family claimed," Jennifer said.

"The Spragues seem to prefer to keep their skeletons in the closet," Michael commented. "Did you learn the specifics behind the charges, Steve?"

"He was standing, his head sticking out of his sunroof, driving with his knees, when he lost control of his car and hit a fire hydrant. His pal in the passenger seat had dared him to try the knee-driving trick. His lawyer argued that it was simply youthful exuberance."

"How old was Kevin at the time?" Michael asked.

"Twenty-nine," Steve said.

"Little old to have such behavior excused as youthful exuberance."

"I don't have to tell *you* that some people never grow up, Michael. Anyway, he paid a heavy fine, received a suspended sentence and a year's probation."

"Was there any indication of other such behavior before or since?" Michael asked.

"A bunch of speeding tickets on his record before his license got suspended. Since his conviction, nothing's shown up on the insurance files. You understand we don't always know everything that goes on, unless it pertains to driving or some other insurance-related event. Which brings me to something odd on Russell."

"About his driving?"

"Home policy," Steve said. "He filed a claim four months ago that raised a red flag. Swore his house had been burgled."

"Did he mention this to you?" Michael asked, turning to Jennifer. She shook her head.

Michael faced his brother-in-law again. "What was unusual about the claim?"

"His home was equipped with a state-of-the art surveillance system, one of the reasons he got a discount on his policy premiums. When the insurance investigator asked why the alarm hadn't gone off, he said he'd accidentally deactivated it."

"The investigator didn't believe him," Michael guessed.

"He might have if that had been the only thing. But when he asked for the surveillance tapes from the system, Russell said he'd taken them out and forgotten to put in new ones. His system has two taping units and is equipped with motion sensors, sound sensors, light sensors, plus video cameras disguised as clocks and lightbulbs. We're talking paranoia here. Anyone that concerned about being ripped off might accidentally deactivate an alarm, but the odds that he would also take out the tapes of both units and forget to put in new ones goes beyond the law of probabilities."

"What happened to the claim?"

"When the insurance investigator called to make an appointment to meet with Sprague at his home," Steve said, "Sprague told him to forget it, withdrew his claim and canceled his policy."

"How much was the claim?"

"Hundred and fifty grand."

"What did he say was missing?" Michael asked

"A coin collection he inherited from his grandfather."

"Did he file a police report on the theft?"

"Yes, but he withdrew that at the same time he withdrew the claim," Steve explained. "He told the police he'd made a mistake— that a friend had borrowed the collection and forgotten to tell him."

"What was the name of the friend?"

"He never gave it. I saw a copy of the police report, Michael. When a detective visited the premises right after the incident, he noted a broken window in the utility room. Friends don't break in. And when the detective asked Sprague if he had a security system, Sprague told him he didn't."

"So what do you think was going on?"

"Hard to say. He produced receipts for all that surveillance equipment when he bought it some six years ago. I checked. The equipment was never returned. If it wasn't installed in his home, my guess is that he used it elsewhere."

"And he dropped a hundred-and-fifty-thousand-dollar claim because he didn't want to admit to you that he lied about installing the security system in his house?"

"Doesn't make a lot of sense, does it?" Steve said.

"You have any idea where he might have installed that surveillance equipment?" Michael asked Jennifer.

"I never knew he owned any," she answered.

"Steve, is it possible to get a list of his surveillance system's various peripherals?"

"I made copies of everything I found on the Spragues. They're in my briefcase. I'll get them for you."

"HAVE YOU SENT IN the documents relinquishing your claim to Russell's estate?" Michael asked Jennifer as he drove her back to the studio for her ten o'clock spot.

"Not yet. I was going to take them to the post office tomorrow and send them certified mail. Why?"

"Until the lawyer has them in his hands, you legally have ac cess to Russell's house. I'd like to get in there. Would it bother you to make the trip after your final broadcast tonight?"

She shook her head. "What do you hope to find?"

"That list Steve gave me of the surveillance equipment Russell purchased contained two recording devices and six peripherals, all disguised as lightbulbs and common household items. Even if he didn't install the surveillance equipment in his home, he may have stored the tapes of what he shot there."

"You think looking at those tapes might be important."

"If he were watching people surreptitiously, he might have found out something that someone didn't want him to know."

RUSSELL'S HOME WAS a showy expanse of chrome and glass—as sleek and ultramodern as the art that covered the walls. A decorator had done it, and Jennifer remembered how proud Russell had been when he'd first shown her around.

She hadn't said anything, but it wasn't a style that she found even remotely appealing. Coming upon it again made her realize how very different their tastes had been.

"Any thoughts as to where Russell might have stored tapes?" Michael asked.

"No idea."

"How about you take this part of the house, and I'll look through the rooms at the back?"

Jennifer nodded as she headed into the kitchen. Opening cabinets brought back memories of the last time she'd been here.

Russell had cooked her dinner—a starchy meal of pasta, thick sourdough bread and aged wine. She'd nearly fallen asleep on the couch afterward. When Russell's kisses had started getting serious, she'd brought the evening to an end without a moment's temptation or hesitation.

Thinking back on it now, she wondered how she could ever have considered marrying someone she didn't love.

Because Michael was lost to you. And Russell seemed to want you so much. And it was better to feel wanted than to feel nothing at all.

Jennifer's search of the kitchen did not turn up the tapes. A perusal of the utility room also brought her up emptyhanded. Her hope revived when she found a hidden wall safe behind one of the splotches that passed for a painting in the living room. She tried using Russell's birth date on the combination lock, but when that didn't work, she gave up.

Wondering how Michael was doing, she wandered down the hall.

She found him in Russell's bedroom—another expanse of chrome and glass—sitting on the edge of a black velvet bedspread, watching something on a wide-screen TV. He looked up when she entered, and immediately hit the pause button.

The expression on his face told her.

"You found the tapes."

He nodded.

"Where were they?"

"On a shelf in plain view, except he'd put false identification tags on them. What I have in the tape machine now was labeled 'Aerobic Exercise #48.'"

"What's actually on it?" Jennifer asked as she approached the bed.

Michael gestured toward the screen. It was a paused view of a nearly nude Russell and Gina in a dental chair. The activity they were engaging in had nothing to do with calisthenics or tooth care.

"He filmed himself having sex with her," Jennifer said, shaking her head.

"And others."

Michael rewound the tape, hit the play button. Another nearly naked woman, one Jennifer had never seen before, was on top of Russell in that same dental chair. Heavy breathing accompanied the footage. The date on the bottom of the film was three months earlier.

Jennifer turned her head away. "So the surveillance system was put in his dental office."

Michael stopped the tape. "There are also hidden cameras here in his bedroom."

"You saw a tape that was shot in this room?" she asked.

He nodded.

"Where are the hidden cameras?"

"My guess would be there, there and there, according to the peripheral inventory that Steve gave me."

He had pointed to the clock on a nightstand, a radio on another, the light fixture in the ceiling. She hadn't noticed before, but none of those items matched the sleek decor of the room.

"What I need to find is the recording machine," Michael said, rising. "Want to help me look?"

"I'll start in the bathroom." She was happy for any excuse to leave the bedroom.

Jennifer didn't consider herself a prude. If two consenting adults really wanted to tape themselves having sex, that was their business. But hidden cameras implied that at least one party hadn't been aware that the taping was going on.

That was an unforgivable betrayal of trust.

Since she'd always used the guest bathroom when she visited Russell in his home, this was the first time she'd seen the master bath. Mirrors covered every wall. She found a half bottle of lubricating ointment and three cases of condoms beneath the sink, one of which was nearly empty. But no tape machine.

When she returned to the bedroom, Michael gestured for her to join him at the entrance to the walk-in closet. He pointed to where he'd pushed aside Russell's shoes, and she saw the opening in the wall.

"The panel was false," Michael said. "When I knocked on it, I could hear the hollow sound. The tape machine is inside there. It was still recording."

"It's been running for more than a week?"

"Unless the tape's extracted when it comes to the end, it automatically rewinds and records over the previous information."

"Where is the tape that was in there?" she asked.

"My pocket. I'd just as soon that the next person who finds the recording machine not know we were here."

As Jennifer watched, Michael replaced the panel and put Russell's shoes in front of it.

"I don't want to leave these tapes here for Russell's parents to find," she said, gesturing toward the shelves when they reentered the bedroom.

"We're not. I'm going to need to check to be sure there isn't something on them that could explain the motive for Russell's murder."

"How many tapes are there?" she asked.

"Close to fifty."

"And you're going to have to wade through them all," Jennifer said. "I don't envy you. Still, I suppose for a man, watching that kind of thing is…not abhorrent."

"Depends on the man," Michael said, stepping into the closet to lift a suitcase off the shelf. He brought it to the bed and opened the lid. "I'll carry the tapes out in this and return it later. Do you mind leaving the door key with me?"

She handed it to him.

He grabbed a bunch of the tapes off the shelf and started packing the suitcase. "I'll get the key back to you tomorrow."

As Jennifer nodded, something flashed at the corner of her eye. She looked over to see that it was the second hand of the clock on the nightstand. The clock that was really a hidden camera. Even knowing that the recording tape had been removed didn't diminish her feeling of being watched.

"You'll find me by the door when you're ready," she said. Then she left the bedroom because she couldn't stand to remain in it a second longer.

MICHAEL FAST-FORWARDED through the last tape, shaking his head in disgust. Russell had filmed himself with more than seventy-five different women during the six-year span represented by the dates on the bottom of the film.

He'd deliberately positioned the women in front of his hidden cameras so he'd be able to view them from different angles later. That none of them had known they were being taped was obvious.

But Russell had been diligent about wearing condoms. And Michael hadn't seen a wedding ring on the finger of any of the women Russell had sex with, either in his office or his home. These weren't blackmail tapes. They were for his personal viewing. And although the women might be incensed to discover they had been filmed, Michael doubted Russell had ever let them know.

In terms of the aberrant sexual behavior Michael had dealt with as a practicing psychiatrist, Russell's voyeurism wouldn't even rate a two on a scale of one to ten. But on a purely personal level, Michael was more than relieved that Jennifer had never slept with the sod.

He ejected the last tape out of the machine and dropped it into the box where he'd placed the rest of them. Then he went over to his shelf and pulled out a tape of his own, slipping it into the machine.

Jennifer's face came on the screen. She was pointing to the weather map behind her and warning of a heavy storm that was brewing off the coast and would be coming inland later that night.

It was a clip of a weather segment from the winter before. Since the moment he'd discovered she'd become KSEA's meteorologist, he'd been taping her reports. Every one of her broadcasts sat on his shelves.

The naked women on Russell's tapes had done nothing for Michael. But simply seeing Jennifer's smile turned him on. When her segment came to an end, he glanced over at the clock. It was after five in the morning. He needed sleep.

But he watched the tape of her next broadcast. And when it was over, the next one. And then the one after that.

IT WAS NEARLY NOON when her doorbell rang and Jennifer saw Michael through the peephole. Smiling, she swung open the door.

"Returning the key," he volunteered, holding it up. "I suddenly found myself in the neighborhood, so I took the chance that you'd be home."

He was in a suit, which told her he'd been at work or was on his way. What had brought him to her neighborhood, she couldn't guess. But she was too happy to see him to question his explanation.

"Would you like some lunch?" she asked. "I was about to have some. I certainly can't offer anything as good as what your folks could, but I'll try to make it edible."

"Yes. Thanks."

They sat in the kitchen at the center island. She'd planned to have a sandwich with some milk. But now that he was here, she made a large green salad with fresh chunks of chicken, avocado, carrots and walnuts, topping it all with currants.

Michael paid the meal the ultimate compliment by cleaning his plate. He also drank three cups of coffee.

Having tasted his mother's wonderful brew, and knowing hers couldn't compare, Jennifer was a bit surprised. Then it dawned on her why he might need the extra jolt of caffeine.

"You were up late watching the tapes," she guessed.

He nodded. "Unfortunately, I didn't learn anything helpful from them."

"Where are they now?"

"Ben's keeping them in the safe at his law offices. Just a precautionary measure in the unlikely event that they could somehow be related to Russell's murder. When all this gets settled, he'll quietly destroy them."

"On behalf of Russell's family and all the women in those tapes, thank you."

She rose, gathered their plates and set them in the dishwasher. "We're back where we started. No viable suspects."

Michael downed the last of his coffee, shaking his head at her offer of another refill.

"How would you feel about returning Russell's ring and the key to his house to Caroline?" he asked.

"As a kind of good-faith gesture so she'll talk to me?"

"You're not bad at this psychology stuff," he teased.

She returned his smile. "What do you want to learn from her?"

"I'm curious about her relationship with Frank Keller. The burglary at Russell's place. Nettie said it was Kevin who requested the back rub for his brother that night. I'd like to hear from Caroline how that happened."

Jennifer gave it some thought. "She'd be hesitant to say anything in front of you, Michael. I'd have to see her alone."

"Would you consider taping your conversation?"

"I can't tell Caroline I want to tape our conversation."

"You don't have to. It's not illegal to record a conversation to which you are a party."

"You mean tape her without her knowing?"

"We're not out to hurt her, Jen. I only want to hear the inflection in her voice when—if—she chooses to talk to you about those things."

"Because you'll know if she's lying, whereas I won't."

"I might be able to hear something you wouldn't. But if there's anything about your conversation with her that you decide you don't want me to listen to, you don't have to give me the tape."

It sounded fair, but Jennifer was still uneasy. "Where would I get this tape recorder?"

"I have a miniature one out in the car that will fit in your pocket. It activates at the press of a button. The tape lasts an hour and switches off quietly and automatically when it gets to the end."

"Is that what you use for your interviews with patients?"

"Yes. It's far less intrusive than taking notes."

"I guess I'm a little sensitive on the issue of people being eavesdropped on without their knowledge after getting a glimpse of Russell's tapes."

"What Russell did was reprehensible, Jen. But the situation here is very different. We're not trying to tape someone in what should be a private act."

"I know, Michael. You wouldn't do anything like that. You're nothing like Russell, thank heavens."

She was standing at the sink and he was sitting in his chair at the center island. He didn't move a muscle, but the sudden flash of emotion on his face had her heart thumping hard in her chest.

"I'll get you that tape recorder and be on my way," he said, rising quickly and loping in the direction of the door. "Lunch was great. Thanks."

"THE LAWYER TOLD US you weren't accepting Russell's bequests," Caroline said as she held the engagement ring and key in her hand. "That was sensitive of you, Jen. It meant a lot to Mom and Dad."

Caroline had invited Jennifer to come to the beauty salon between her six and ten o'clock broadcasts. The moment Jennifer knocked at the back door, Caroline had swung it open, ushered her into the office and gotten them both a cup of tea.

That Caroline had gone through a change of heart since the will reading was quite evident.

"Do your folks still think I killed Russell?" Jennifer asked.

"They'd much rather think it was Elissa, but that detective says she has an alibi."

"Have you always known about Elissa?"

Caroline frowned at Russell's house key as she rubbed it with her thumb. "It caused a big stink in the family when she got pregnant and said the baby was Russell's. He swore it couldn't be. Even bet Kevin the paternity test would come out negative. I've never seen him so mad as that day he learned he was the father."

She looked up and met Jennifer's eyes. "Russell wanted to wait until you were pregnant before explaining about Elissa and Jamie. He believed that as his wife, you'd feel more secure and understand that you and your baby would always be first with him. He was only thinking of you, Jen."

Jennifer was certain Caroline meant her words to be kind ones, and made no comment. "How did Russell seem when you saw him that night in the hospital?"

"His only complaints were that he had a headache and we were all a little blurry."

"His eyesight was affected by his injury?" Jennifer asked.

"No, he wasn't wearing his contacts. They were in a lens solution on the stand next to his bed, and he didn't have his glasses. We all watched that interview KSEA did with Frank where he described how brave you were that night, running into the wreckage to be by Russell's side. You must have loved him so much. Frank told me right from the start that there was no way you would have killed him."

"Have you and Frank been seeing each other long?"

Caroline's cheeks flushed. "How did you know we were seeing each other?"

"I'm sorry. I didn't realize it was a secret."

"It's not…exactly a secret. I just haven't told my folks yet."

"You think the age difference will bother them?"

Caroline sighed. "He could be ninety and they wouldn't care, as long as he had money and position. Problem is, he has neither. They're going to be even more disappointed in me than they already are when they find out."

"Then they're very foolish. You're terrific, Caroline. And everything I've seen of Frank tells me he's a really good guy. Did you meet him at Russell's dental office?"

"No, his wife used to be a customer of mine. She died suddenly of a stroke a couple of years back. It was a really rough time for him. I came out of the shop one night a few weeks afterward and there was Frank sitting in his car, waiting for her just like he used to, tears streaming down his face. I took him out for a drink and somehow things clicked between us. I can't explain it."

"You don't even have to try," Jennifer said. "When it's right, you know."

Caroline sent her a smile. "Nothing like that had ever happened with the stiffs Mom and Dad kept setting me up with. I asked Frank if he wouldn't mind becoming a patient of Russell's, because I thought once my brother got to know him, he'd help us pave the way with my folks."

"How did that work out?"

"At first Russell wasn't too pleased. Kept insisting I could do better. But when I explained to him that I was in love with Frank, he told me if I really wanted him, he'd do his best to help. His suggestion was that I wait to tell our parents until your wedding day. He thought they'd be really happy then and would take the news better. Jen, I still can't believe he's dead."

Caroline's voice caught and Jennifer gave her arm a squeeze.

"Do you have any idea who would have wanted to kill him?" she asked.

Russell's sister shook her head. "Most people really liked him. You know that. Except for Elissa, of course. But she was…a mistake. And, Jen, that thing with Gina, it didn't mean anything to him. She seduced him, I know it. He loved you. You were the only woman he'd ever asked to marry him."

The last thing Jennifer wanted to do was challenge Caroline's image of her brother.

"Did he tell you about a burglary he had at his home a few months ago?" she asked.

Caroline looked back at the key in her hands. "It wasn't a real burglary. Kevin was the one who broke in."

"Why would Kevin break into Russell's place?"

"It was that bet Russell made with him that Elissa's child wouldn't be his. Kevin put up his classic car and Russell bet Grandfather's coin collection, which had been promised to him. But Grandfather hung on a few more years than expected, and when he passed and Russell got the collection, he didn't want to give it up. He'd been coveting those coins since he was a boy."

"Did Kevin need the money?"

"Oh, hell no. Grandfather was generous with him as well— left him three million in stocks. Besides, Russell offered Kevin money in place of the collection and Kevin said no. He demanded Russell make good on their bet. Russell told Kevin that he could stuff it. So Kevin broke in and took the coins."

"And Russell knew this?"

"Not at first. Wasn't until he'd brought in the police that Kevin told him he'd smashed the window and taken what was his."

"How did Russell react to that?"

"He let it go because he knew that Kevin was right. Had Russell won the bet, he would have taken Kevin's favorite car. Kevin didn't really want the coin collection, of course. Once it was in his possession, he sold it and refused to tell Russell where."

"Seems mean."

"It's just a guy thing. They did this kind of stuff a lot when they were growing up. Goading each other into staking something they didn't want to lose in some silly bet. Ninety-nine percent of the time it was Kevin who ended up losing and getting pissed. That coin collection was one of the rare occasions he won."

"I understand Kevin asked the hospital volunteer to give Russell a back rub," Jennifer said. "That was a nice gesture."

"What are you talking about?" Caroline asked.

"The hospital volunteer who saw Russell later that night told me that his brother had requested a back rub for him."

Caroline shook her head. "The volunteer was wrong. I picked Kevin up and drove him to the hospital. We were together the whole time. No one told us about any hospital volunteer, and he made no such request. After we left the hospital, I dropped him back at his friends' house."

"Could he have returned to the hospital?"

"I know what you're thinking, Jen, but Kevin didn't do it. Yes, he's done some dumb stuff. And he and Russell definitely had that sibling rivalry thing going. But he's never been violent. And since Russell's death, he's acted so much more responsible."

Because he'd finally broken free of his older brother's image of him as a screwup?

"Besides, the police checked," Caroline continued. "Kevin's friends said he was playing poker with them until two in the morning, when they all passed out."

So Batton had suspected Kevin enough to check out his alibi.

"Did you see Frank that night?" Jennifer asked.

"I had to come back here for an emergency makeover on a very important client. Frank was waiting for me out front when I closed the shop around eleven. We went back to my place together. Wait. You're not thinking that Frank or I—"

"No," Jennifer interrupted quickly. "All I was thinking was

that after the shocks of the evening, I'm glad he was there to offer you comfort."

"That's the reason you spent the night with Dr. Temple, isn't it?" Caroline asked. "Because after learning what Russell had done with Gina, you needed…comfort?"

Caroline wasn't asking the question out of spite. She wanted to understand. And after all the questions Jennifer had asked, it wouldn't have been right not to answer.

That her response wasn't going to be accurate didn't particularly bother Jennifer. It was what Caroline wanted—needed—to hear.

"Yes, that's why I spent the night with him," Jennifer said.

CHAPTER ELEVEN

MICHAEL WORKED at his home on case notes throughout the evening, waiting for a call from Jennifer. When it still hadn't come after her ten o'clock broadcast, he closed down his computer and headed for the shower.

Turning up the hot water, he put his head underneath the spray and let it stream down his neck, hoping it would relax him enough for a good night's sleep. He couldn't remember the last time he'd had one.

Yes he could. It was before he'd made love to Jennifer. Ever since then, he kept reliving the incredible time they'd shared instead of sleeping.

The hot water didn't seem to be such a good idea, after all. He switched the knob to cold.

Emotional restraint had always been a big part of Michael, integral to his identity, an absolute necessity in his profession. Yet every time he got close to Jennifer now, he felt like a smoke detector going off because a candle was lit.

Had a patient come in with such a problem, he would have suggested developing a strategy to avoid those situations that led to temptation. In his case that meant controlling the urge to drop by her place. Not inviting her over to his. Making sure that wherever they went, there were other people around. Simple, basic steps. It was time he took them.

As soon as he switched off the water and stepped out of the shower, the phone rang. He made a dash for it.

"Hi," she said.

His pulse jumped. "Hi."

"Is it too late to bring the tape by?"

Her. Here. Now.

Don't do this to yourself. Tell her you'll pick it up tomorrow.

"No, it's not too late. How soon will you be here?"

"I'm downstairs at the gate. Buzz me in?"

You can still stop her from coming up. Tell her your other line is ringing. Put her on hold. Then you can come back on the line and tell her a patient just called and has to see you.

Michael walked over to the wall unit and hit the button to release the lock on the front gate.

"Thanks," she said. "I'm on my way."

He hung up the phone, aware that his heart was beating far too fast. Taking several slow, deep breaths, he centered himself.

When the doorbell rang, he started sedately toward it, realized he was both wet and naked, and did a one-eighty run for the closet.

JENNIFER WAS A LITTLE surprised when Michael didn't immediately answer the door. She was wondering whether to ring the bell again when the door suddenly opened and she found herself staring at the smooth, wet muscles of his bare chest.

"Sorry, I just got out of the shower when you called," he said, hastily slipping his arm into a shirtsleeve. His feet were bare and his hair was damp and disheveled. A pair of jeans hugged his long legs.

Whatever thoughts had been in her head took a trip.

"Come in," he said.

She must have, because the next thing she knew, she was in the living room sitting on the couch, a glass of wine in her hand. He stood before her, buttoning his shirt.

When she realized she was staring at bare flesh disappearing beneath his hands, she took a quick sip of the wine and focused on the blank wall behind him.

"How did it go with Caroline?" he asked, picking up his wineglass from the coffee table as he sat on a chair across from her.

Caroline. The tape. Well, at least now Jennifer remembered what she was doing here.

She reached into her handbag and lifted out the miniature recorder. She'd planned to give it to him at the door and leave. So much for good intentions.

"Caroline answered my questions easily enough," she said. "But I don't think I learned anything that puts us closer to who killed Russell."

Taking the recorder from her hand, Michael hit the rewind button. "Mind if I listen to it now?"

Setting down the wineglass, she made to rise. "I'll leave you to it."

"Please stay," he said. "I might have questions and it would be much easier if you were here to answer them. Besides, you haven't finished your wine."

Probably wouldn't hurt to do that. It wasn't much wine. Half a glass. Not like downing three strong drinks. She settled back on the couch.

Michael set the recorder on the table and hit the play button. As he listened to her conversation with Caroline, he swirled the wine in his glass, stared thoughtfully at the changing patterns. At a couple of places he stopped the tape, rewound it and played a segment again before going on.

Jennifer finished her wine, then left the living room to rinse out her glass in the kitchen sink. When she returned, the tape had come to an end and Michael was standing beside the machine, an unreadable expression on his face.

"Well, what did you learn about Caroline?" she asked.

Downing the last of his wine, he set the glass on the table. "That she's still in desperate need of her parents' approval, even at her age. If they don't give it to her, she'll end it with Frank, no matter what she feels for him."

"How do you know?"

"There was fear in her voice. When I talked with Frank after the plane crash, I wondered why he was so concerned about offending Russell. Now I understand. Both Frank and Caroline were counting on Russell's support when it came time to tell Caroline's parents about them."

"So Caroline and Frank would have had every reason to want Russell to remain alive."

"Yes," he said.

"That's a relief. I didn't want to think either of them was involved."

"From what I've seen and heard of the members of the Sprague family, I doubt any of them killed Russell."

"Not even Kevin?" Jennifer asked.

"Caroline firmly believes Kevin didn't. The thought struck her as ludicrous. And although he's been an emotional adolescent, giving in to urges without much, if any, thought, I believe she's right. He's the type to act impulsively—not with the kind of deliberation that this killing took."

Jennifer mentally revisited the possibilities. "We eliminated Elissa, Dorie and Harvey because they have alibis. Gina?"

"Gina was incensed that Russell could so easily write her off, but I'm convinced that she didn't intend to kill him when she went to see him that night. Whoever did this came prepared."

"So you're thinking it had to be Don?"

"Hardrick learned of your ice-water incident in the E.R. before he went up to see Russell. When he got to Oncology, Gina was coming out of Russell's room. Hardrick had to have realized that your relationship with Russell was already circling the drain. Waiting until the time was right to make a play for you strikes me as being more his style."

"Michael, that doesn't leave anyone. Unless there was another woman in Russell's life? Someone we don't know about?"

"Russell collected sex partners. But there was only one woman in his life. That woman was you."

"You seem so certain."

"When it comes to human nature, nothing is ever certain. But Caroline was closest to Russell and the one most likely to have known him best. That tape I just listened to tells me that she had no doubt of her brother's love for you."

"You could tell all of that by simply listening to her talk?" Jennifer asked.

"Sometimes it's easier to see past the mask we all wear and tune into someone's thoughts when you're focused only on their voice."

The message in Michael's words made Jennifer immediately uneasy. "Remind me never to talk to you on the telephone again."

He blinked in what looked like genuine surprise. "Why?"

She got up. "Why do you think?"

He came to his feet and stood before her. "I have never been a psychiatrist with you. The truth is I could never be, even if I tried. All I can ever be with you is a man—and most of the time only a half-sane one at that."

His words had not been spoken lightly, but with a self-deprecating seriousness that tugged at her heart.

She made a point of looking at her watch. "It's late. I have to go."

"Before you do, I need to ask you something."

"Which is?"

"Did you mean what you said to Caroline?"

His question confused her. "About what?"

"About sleeping with me only because you needed comfort that night?"

Oh, hell. She'd forgotten that was on the tape. Why hadn't she had the sense to erase that part?

"Did you mean it?" he repeated.

He was watching her intently, waiting for an answer.

"You agreed we could leave that night in the past," she reminded him.

"I thought I understood why you wanted to. Then. Now... Did you mean what you said to Caroline?"

She wanted to tell him yes. That would be the easy answer. But the pain of the truth twisted tight inside her, and wouldn't let her lie.

"What did you expect me to tell her, Michael? That even after five years you were still the one I wanted? That I could never feel for her brother what I felt for you?"

Jennifer heard the angry echo of her unhappy words banging against her ears. Tears filled her eyes as she blindly started for the door.

Michael caught her before she'd gone a step.

"Jenny, forgive me. I had to know. God, please don't cry. Just when I think I can handle anything the world sends my way, I see your tears and I'm lost."

He cupped her face, gently kissed the wet trail down her cheeks, softly brushed her mouth with his. The tenderness of his touch reached inside her, loosening the tight coil of pain like nothing else could. With a shaky sigh, she gave up all resistance and sank into the warmth of him.

His arms banded tightly around her, snatching the breath from her lungs.

"Jenny, that last night of the seminar when you kissed me, you'll never know how hard it was for me to let you go. Not a day's gone by since that I haven't thought of you. All these years I kept telling myself that I'd be happy for you if you found someone to love. But it's been torture for me to think of you with another man."

Her voice was barely more than a breath. "I haven't been with another man."

He burned a kiss on the side of her neck. "I know. And I haven't been with another woman. I haven't wanted to be with anyone until that night I was with you."

His next kiss was not soft and gentle. It was deep and hot, full of the intimate knowledge of a lover. When he finally released her mouth, her body was humming and she was struggling for air.

He was breathing hard as well, his voice a whispered warning. "You said you couldn't let Saturday night happen again. I'm going to do everything in my power to make it happen right now if you don't push me away."

"I can't push you away."

He drew back to look into her eyes. "Do you want to?"

"No."

His smile was raw with relief and need before he took her mouth once again with his.

MICHAEL COULDN'T REMEMBER the last time he'd slept so well. Or felt this good. He'd made love to Jennifer yet again when they'd awakened this morning. That had been an hour ago, yet here they lay, still entwined in each other's arms.

"I can't get enough of you," he said. "I don't think I ever really understood the power of an addiction until now. Makes me feel like I should be apologizing to some patients."

She made a contented sound against his neck and snuggled closer. "If this is an addiction, I'm not looking for a cure."

His hand caressed her bare shoulder as the words filled his heart. The thought of calling in sick, spending the day in bed with her, suddenly became compelling, irresistible.

Except there were patients he should see. Also, the ethics committee met the day after tomorrow. Ben had scheduled an early appointment with Michael this morning to review the legal options available in the event that they ruled against him. It was neither practical nor wise to miss that appointment.

Screw it. He didn't want to be practical or wise. He wanted to be with her. Last night he'd told her that he was only half-sane around her. That had been a gross understatement. He wasn't sane at all.

Both nights they'd been together they'd had unprotected sex. Considering Jennifer hadn't slept with Russell and had intended to start a family as soon as they were married, Michael was fairly certain she wasn't on birth control.

What if he'd gotten her pregnant?

The surprising thrill of the thought was so strong it stunned him.

He'd had no choice but to give up all plans to have children after Lucy's accident. Now, suddenly, the possibility was here, right here in his arms.

"Jenny, can I ask you something?"

Her fingertips lightly traced his collarbone. "Just about anything."

The way she touched him, the silky sound of her voice—normally these things would have drained every thought out of his head save the one to make love to her again.

But at the moment, the need to know overrode even that desire. "Are you taking oral contraceptives?"

There was a full—one might say pregnant?—pause. "No."

He was glad she couldn't see his smile as he planted a proprietary kiss on the top of her head. "We've tempted fate quite a few times now. Have you thought about what you would do if—"

"I know all about the morning-after pill," she interrupted.

Michael fought an overwhelming disappointment as he tried to reason with himself. After their first night together, she'd learned he was still married. That had been a terrible shock. Besides, she'd made no secret of the fact that she had fully intended to wait until she was married before having sex, much less children.

He was still struggling beneath an avalanche of unaccustomed emotions when he realized that she was drawing away.

"Look at the time!" she said. "I had no idea it was so late."

She slipped out of his arms, out of the bed, so quickly that he felt the flash of cool air against his skin where her warm bare body had been.

"Where are you going?" he asked.

She grabbed her clothes off the chair. "I have to get home. Sorry to run like this, but there are a bunch of things I need to take care of today and I'm already late. No, don't get up. No reason for you to. Call me later when you get a chance?"

She sailed out of the bedroom so fast he had no time to blink, much less respond.

AS JENNIFER LET HERSELF out of the gate surrounding Michael's condo complex, she saw the newspaper reporter parking her car across the street. Thankful her own car was in a grocery store lot a block away, Jennifer quickly sprinted down the sidewalk and around the corner before the reporter opened her door.

Out of sight behind a bush, Jennifer watched the woman approach the gate to the condo complex and ring the buzzer to Michael's unit. When she didn't get an answer, she returned to her vehicle and drove away.

Jennifer got out her cell phone and tried Michael's number

so she could warn him. When it rang five times, she figured he was probably in the shower. Disconnecting the line, she made her way to her car.

As she pulled out of the lot, her own cell phone rang. She dug it out of her bag and answered.

"It's all over the morning newspaper," Liz said.

"What is?" she asked.

"Your dumping ice water on Russell. Your being seen dancing with Dr. Temple afterward at the Courage Bay Bar and Grill. The fact that he's been asked to appear before the hospital's ethics committee."

So that's what the reporter was doing at Michael's condo—trying to get him to comment on what had been printed. Jennifer let out a few cuss words she wasn't in the habit of using.

"Yeah, my sentiments exactly," Liz said. "I need you to come into the studio. We're going to have to see what we can do in the way of damage control. How soon can you be here?"

Jennifer was in the same clothes she'd worn the day before. There was no way she was going to arrive at KSEA in them and broadcast the fact that she hadn't spent the night at her place.

"I've just bought a bunch of perishables at the grocery store on the other side of town," she said. "I'll have to get them home and put away first. Give me an hour."

"Okay. See you then."

Jennifer disconnected the line and dropped the phone back into her purse. For someone who didn't consider herself a liar, she'd told a couple of whoppers this morning.

BEN HAD THE MORNING PAPER on his desk when Michael walked into his office. He pointed to the prominent display of two pictures on either side of the page one article. Michael snatched it up.

They'd used the photograph off the dust jacket of his book and one of Jennifer's publicity shots. Sinking onto a chair, Michael quickly scanned down the column. Nothing in it came right out and said that he and Jennifer were suspects in Russell's murder. But after a quote from Batton that claimed he was "working on some promising leads," the article described the ice-water incident, Michael's dancing with Jennifer, and finally the fact that he'd been asked to appear before the hospital's ethics committee—all of which made the implication clear.

He dumped the paper back on Ben's desk.

"The timing on this couldn't be worse," Ben said, "what with the committee meeting on Friday."

Michael didn't need the reminder.

"Even if they wanted to give you the benefit of any doubt, this kind of publicity is going to put the spotlight on them. If they rule in your favor, they're going to have to know that their decision will be scrutinized, up for criticism."

"Any suggestions?" Michael asked.

"Let me see if I can get a postponement," Ben said after giving it a moment's thought.

"On what grounds?"

"I'll tell them a conflict has come up in my schedule."

"Won't that be a lie?"

"The legal terminology in such a situation is called retreat and regroup. I'll see if I can talk them into rescheduling in a few weeks when the climate is more amenable to a fair evaluation of the facts. I wish you'd stop being so stubborn, and let me ask Jennifer Winn to appear on your behalf. She would be the best one to assure the committee of her nonpatient relationship with you."

"I'm not dragging her into this."

"This isn't only your job at the hospital that's at stake here," Ben reminded him. "Your license could be revoked if this thing goes south."

"Ben, if she appears before the ethics committee, they'll have the right to question her about everything that's ever happened between us. I'm not going to put her in the position of having to reveal her personal life to a bunch of strangers. Bad enough I have to."

"Am I reading this right? Have you fallen for her?"

Michael met his friend's eyes. "The psychiatric terminology in such a situation is head over heels."

"Well, I'll be damned. You of all people. Michael, you do realize it's only been a week and a half?"

"It's been five years."

Ben stared at him, then nodded in tardy understanding. "Since you met her in the seminar. But you didn't have a relationship with her then."

"No."

"That's a hell of a long time to have felt a flame burning and done nothing about it."

"Thanks for that insight. I might have missed it."

Ben's smile came and went. "How does she feel about you?"

"I think—I hope—the same."

"You *think?* You *hope?* You don't know? Geez, have you forgotten you're a psychiatrist?"

"I haven't forgotten that I have the legal power to sign an emergency order of commitment to a psychiatric hospital for an irritating lawyer who used to be my friend, if that's what you mean."

Ben chuckled. "Okay, I get it. You're as clueless as the rest of us guys. Actually, that's kind of comforting to hear. Does she know about Lucy?"

"She knows about Lucy."

"And the beautiful TV meteorologist still wants to be with you? Maybe she needs to see a shrink."

"She is seeing a shrink."

Ben grinned. "When are you going to find out how the lady feels?"

"I'm trying not to rush her. She's still dealing with her fiancé's betrayal and death, not to mention being a prime suspect in his murder. And, as you say, she and I have only been seeing each other for a week and a half."

"Your life is getting pretty damn complicated, Michael."

"Thank you for pointing that out."

"I'm not just pointing it out. I'm asking. Do you know what you're going to do about it?"

"I HAVE TO TAKE YOU off the air," Liz said. "I have no choice."

Jennifer was sitting across from the news director in her office. The message wasn't easy to take, but it didn't surprise her. For the past twenty minutes, Liz had been telling her about the emergency meeting she'd had with the station manager that morning.

They'd been bombarded by negative phone calls and e-mail because of the newspaper article. And that wasn't all. An administrator from the school where Jennifer was scheduled to appear next month had called to cancel her talk on meteorology to the children.

All the positive feedback generated by her interview with Hardrick had fizzled. The fact that she hadn't been charged with anything didn't seem to matter. In the minds of many viewers, she was a prime suspect in the murder of her fiancé.

Her boss was only doing what she had to do.

"Thanks for telling me in person," Jennifer said, coming to her feet. "Getting canned by phone or fax would have been a lot harder to take."

"Jen, you're not fired. We just can't renew your contract."

Softer words. Same effect.

"Damn, I don't want to lose the best TV meteorologist Timeright has ever had," Liz lamented. "This is going to get cleared up. There are still two weeks left on your old contract. I want you in here every night getting the forecast together so Wally can read it in front of the camera. This couldn't have come at a worse time, what with Ratings Book next week."

They were in one of the four months during the year when viewers filled out a "book," or list, of the shows they watched. Getting in that book was what it was all about in broadcast news.

"I've convinced Andrew and Ursula to let us announce their engagement next week," Liz said. "That should get viewers tuning in. We'll throw a party for them between the six and ten o'clock spots on Monday. I'll call the Seacrest Café and get them to provide a spread for the celebration. Thanks for recommending them. The owner brought by some samples the other day that were to die for. Oh, I almost forgot."

Liz pulled a bag out of her desk drawer and handed it to Jennifer. "She dropped off this bag of roasted coffee beans for you this morning and asked how you were. She seemed very upset when I told her I might have to put you on a leave of absence from the air for a couple of weeks."

Alice Temple wasn't the only one upset. TV personalities did not take leaves of absence. They were either on the air or out of work. Jennifer thanked Liz and left her office, fully aware that she was facing the end of her career in weather news.

AFTER HIS THIRD unsuccessful try to reach Jennifer on her cell phone, Michael left another message on her voice mail and continued his rounds.

The ethics committee had denied Ben's request for a postponement. They had advised him that, represented by counsel or not, Michael was still scheduled to appear before them Friday morning.

After reviewing test results and adjusting medications where required, Michael made sure his chart notes were detailed in case the ruling went against him and his patients were assigned to a new doctor.

He didn't have a specialty that was amenable to the quick fixes of a scalpel or a two-week course of antibiotics. For the most part his methods took time, plus a great deal of courage, commitment and trust from those he treated.

Gaining trust wasn't easy. Several of the female patients he'd had to relinquish to other psychiatrists had suffered setbacks. A sudden change of doctors could prove detrimental for some of his male patients as well.

Walking into Gary and Leon's room, he found the drape drawn between their beds. One look at Gary—bunched up and angry—and Michael retreated out the door.

He found Hazel at the central desk.

"I don't know what's wrong," she said. "They were getting

along great before morning visiting hours. After their families and friends left, I came in to ask what they wanted for lunch and found the curtain drawn between them. Haven't been able to get a word out of either since."

Michael thanked Hazel and used the phone on her desk to call down to X-ray. A couple of minutes later a technician stepped off the elevator and rolled a wheelchair over to him.

"Who's the patient to be x-rayed, Dr. Temple?"

"Warren, I need you to do me a favor. Take Gary down to X-ray and keep him there for the next hour. Sit him in front of the TV in the waiting room and hand him the remote. I'll call and let you know where to take him from there."

Warren shook his head. "You practice some of the strangest psychiatry I've ever seen. But what the hell. Always seems to work. Sure, I'll baby-sit your boy for a while."

Michael thanked Warren and watched as he collected the sullen Gary from his room and rolled him onto the elevator.

Their families and friends had visited several times since Leon and Gary began sharing a room. There'd never been a problem before. But something had happened that morning to set the two men at odds.

Leon had always been more open in expressing himself. Michael was counting on that to still be true. But he needed him to feel secure that whatever he said, Gary would not hear. And that was why Michael had made sure Gary would be gone for the next hour. Leaving word at the nurse's station that he and Leon were not to be disturbed, Michael let himself into the room.

"No need to get up, Leon, it's just me," Michael said jokingly to the young man with only one leg as he closed the door behind him.

EVEN BEFORE NOTING the collecting clouds on the satellite link and the downward march of millibars being recorded out in the Pacific, Jennifer sensed the impending storm.

She turned to her instruments in the weather center, consulting them as she made her predictions. In about forty-eight hours, Courage Bay was going to see some serious wind and rain.

After completing the maps for the next two days' forecasts and the copy for the weather spots that night, Jennifer stood behind the camera and watched Wally fumble through the six o'clock report.

She called in her forecast to the radio station, only to discover that they had no plans to put her on the air, either. Disheartened, she headed for home. As soon as she veered onto the canyon road, her cell phone rang.

"Hi," Michael said.

Just the sound of his voice lifted her spirits. They'd been missing each other's calls all day, but she'd smiled every time she'd listened to his messages.

"No doubt you've seen the newspaper?" he asked.

She let him know about Liz calling her in and taking her off the air.

"Are you okay, Jen?"

"There's always the National Weather Service," she said blithely. "That woman newspaper reporter was outside your place this morning when I was leaving. Fortunately, she didn't see me. So, what are they doing to you? Padded cell? Strait jacket?"

"They'll never commit me. I know all the answers to their trick questions."

She chuckled, feeling better by the second.

"Since you don't have to appear for the second broadcast tonight, how about inviting me over?" he suggested.

"I'm about ten minutes from home. When should I expect you?"

"About ten minutes. I'm right behind you."

Jennifer saw the blink of headlights in her rearview mirror.

"How long have you been following me?"

"Since you pulled out of KSEA's parking lot. When I couldn't reach you by phone, I decided to swing by. I brought dinner. Hungry?"

"Starved."

"Damn. I guess that means we'll have to take time out to eat."

Laughing, she disconnected the line.

The emotional commitment she was making should scare her. It did. By choosing to be with an unattainable man, she was closing the door on marriage. That had been a hard decision. But giving him up would be harder.

She hadn't lied to Michael when she'd told him that if the need to be with him was an addiction, she didn't want a cure.

IT WAS A COUPLE OF HOURS later when Michael finally brought the assortment of finger sandwiches, salads and containers of whipped chocolate pudding to Jennifer's bed. They snuggled against each other and ate contentedly.

They hadn't talked about the new problems that faced them. They hadn't talked at all. What they had been doing had put all thoughts out of Jennifer's head. She hadn't been the only one who'd bought condoms today.

"This food is too good to have come from anywhere but your parents' place," Jennifer said as she licked the last of the chocolate pudding off her spoon. "Makes me wonder why you ever left home."

Taking the empty container from her hand, he set it on the tray with the other discarded remnants of their meal and drew her to him. "Man does not live by food alone."

"Really?" she said, feigning surprise. "And what else could he possibly need?"

Michael was eager to show her, yet again.

As she lay beside him afterward, she felt too happy to worry about anything. The words to an old song kept playing through her head, the meaning of which had never really resonated with her until this moment.

Sometimes, all I need is the air that I breathe and to love you

"What is that you're humming?" Michael asked.

She didn't realize she had been. "Sorry, it's copyrighted."

"Ah, let me see if I can guess. An old or new song?"

"Very old."

"'Folsom Prison Blues'?"

She laughed. "No need to ask what you've been thinking about. Any new thoughts on the murder?"

"Maybe one or two. Remember when Caroline told you she drove Kevin both to and from the hospital that night and that he was with her the entire time?"

"Yes."

"If he didn't return to the hospital as she and his poker-playing buddies contend, how did the back rub request for Russell get on Nettie's list?"

"That's a very good question. Do you think it might have been a mistake, a confusion of room numbers?"

"I think it's something we should make an effort to find out about. Are you tired?"

"Not at all."

He glanced at the clock on the nightstand. "How would you feel about driving over to the hospital and talking with Nettie about it now? It's late enough that Batton and Chaska shouldn't be around."

She nodded as she swung her legs off the bed. "Would you like to come back here afterward to spend the night?"

"Every time I'm asked," he answered, catching her before she could get up, and punctuating his words with a mind-numbing kiss.

He's giving me everything he can. Maybe it will be enough.

CHAPTER TWELVE

"NETTIE HASN'T COME IN yet," Vivian told Michael and Jennifer when they arrived at Oncology. "She called around eight, said she was going to take a later bus."

"Did she say why?" Jennifer asked.

"The ingredients for a lotion she'd been out of for more than a week had just been delivered to her home. She wanted to re-fill the bottle before coming in so she could put it in the store-room with the others."

Vivian turned to Michael. "Speaking of bottles, Clarence Cas-tle died in his sleep on my shift yesterday. Thanks to that nonal-coholic beer you sent down to me, his last few nights on this earth were a great deal more pleasant for us all. You should have seen him smile when I sneaked the bottle to him each night for what he thought was a belt. Not even Nettie's massage made him happier."

Michael acknowledged the words with a smile.

"Nettie told us that you give her a list of patient requests when she arrives each night," he said. "When do you compile the information for the list?"

"The patients let me and the other nurses know what they want when we make our initial rounds. That's if they haven't already passed the information to the day staff."

"And the new patients?"

"I tell them about Nettie and what she offers."

"When do family members make requests on behalf of a pa-tient?" he asked.

"Generally during visiting hours. The nurses give the slips to fill out, like those on the desk." She pointed toward the pad o' slips and the box labeled "Nettie" where the completed slips had been placed.

"On the night that Russell Sprague died, did any of his family members make a request for him?" Jennifer asked.

Vivian shook her head. "I didn't even have time to tell them about Nettie, much less take requests." Her eyes went to the wall clock. "She should have been here by now. There might be a problem with the bus. It's been late before."

"Want to try to reach her at home?" Michael suggested.

The nurse nodded and went to the phone on the desk. After consulting a list of numbers beside it, she located and punched in Nettie's. She listened quietly for a minute before hanging up the receiver.

"No answer."

"Do you know what bus she takes?" Jennifer asked.

"The schedule should be here someplace," Vivian said as she leafed through some papers on the desk. "A couple of the nurses' aides ride the buses, as well. Here it is."

She lifted the schedule out of the pile, scanned down the list and pointed at a number two-thirds of the way through. "That's the bus Nettie takes. Number nine. It runs every half hour."

One of the call monitors on the desk began to beep. Vivian raced off to check on the patient.

Referring to the number at the bottom of the bus schedule, Jennifer entered it into her cell phone. After wading through a long automated phone tree, she finally got a recorded announcement saying that the bus she was inquiring about was on time.

"It's not a bus problem," she said, flipping the phone closed.

"If an emergency came up involving her son or grandkids, she may have had to leave suddenly," Michael suggested.

"Yes, but I still think she would have called to let Vivian know," Jennifer said. "The patients here seem very important to her."

Michael nodded. "Let's swing by her house."

NETTIE DIDN'T ANSWER the bell or respond to Michael's knock. But he could hear what sounded like a radio and see light coming from within. Off to the side was a gate leading to the backyard.

"I'm going to take a look around," he called to Jennifer over his shoulder as he started toward the gate.

When he'd reached it, he found she'd followed him.

"Jen, if a neighbor is watching and decides to call the police as I go through this gate, I'd like to think you'd at least be free to bail me out of jail."

"Think again. If you're going to jail, I'm going with you."

She bent forward to unlatch the gate. "Ladies first," she said, before stepping in front of him and sweeping inside.

Wearing an appreciative grin, Michael followed her through and closed the gate behind them.

Jennifer was already on her tiptoes, trying to peek into the high window of the lighted room at the back of the house, when he reached her.

"I can't see much," she said.

Stepping up to the window, Michael surveyed the room from the advantage of his greater height.

Countertops were layered with pans of cookies. Off to the side was an open door leading into what looked like a bathroom. The music coming from the out-of-view radio was a soft instrumental.

"The kitchen appears to be deserted," Michael said. "She may have gotten a call from a family member and left in a hurry."

"I would have automatically turned off the lights and music on my way out."

"Leaving them on could be her attempt to let a potential burglar think someone's at home when she's away."

"If that's what she intended, she would have left the light on in an interior room where someone couldn't see into a window and she would have tuned the station to a talk show so muffled voices would be heard."

"And here I thought you were just a brilliant meteorologist," Michael said, aware that her logic was dead-on. "How did you come up with that so quickly?"

She winked at him. "Single Woman Living Alone 101. Some thing feels wrong about this. I'm going to try the back door."

Jennifer knocked first, called out second and finally twisted the knob. The door was locked.

Michael located an empty orange crate between two bird-of-paradise plants and set it beneath the screened window. Standing on the crate, he slowly scanned the area beneath the countertops that was previously hidden from view.

Nettie's monthly planner lay on a small table in the center of the room. On the floor at the entry to the bathroom, he caught sight of a shoe and the top of a white sock.

"Jen, get back."

Michael tore away the screen and threw it to the ground. Yanking off his jacket, he wound it around his right arm, shielded his face and crashed sideways, shoulder first, through the window.

He rolled off the kitchen counter and landed on his feet. Nettie was where her shoe and sock had told him she would be—lying on the floor between the bathroom and kitchen.

Dropping to her side, he groped for her pulse and rested his ear against her chest. Her heartbeat was dangerously slow, arrhythmic.

She was alive, but not by much. He was about to pull out his cell phone when he heard Jennifer on hers asking the 911 operator to send an ambulance.

As NETTIE WAS BEING rushed to the hospital, sirens blazing, Jennifer returned to the kitchen to find Michael at the sink, talking on his cell phone.

"Check for nicotine poisoning, Brad. No, not ingested. Absorbed through the skin. Right. I'll be there as soon as I can."

He flipped the phone closed and faced Jennifer.

"Nicotine poisoning?" She repeated the words with a sense of dread.

He nodded. "Look at this."

Drawing closer, she saw that he was pointing to a rose-aphid insecticide sitting on the shelf beneath the sink.

"The main ingredient in the stuff is nicotine," Michael said. "And notice the bottle in the dish drain."

According to the handwritten label, the empty bottle had contained peppermint lotion.

"Looks like Nettie washed out the bottle tonight in anticipation of filling it up again," Michael said.

Jennifer's eyes went to the table, where a blender and several dishes sat. She stepped toward them, bent down to the bowl and smelled the freshly crushed peppermint in the paste.

"It was a peppermint lotion that Nettie told us Russell's brother had requested for his back rub," she mused, straightening. "But Vivian said she never mentioned Nettie to the Spragues. And Caroline swears Kevin never returned to the hospital. Nettie was the last one we know of to see Russell alive. You're thinking that the lotion she rubbed on him contained the nicotine."

"I'm thinking I need to stay in this kitchen and make sure nothing is touched until the right people have a chance to evaluate exactly what went on here," he said, pulling the keys out of his pocket and holding them out to her. "Take my car and follow the ambulance to the hospital, Jen. I'll catch up with you there."

JENNIFER WAS IN THE E.R. waiting room when Michael finally joined her nearly an hour later. Before she could ask him what he'd learned, Brad appeared at the entrance to the room and walked up to them.

"It was touch and go there for a while, but she's going to make it," Brad said to them both.

He turned to address Michael directly. "Good thing you got her in here when you did and told me what to look for. Without positive pressure ventilation of her lungs with oxygen, her respiration could have easily arrested."

"You confirmed it was nicotine poisoning?" Michael asked.

Brad nodded. "The tox screen revealed the alkaloid salts and cotinine metabolites. Not something we would have thought to look for. How did you know?"

"A guess," Michael said.

Brad eyed him closely. "You know, if this was a deliberate poisoning, I have to report—"

"I've already talked to Ed," Michael interrupted. "But at the moment, I have no evidence that this was intentional. Do me a favor and don't discuss the real reason behind Nettie's close call tonight with anyone else until he can find out what's going on."

"I take it Ed's waiting for me to verify what I found on the tox screen?"

Michael nodded.

Brad glanced at Jennifer, then back to Michael. "Does this have anything to do with Russell Sprague's death?"

"If I answer that I could put you in a difficult position should Detective Batton ask any more questions."

Brad nodded. "Enough said."

"Can we see Nettie?" Jennifer asked.

"She's on her way to the ICU," Brad said. "No visitors until tomorrow, and then, officially, only family. Which reminds me. Do either of you have a name or number of Nettie's next of kin?"

"This was beside the phone in her kitchen," Jennifer said as she held out an address book. "I found her son's name in it. He lives in Sacramento. I've already given him a call. He's on his way."

Brad thanked Jennifer, took the address book and excused himself to phone Ed.

"I spoke to Vivian a few minutes ago," Jennifer told Michael as they left the E.R. "I explained that we found Nettie collapsed on the floor and she'd been taken here by ambulance."

"When we get out to the parking lot, I'll call her with an update."

"Are you going to tell her about the nicotine poisoning?" Jennifer asked.

"Only that Nettie was having trouble breathing and her heart rhythm was erratic. Until Ed has a chance to check things out, I'd prefer to keep the particulars quiet."

"That reminds me," Jennifer said as they stepped outside, "who's Ed?"

"Detective Ed Corbin, my friend in the police department. He's also Brad's brother-in-law."

Jennifer understood Michael's intention was to keep things among friends. "I can't believe Nettie would do something like this. She didn't even know Russell. What possible motive could she have?"

"Remember when Vivian told us they'd been losing a lot of patients recently?"

"And she said for some it was a blessing."

"Exactly," Michael confirmed. "Nettie's been watching people suffer in that ward for more than a year. It's conceivable she got it into her head that by ending their lives quickly, she was doing them a favor. Rubbing nicotine onto their skin would be a fast and fairly painless death compared to what many of them are facing."

"And because they're already terminal, no autopsy would be done when they died," Jennifer said as the possibilities became clear.

He nodded. "Even if one was, all a normal autopsy would show is the organ damage the patient had already sustained from his or her cancer. The inference would be drawn that such damage had caused their heart to stop."

Nightmarishly clever and, if true, unbearably sad. Jennifer felt the weight of the sinister scenario dragging her down.

They reached the car and she handed Michael his keys. Before they drove away, he called Vivian to let her know that Nettie was all right.

Several miles down the road, Jennifer gave voice to the other possibilities bouncing through her mind. "Michael, if this is what happened to Russell, that means others…"

His somber expression told her he'd considered that possibility, as well. "Ed's going to see if he can get hold of Clarence Castle's body for an autopsy, since Vivian mentioned Nettie gave him a massage as well. Tomorrow, he's going to get a court order for the records of all those in the ward who have died recently."

"Nettie thought Russell was a cancer patient until you told her he was there because of a concussion," Jennifer said. "Could tonight have been a suicide attempt brought on by remorse for having killed a healthy man?"

"Even assuming the mercy killing motivation is accurate, I'd say tonight was much more likely to have been a mistake. She forgot to wear gloves when she cleaned out the bottle laced with the nicotine, and enough was absorbed into her skin to cause her to collapse."

"Because if she really were intent on committing suicide, she'd know how much to take for a lethal dose," Jennifer said.

"Ed has a crime scene unit at her place now. They'll analyze the lotion bottle for residue, the new lotion she'd prepared, and take a close look at that insecticide as the possible nicotine source."

"Even imagining a person could do such a thing is terrifying. How do you deal with such matters every day and keep your sanity, Michael?"

"By remembering my humanity. Abnormal behavior grows out of a natural survival instinct that has become distorted, Jen. Paranoia, phobias—these have roots in our basic need to be cautious with things that we perceive as causing us harm. Our ability to love is why we suffer depression when we lose someone or something we value. Whatever my patients are feeling—anger, anxiety, hopelessness, fear—I can understand because I have felt all those things myself."

"If I ever had to see a psychiatrist, I'd want him to be exactly like you. Except not half as handsome or a tenth as sexy, or I'd forget why I came to him."

Michael pulled over to the side of the road, shoved the gearshift into Park and reached for her. "Jenny, you can't say things like that to me when I'm driving. You'll get us killed."

She laughed as she undid her seat belt. The next moment she was in his lap, kissing him. When she heard the engine revving, she realized his foot was flooring the gas pedal.

"Okay, fair warning," he said, his voice husky. "I'm going to make love to you in ten seconds, right here on the shoulder of this highway, with cars whizzing by, and without a condom."

She munched on his earlobe. "Would you really?"

"Nine seconds. Eight. Seven."

She slipped off his lap. "Maybe we'd better wait. We're what? Fifteen minutes away from my place?"

He made it in nine minutes flat.

ED WAS A LITTLE bleary-eyed after his all-nighter. Rising from his desk, he picked up his empty cup and headed toward the coffeemaker in the corner. He'd just gotten his refill when Batton charged into his office.

"Hand over the Nettie Quint file," Batton said. "Guthrie just gave me the case."

"Why would the chief give you my case?" Ed demanded. "I haven't even briefed him on it yet."

"Because I briefed him on it. All of the evidence shows that it's an extension of mine."

"And what evidence is that?"

"The lab guys found nicotine in Nettie Quint's lotion bottle. That's the same stuff that killed my dentist. The hospital volunteer was in the ward that night my vic bought it. She had both means and opportunity."

Ed did some serious, silent cursing. The lab technicians knew better than to go blabbing about their findings to anyone except the detective in charge of the case. Problem was that when a guy had been around as long as Batton, there were a lot of people who owed him favors and would bend the rules.

"There's been nothing in the briefing sessions about your being on a nicotine-poisoning case," Ed pointed out.

"That's because it was on a need-to-know basis," Batton said. "You didn't need to know."

"We should work together on this," Ed suggested as he sat on the edge of his desk.

"I've already got one useless partner. Don't need another. Stop stalling and hand it over."

Knowing he didn't have any choice, Ed scooped up the folder containing what he'd compiled over his long, sleepless night.

Batton grabbed it out of his hand. "You should be thanking me. If I end up pinning the dentist's murder on this old broad, your buddy and his lady friend will be off the hook."

"My buddy?"

"Don't play coy with me, Corbin. I know it was Temple who found the Quint woman passed out in her kitchen, and contacted you. You've been tight with him ever since he pulled your bacon out of the fire on that domestic dispute three years ago. Be thankful I don't go after him and that meteorologist for interfering with a murder case. They had no business going near that hospital volunteer and you know it."

Batton sent Ed a triumphant smirk as he exited the office and barreled down the hall.

Ed waited until the senior detective was out of sight before standing and retrieving Nettie's monthly planner, which he'd purposely sat on.

Batton had demanded the file and he'd given him the file. But he was too angry at the senior detective's underhanded methods to feel like cooperating in handing over that piece of evidence. Let Batton have fun looking for it.

Ed slipped the planner into his desk. After locking the drawer, he pocketed the key.

"THIS COFFEE IS incredible," Michael said as he sat in Jennifer's kitchen and swallowed what remained in his cup.

"It's your mother's," Jennifer told him as she folded over the cheese and vegetable omelette she was cooking. "She was nice enough to leave a bag of her special blend for me at the station when she brought by samples of food for everyone to taste."

"Only time she gives me some of her special blend is on my birthday. How do you rate?"

Jennifer slipped half of the omelette onto each of two plates, then took the chair beside him. "Maybe she likes my weather forecasts."

More likely she knows I'm crazy about you. Never could keep a secret from her.

Michael leaned over, kissed Jennifer's cheek. "Now, why didn't I think of that?"

She looked so beautiful this morning, her long hair loose around her shoulders, the blue silk of her dressing gown slipping over every curve each time she moved. None of his fantasies of her over the years could match the sweetness of this reality.

The omelette tasted great, as did the hot biscuits and fresh fruit Jennifer served with it. But she could have handed him a bowl of cold cereal and he still would have been happy.

They had finished their breakfast and she was refilling their coffee cups when the telephone on the wall rang. She picked it up.

Michael was in the process of swallowing more coffee when he heard her say, "Yes, he's here."

He took the receiver out of her hand and answered with his name.

"I've been trying to get you for the past hour," Ed said, clearly not pleased. "Why did you turn off your cell phone?"

Considering that Ed had eventually figured out where to find him, his friend shouldn't have to ask that question. The fact that Ed's irritation was showing told Michael that something had happened to make him lose his normal cool.

"What's up?" Michael asked as he fished his cell phone out of his pocket and turned it on.

He listened, thanked Ed for calling and replaced the receiver on the hook.

"Is something wrong?" Jennifer asked.

"Batton found out Nettie's lotion contained nicotine. He's tied it into Russell's murder and taken over Ed's case. Ed's a little ticked about it."

"So the police lab confirmed the nicotine was in that jar you found in the dish drain?"

"Yes. Microscopic traces of the nicotine were discovered along with the peppermint lotion residue. Batton will be pursuing her involvement in Russell's murder."

"I know I should be glad the spotlight's off us."

Moving behind Jennifer, Michael wrapped his arms around her. "But you wish the number one suspect hadn't turned out to be Nettie."

She nodded, resting her head on his shoulder. Her body was invitingly warm, her hair soft against his chin. She smelled of sweet bath soap.

Michael's cell phone rang. Reluctantly, he pulled it out of his pocket and answered with his name.

"Dr. Temple," Hazel said, "I know you don't come on shift for another hour, but I thought you'd want to know. Leon got into a shouting and pushing match with the physical therapist who was trying to measure him for an artificial leg this morning. We've had to restrain him in his bed."

"Thanks for calling, Hazel. I'll be there in about forty minutes."

He flipped the cell phone closed as he released Jennifer.

"Trouble?"

"A young man I've been treating."

"Will he be all right until you get there?"

"I don't know."

Jennifer wrapped her arm around his waist. "What happened?"

Michael drew her close. "I put him together with another young man because their devastating physical losses had left them both angry and deeply hurt. The growing friendship between them was integral to their healing. Now it's fallen apart and neither will tell me why."

"What are you going to do, Michael?"

"Separate them. Start over. Try to find something else that will work."

Her free hand slid across his chest. "You will."

The absolute certainty in her voice warmed him in ways nothing else could. His cell phone interrupted again, making him regret he'd turned it on. Working to keep the frustration out of his voice, he answered.

"Dr. Temple, it's Trish, Leon's girlfriend?"

"Yes, Trish, I remember you. Do you mind telling me how you got this number?"

"I saw your nurse refer to the list it was on a moment ago when she called you. As soon as she left, I copied it down. Look, I'm sorry to bother you like this, but I need to talk to you about Leon."

"Where are you now?" Michael asked.

"In the psychiatric ward waiting room."

"Stay there. I'll be in soon."

Michael disconnected the call and faced Jennifer. "I have to go."

"I heard. Call me when you can?"

He nodded, gave her a quick kiss and was out the door.

"I KNEW BATTON WOULD wise up sooner or later and find Russell's real murderer," Liz said over the phone.

Michael hadn't been gone twenty minutes when Liz had called to say she'd heard about Nettie becoming the new number one suspect. It sometimes amazed Jennifer how fast such things got picked up in the newsroom.

"Don tells me that the police found the same kind of poison that killed Russell in some lotion the volunteer used on him. This time it sounds like Batton has some pretty strong evidence to go on, not just suspicion."

"Where did Don learn about the lotion?" Jennifer asked.

"He didn't say, but he rarely passes on his sources."

"Does he know what poison was used?"

"Not yet. But if he can weasel his way in to see this Nettie Quint in the ICU, I bet he finds out. Do you know what it would mean if it really does turn out that we have a serial mercy killer on our hands?"

"Let me guess. Andrew and Ursula will have to postpone the announcement of their engagement until the other story is all played out?"

Liz laughed. "A year in broadcast news and you're already a pro. Jen, it also means that I'll be able to put you back on the air. Come into the studio early tonight and let's get started on that contract renewal. I'll call the Seacrest Café and have something special sent over. It's celebration time."

Jennifer thanked Liz and hung up. But she didn't feel much like celebrating.

She kept seeing the sweet woman who had welcomed them into her home. And she kept hearing the sadness in Nettie's voice as she spoke about the patients she baked cookies for and took a long bus trip to the hospital to see almost every night.

TRISH HAD PRETTY RED HAIR and sad brown eyes. Michael found her biting her nails down to the quick in the waiting room of the psychiatric wing, dark half-moons of tear-smeared mascara on her cheeks.

He took her to his office and sat in the chair across from her.

After waiting several moments for her to begin, he asked, "Do you want to tell me about it?"

She let out a deep sigh. "No, but I know I have to. Before Leon got sick, we were dating, but there wasn't a commitment or anything between us. Then he got the diagnosis and they had to hack off his leg, and it was like I *had* to be with him, because otherwise he was going to think I was dumping him just because he only had one leg. You understand?"

"Yes."

Trish gnawed at a nail. "I know he didn't do anything to de-serve getting sick. But I didn't do anything to deserve getting tied to a sick guy. And he got so down and stuff after the surgery that I really didn't like being around him. But I still kept coming to see him, kept smiling."

She put on one of those smiles. Michael had no doubt it was as painful as it looked.

"Then these past couple of weeks, Leon really perked up. I figured that now he was better, I could fade out of the picture. Only suddenly he starts talking about us moving in together when he leaves the hospital." Trish attacked another nail.

"Did you tell him you didn't want to?" Michael asked.

"That would have hurt him. I didn't want to hurt him. I thought if I showed Leon I was interested in other guys, he'd get the hint and I wouldn't have to spell it out and make a scene or anything. So yesterday when I visited, I smiled a lot at this Gary in the next bed, laughed at his lame jokes, even touched his arm."

She muttered a frustrated oath.

"What happened?" Michael asked.

"Leon's face got so red he looked like he was ready to ex-plode. He pushed himself out of bed and hobbled toward Gary, then he raised his cane to strike him, only he fell flat on his face because he forgot he's only got one good leg."

Her shoulders slumped and she collapsed back against the chair.

It was clear to Michael now why the friendship between the two young men had fallen apart.

"Trish, I know you've been trying to be a kind person and stick by Leon," he said gently. "Your intentions were good. But put yourself in his place. If you had to have a leg amputated, would you want Leon to come around pretending affection for you that he didn't feel?"

She shook her head.

"Leon can face the truth, Trish. But neither of you can live with this lie any longer. We aren't meant to be liars. Our nervous system, digestion, metabolism—everything inside us rebels when we're not presenting our authentic selves to the world. Tell me. How do you feel right now?"

"Awful."

"Listen to your body, Trish. It's letting you know that what you've been doing isn't working. Tell Leon how you really feel. Be who you are. It's the right thing to do. For you. And for him."

JENNIFER WAS GETTING OUT of her car in the KSEA parking lot when she was startled by a man's voice coming from behind her.

"Jennifer Winn?"

She whirled around to see a tall stranger not two feet away. Jennifer took a step back, colliding with the side of her car.

"I didn't mean to frighten you," he said quickly. "I'm Roy Quint. Nettie's son. You telephoned me last night when you found her."

Jennifer let out a relieved breath.

"I'm sorry to just show up like this," he said. "I wanted to call you, but I didn't have your number and the TV station wouldn't give me any information. I really need to talk to you. Is there someplace we can go?"

Jennifer checked her watch. She'd arrived early as Liz had asked her to. She could spare a few minutes.

"There's a coffee shop across the street," she said.

"Thank you."

When they arrived at the coffee shop, the tables were all occupied. They sat at the counter.

"How is Nettie?" Jennifer asked when their coffee had been delivered.

"She's doing better. The doctor said he'll probably be moving her out of the ICU tomorrow morning."

"I'm very glad to hear it."

Despite the good news, Roy continued to frown. "Ms. Winn, there's a Detective Batton who keeps pressing the doctor to let him see my mom. He told me that she's a suspect in your fiancé's murder. Do you know what the hell he's talking about?"

Jennifer understood she had a couple of choices at this moment. The easy, safe one was to profess ignorance. But it wouldn't be the honest one. And as she looked at the man's worried face, she knew it wouldn't be the right one.

"You know how dedicated Nettie is to caring for people in the hospital's oncology ward," she said.

"It's kept her going since my dad died."

"Detective Batton thinks she may have ended my fiancé's life because she thought he was a terminal cancer patient, and was trying to spare him any more discomfort."

Roy stared at Jennifer in absolute horror. "What? No. Never!"

"She had to watch your dad die," Jennifer said softly. "And so many others over the past year. That must have been terrible. The hope that she might be easing their suffering—"

"No, I don't believe it!" Roy said. "I'll never believe it. You don't know her, Ms. Winn. My dad was in terrible pain those last months and she suffered right along with him. One night when I stood at the door to his hospital room, I heard him beg her to turn up the IV drip on his pain medication and give him an overdose to put him out of his misery. But she cried and said she couldn't. Then she crawled into the bed beside him, held him in her arms and sang him a love song."

Tears came into Roy's eyes. He wiped them away with the back of his hand. "She couldn't do it for my dad, whom she loved with all her heart. She sure as hell couldn't do it for a stranger."

CHAPTER THIRTEEN

"I DON'T THINK Nettie did it," Jennifer said.

Michael had phoned the moment he'd checked his voice mail and gotten her message. Resting back in his office chair, he listened to her relate the details of her conversation with Roy Quint.

"I know the fact that nicotine was found in her lotion bottle is damning evidence," she said. "But if you could have heard how Roy described Nettie with his dad, I think you'd be seriously questioning her guilt in Russell's death."

"Do you have Roy's number?"

"He's staying at a motel a few blocks from the hospital until the police let him into his mother's home."

Michael wrote down the number of the motel as Jennifer recited it. "Where are you now?" he asked.

"I'm at the station. Liz requested I come in early so we can begin negotiations on a contract renewal. She's waiting for me now, so I have to make this short."

"You're back on the air?"

"I'll be giving the six o'clock report. Station management seems satisfied that the new evidence in the case has taken us off the suspect list. They've even insisted that I make an appearance with the rest of the news team at the ceremony giving Batton his Investigator of the Year award tonight."

"I'm happy for you, Jen."

"I'd be a lot happier if my good fortune wasn't due to Nettie having become the prime suspect. Is there any way we can help her?"

"For a start, I can talk to Roy, see if she has good legal counsel."

"Is it possible someone else could be performing mercy killings in Oncology?" she asked. "Maybe someone on staff at the hospital who had access to Nettie's lotion and made out that bogus back rub slip for Russell?"

"It's a possibility," he agreed.

"I know we're off the hook here, and normally I'd be happy to let the police handle it. But Batton was wrong about us, and now I believe he's wrong about Nettie. If we don't try to find out the truth, we could be letting an injustice occur."

"I'll do some checking, see what turns up," he said. "Where can I reach you?"

"Looks like I'll be at the station the rest of the day, settling this contract business, so calling my cell number would be the easiest way."

"And tonight?"

"The weekend anchors are coming in to do the ten o'clock broadcast, since the Monday through Friday team will be at the awards dinner. After I get the forecasts completed and appear on the six o'clock spot, I'll be swinging by the house to get ready. It's a formal affair, being held at the Grand Hotel of all places."

"Not in the reception hall where the plane crashed?"

"No, the second floor is still being repaired. The ballroom on the first floor is where this event was booked. Apparently it's both structurally sound and open for business."

"Are you comfortable going back there, Jen?"

Her pause was a little too long. "I'll be okay."

"I have a tux. Love to be your date."

"It's going to last well after midnight. Don't you have to appear before the ethics committee early tomorrow?"

"I'll bring a change of clothes, leave from your place."

"Let me check with Liz to see if I can bring a guest tonight. How did it go with the two young men you told me about?"

"Things are looking up, thanks to a misguided but well-meaning young woman who came clean with them both. They're currently bonding over their disappointment in the entire female sex. It'll probably last until tomorrow, when they get a look at some of the cute new candy stripers who'll be helping out in the ward."

"Ah, the inconstant male heart," Jennifer said.

"Some of us are very constant. I have a cabin in the mountains in a small community a few miles from Lucy's sanitarium. Hiking trails in the nearby woods. Big fireplace. Drive up there with me Friday night after your broadcast, and I'll have you back at the station on Monday in time for the six o'clock spot."

"Whole weekend, huh?"

"Tell me you'll consider it," he said.

"Your name is at the top of my list."

"Wait a minute. There's a list?"

She chuckled in his ear—a soft, warm sound. "Talk to you later."

Smiling, Michael disconnected the line.

After a few minutes, he forced his mind back on business. Facing the computer, he began clicking keys. A mathematical analysis would tell him if there had been a statistically significant rise in deaths among cancer patients over the past year.

"So I HEAR YOU AND TEMPLE were the ones who found the Quint woman," Hardrick said as he sauntered into the weather center, where Jennifer was working.

Jennifer nodded, having no doubt that the paramedics had filled him in.

"You could have given me a call," he said. "We do work for the same news team."

"And told you what, Don? That an elderly hospital volunteer had collapsed? Is that the kind of earth-shattering news you're looking for?"

"You know Batton has the old lady pegged as the one who killed Russell."

"I only learned that this morning when Liz called me. And she says you won't reveal your source on that particular piece of information."

Hardrick sat on Jennifer's desk. "Knowing Liz's history with Batton, I don't like rubbing it in when the guy helps me out."

"Batton told you?" Jennifer asked, surprised.

"He can be cooperative when it suits him. Of course, everything is 'off the record,' so it doesn't come back to bite him in the butt if he's wrong. The way he was about you. Something I told him from the first, even though he wouldn't listen."

"Thank you for trying."

Hardrick picked up a pen and tossed it into the air. "Like I said, we're on the same team. We've been running news bites of Batton's latest lead all day and will again tonight. I'm staying on this story until he gets what he needs to arrest Quint. Once that happens, you and I will do a follow-up interview on your reaction to the murderer of your fiancé being caught. It'll bring home your innocence to the viewers."

"Don, I appreciate what you're trying to do. But you might want to be careful. I think Batton is wrong about Nettie Quint."

"Based on what?"

"On having met and talked with her. And her son."

"No offense, but in light of Russell and Gina, I think that personal veracity meter you use could do with a major overhaul."

Even if he'd meant no offense, Jennifer still felt the sting of his words. Michael was the real professional when it came to reading people. Not once had he put her down for having made a mistake with Russell or Gina.

And he would never have dismissed her opinion with such condescension. Quite the contrary. He gave her and her ideas respect.

"Dr. Temple isn't so sure Batton's right this time, either," Jennifer said evenly.

"More likely he's humoring you."

"Excuse me?"

Hardrick stopped tossing the pen and looked at her pointedly. "For all the obvious reasons."

"Are you trying to be offensive?" Jennifer asked.

"I prefer blunt honesty to B.S.," he said, dropping the pen onto her desk and bending toward her. "Give it a try. You might discover you prefer it, too."

Jennifer understood what he was suggesting. Intent on making sure that the subject was closed once and for all, she said, "That's never going to happen."

Hardrick straightened, seemingly unperturbed. "Liz said you asked her if you could bring a guest tonight. She's not comfortable with who you have in mind."

"I didn't tell her who I have in mind."

"You didn't have to. Look, I give Temple points for sticking by a wife who's locked up in a loony bin. But married is married. And just in case you missed it, there's a morals clause in that contract you signed this afternoon. This is not something either of you can keep quiet. You're too much in the spotlight. Neither your viewers nor this station's management is going to condone your having an affair with a married man."

"My personal choices mean more to me than this job."

Hardrick fixed his eyes on her. "And what about *his* job?"

"What are you talking about?"

"Do you know that Temple is being pressured to resign as president of the California Psychiatric Association?"

"Since when?"

"Since they heard he slept with a patient. A direct violation of item one, section two of the American Psychiatric Association's Code of Ethics."

"I wasn't his patient."

"He was called in to evaluate you as a psychiatrist and he filled out a patient chart," Hardrick said. "Pretty cut and dried. And more than sufficient grounds for his license to be revoked."

Why didn't he tell me how serious things were for him?

"Even if the ethics committee doesn't can him on Friday," Hardrick said, "a continuing affair with you will eventually force them to ask him to resign. The hospital can't ignore one of their psychiatrists—a guy they'd hope would have his id under control—carrying on a blatantly adulterous affair with a media star."

Jennifer shook her head, a jerk of denial mixed with fear.

Hardrick leaned closer. "After tonight's broadcast, the hospital is going to be taking some heavy hits for having let this Quint woman around their patients. They're not going to be able to afford any more bad press. You and the doc keep it up, and you won't be the only one out on your ass."

Sliding off her desk, Hardrick ambled out of the weather center.

Jennifer jumped as a monitor beside her began to beep. Her eyes swung to the gauges. The local barometer was dropping fast. The storm was on its way.

MICHAEL FLIPPED ON HIS TV set at home to watch the six o'clock news. The number one story featured an interview with Batton by Don Hardrick. The detective talked about a promising new lead in the murder of Russell Sprague, stating that the latest and most compelling evidence had led police to question a hospital volunteer in connection with the dentist's death.

"We believe that this crime may well have been committed by someone who did not know the victim personally," Batton said.

Although the film did not show Nettie, it gave a shot of Courage Bay Hospital and even a few frames of the oncology ward. Anyone who had been in the ward over the past year would no doubt know that Batton had been referring to Nettie.

Following Batton's interview, the news anchor spoke about the detective's exemplary record for solving crimes, and how he had been selected to receive the prestigious award of Investigator of the Year at a ceremony that evening.

Michael muted the rest of the news, waiting until Jennifer appeared to give the weather. She was as lovely as ever, but there seemed to be a tenseness surrounding her that he hadn't noticed before.

When she warned of the coming storm that would hit the coast that night, an odd feeling of alarm skittered through him.

He'd received two messages from her on voice mail. The first had invited him to the dinner that night. The second had canceled the invitation. After listening to the second, he'd called and left a message. She hadn't called back.

It was a half hour later when he tried again. This time she answered, her voice sounding slightly off-key.

"Are you okay?" he asked.

"A bit rushed. You caught me in the car headed for home. I need to put myself together for the shindig tonight. How did things go for you today?"

"I ran a computer analysis to see if there was a statistical trend to support a possible mercy killer. It came up inconclusive. Then I went to see Nettie."

"How is she doing?"

"Not too well after a very upsetting interview with Batton. She's horrified she's being suspected of a mercy killing. I also talked to her son, Roy. You were right, Jen. I can't see her doing this."

"Thank you, Michael."

"No reason to thank me. You're the one whose instincts were on the money. I put Roy in touch with Ben."

"Ben's going to represent Nettie?"

"No, Ben's representing us in this matter until it's resolved. But he's referred Roy to a very good criminal lawyer who will handle Nettie's interests and make sure Batton doesn't talk to her again without legal counsel present."

"That's a relief," Jennifer said.

"I also talked to Ed earlier this afternoon. He says the police lab has determined that the nicotine in the washed peppermint-lotion bottle in Nettie's sink didn't come from the insecticide we saw. They're sure of this because the lotion bottle didn't contain the other ingredients in the insecticide."

"So it wasn't Nettie's rose-aphid insecticide that was used."

"The technicians also found that none of her lotions from the storage room at the hospital had any nicotine in them."

"Then just the peppermint lotion was poisoned?" Jennifer asked. "Yes."

"When Nettie read out of her monthly planner," Jennifer said, "she told us Russell's brother had specifically requested the peppermint lotion be used. I wonder how often she got requests for specific lotions?"

"Since January, only eight times."

"You have her monthly planner?"

"Ed does. When I talked with him earlier, he faxed me a copy.

Of the eight times that Nettie received a request for a specific lotion to be used, five times it was for the patient in the first bed of room 423. All five times, the lotion requested was peppermint."

"Then the doctored peppermint lotion could have been meant for that other patient," Jennifer said. "Who was he?"

"I accessed the hospital's records a few minutes ago and learned his name was Oscar Rubio. He was in the final stages of lung cancer. Just minutes before Russell was admitted to the hospital, Rubio's vital signs went critical and he was rushed to the ICU. He lapsed into a coma, died the next day."

"If he'd been poisoned by nicotine, he would have died much sooner."

"With his compromised immune system, in minutes," Michael confirmed. "Which tells us that he probably did succumb to complications from his cancer."

"Michael, if Oscar Rubio was the intended victim, that means Russell was simply in the wrong bed at the wrong time. Have you talked to Ed about this?"

"He's out on another case at the moment. I left a message on his voice mail to contact me when he gets a chance."

"Why would someone want to murder a man who was already so close to death? Was this a mercy killing by Oscar Rubio's brother?"

"Rubio's medical records were sketchy when it came to personal information," Michael said. "He was retired, no previous profession given, and the only relative listed was a wife from whom he was separated."

"So finding out who his brother is won't be easy."

"Rubio's wife responded yes to the hospital's offer of a grief counselor when her husband died, so I took the opportunity to call her. We'll be meeting tonight right around the time you're eating caviar and drinking champagne. Maybe she can shed some light on things."

"I appreciate your doing this, Michael."

"Did you decide to go to the dinner with someone else on your list?"

"Considering it's Batton who's being honored, I want to make a quick appearance and get out of there. It'll be easier without a date."

He'd asked the question playfully, but she'd given a serious answer. A quiver of unease rolled down his back. "We can meet at your place after the awards banquet."

Her response came after a long pause. "I…won't be able to."

"Is something wrong?"

"Michael, you've been wonderful through all the problems we've faced during the past couple of weeks. Really wonderful. And I've enjoyed being with you very much. But there are clauses in my new contract that prohibit… I can't see you anymore."

He'd felt something coming ever since she'd told him she was going to the banquet alone. "What's happened?"

"Now that my job is back on track, I don't want to do anything to jeopardize it. I'm sure you can understand."

He didn't believe for a second that concern over her career was the reason. Something else had her suddenly backing away. The fact that she wasn't being honest with him told him just how serious that something was.

"I need to see you tonight," he said as calmly as he could. "To talk about this."

The pause on the other end of the line seemed to last an eternity.

"I can't," she said. "I want to know what happens with the ethics committee. And I'd like to know if you find out anything that could clear Nettie. But if you'd prefer not to call, I'll understand. Take care. Goodbye."

Before Michael could say another word, the dial tone was blaring in his ear.

THE GRAND HOTEL'S downstairs ballroom was red and silver. With marble floors and two-foot-thick marble pillars, it was a showcase of opulent splendor.

A couple of KSEA news cameramen roamed the room, as well as a newspaper photographer. Most of their shots were of the head table, where Mayor Patrick O'Shea, Police Chief Max

Zirinsky and Chief of Detectives Adam Guthrie rubbed shoulders with Batton, the guest of honor.

Jennifer sat at a table reserved for the KSEA news team, with Liz on one side, Hardrick on the other. Andrew and Ursula were across from her, talking about their upcoming nuptials and where they would honeymoon, partly rehearsing what they would say on the air during Ratings Book week. Jennifer tried to nod and smile at all the right places.

The food must have been good. Everyone around her had quickly consumed it. But most of what she'd been served remained on her plate as the waiters removed the dishes. She didn't want to be here. She wanted to be with Michael. But the reality was Hardrick was right. For her to continue her relationship with Michael could ruin him professionally, if it hadn't already.

When Zirinsky rose to make his speech, the din in the ballroom quieted as all eyes went to the head table. The police chief talked about the case that had caused Batton to be selected for the Investigator of the Year award. How it was Batton's unerring cop instinct and perseverance and only the faintest of forensic evidence that had enabled him to track the murders of four unrelated people to a telemarketer who had become enraged when they'd cursed him out for calling at dinnertime. The telemarketer had pleaded guilty to four counts of murder and was facing a life sentence.

Batton got up, took the offered plaque and thanked everyone. When he sat down without making a speech, Jennifer found herself applauding with the rest of the room because she was relieved she wasn't going to have to hear anything the man had to say.

As soon as it was decently possible, she got up and walked over to the refreshment table. The bartender offered champagne and seltzer. She took the seltzer. Champagne spoke to her of celebration. She had nothing to celebrate tonight.

Liz strolled over and selected a glass of champagne. She eyed Jennifer as she sipped it. "I'm glad you decided against bringing Temple. I could have edited him out of our tape, but there's no controlling the newspaper photographer here tonight."

Jennifer said nothing.

Liz blew out a frustrated breath. "Damn, I knew it. Your glum face is because he isn't here. Jen, he's going to hurt you."

"Michael wouldn't hurt me."

"Look, if you'd loved Russell, you wouldn't have kept him dangling for a year. When you finally said yes, I knew it wasn't to him. It was to marriage. A husband. Babies. Family is what you've been missing ever since your folks died. That's what you want. And that's why this married psychiatrist is going to hurt you."

Jennifer noted the genuine concern on her friend's face. She was very touched to see how much Liz cared. "Don't worry. I've ended it with Michael."

"Judging by the way I saw him look at you, he's not going to let you go easily."

"If I were doing this for me, he might be able to talk me out of it. But I'm doing it for him. Nothing he can say will change my mind."

Liz didn't look convinced. "With Ratings Book next week, I need your face in front of the camera. But I'll transfer you out of state tomorrow to one of Timeright's affiliated stations back east if that will help."

"Thank you, Liz. You're a true friend. But a transfer isn't necessary. I'll be okay."

Hardrick approached, took a glass of champagne and addressed Jennifer. "Batton's located the mate to the earring found in Russell's hospital room. Russell's mother told him the earrings belong to you. He's agreed to give you the set on camera."

"I don't want the earrings," Jennifer said. "And if I get anywhere near Batton, I'm going to tell him what he can do with them."

"Don, could you give us a minute?" Liz asked.

With a shrug, Hardrick strolled off.

Liz turned to Jennifer. "Batton admitted to me that he made a mistake suspecting you. For him, that's a lot. Try not to take the other stuff personally."

"You can say that after what he did to you?"

"He slept with me a few times and talked me into doing things I shouldn't have. But at least he didn't blab about what I'd done."

"Don seems to know about you two."

"All I've told Don is that Batton and I went out a few times and that Batton dumped me. Romantic humiliation I'm willing to endure. But never a breach of professional ethics. This prestigious award has put Batton in the limelight. We're not out of the woods yet on the bad publicity surrounding Russell's murder. Your reputation could use some positive PR."

"Only because Batton did his best to ruin it. And Michael's."

"Do this for me, Jen. Sit next to him. Have a drink. Smile at the bastard."

"All right. For you, Liz. But I'm ordering extra ice in my drink. And if he makes one crack about me or Michael, he's getting it dumped over his head."

SYLVIA RUBIO WAS in her middle fifties, with a face that said her road had not been an easy one. When Michael had called earlier in response to her request for a grief counselor, she'd been eager to meet with him. At the door, she didn't even glance at his offered credentials as she showed him into her living room, which was full of boxes.

"Sorry for the mess, but these are the things from Oscar's apartment that I wanted to keep. Haven't had a chance to unpack them yet. Please, sit. I saw you a couple of times in the ward when I came to visit Oscar."

"Forgive me, Mrs. Rubio, I don't remember meeting you."

"We never met. You were there to see other patients. I just caught a glimpse of you, is all. It's good of you to answer my request."

She gestured him toward a chair and sat on the couch. "I've read those books that give you a list of the steps you need to take to get past the pain of a devastating loss. But it's not like grief is this tangible corridor you can walk through to get to the other side. Those books didn't help at all."

"Tell me what would help, Mrs. Rubio."

"I don't know. Maybe simply to talk. There's no one left to talk to now."

"I'm here."

She nodded, leaning back against the couch as though she was bone weary. "Oscar was once such a strong, robust man. I was at his side every day during his three-week stay in that awful ward, watching him weaken, fade away. We were legally separated, but I still loved him, you understand. We'd shared a life together."

Sylvia focused on the open box beside her. Michael saw the picture there. Leaning forward, he picked it up. "You and Oscar. And the girl's your daughter?"

"Nell," Sylvia confirmed. "She'd just graduated high school. That was four years ago. Nell would be graduating from college now if…" Sadness swept across the woman's face.

"What happened?" Michael asked gently.

"Nell was so bright, so pretty. Her junior year in college she was urged to become a contestant in a local beauty pageant. But things started to change for her then. She lost interest in her studies, got moody. I thought it was the competition of the contest."

"What was really going on?" Michael asked when Sylvia paused.

"She'd begun experimenting with that drug ecstasy. One night she hallucinated from the stuff, jumped off a roof to her death."

So it wasn't only her husband's death that Sylvia was still grieving. Michael gave the woman what he knew she needed at that moment. His complete attention and silent understanding of the pain she had endured.

Her sigh was heavy as she stared at the picture in his hands. "Not that Oscar would believe his little girl was at fault," she said after a moment. "He was certain that the blame was with the guy she'd been dating. Nell had been real secretive about him. Hadn't even told us his name."

Having worked with young people on drugs, Michael knew they often wore allegiance to their fellow users and pushers like a badge.

"Oscar became obsessed with revenge," Sylvia said. "Spent every night looking for the monster who he said had ruined his daughter. I finally couldn't take any more."

"Was that when you separated?" Michael asked.

Sylvia nodded. "When he wouldn't listen to me and get help, I had no choice but to leave. My own grief was bad enough. I couldn't watch the hatred kill him."

She stopped and rubbed her eyes. "He came to get some of his things a few weeks afterward. I fixed him dinner, and for a while that night, I thought maybe we could patch things between us and get back together again. Only then he saw the envelope."

"What envelope was that?"

"I'd found it the week before in one of Nell's old purses. The front had an imprinted post office box number. Inside was a scribbled note from the mysterious boyfriend. Oscar said it was the lead he'd been looking for, and left. I knew then that the hate had won."

Sylvia reached for the photo of her lost family and cradled it in her hands. "He stopped smoking five years ago. We thought…hoped his lungs would heal. I only learned he had cancer when the doctor on the ward called to say he'd been admitted. I think it was the anger over Nell's death that brought it on. Is that possible?"

"Our feelings of happiness or despair can often mean the difference between health and illness," Michael said gently.

She nodded. He wasn't telling her anything she didn't already know. But validating her feelings was important.

"You said earlier that the ward was terrible?" Michael asked.

"I don't mean they treated him terribly, just that so many of the patients there were very sick, and that was difficult to see. The staff was so good to Oscar. And after visiting hours, he told me, a nice older woman would come by to give him back rubs. He liked the ones with the smell of peppermint."

"Was there anyone in your family or Oscar's who was there to help you in his final days?" Michael asked.

"A distant aunt of Oscar's came by. My older sister. A cousin.

They told me to contact them if I needed anything. But that's the kind of thing people say at those times. They hope you'll never make that call."

"Then you were the only one by Oscar's side," Michael said.

"Vern, his long-time partner, would drop in. That helped. Oscar and Vern were as close as brothers. Toward the end, Oscar asked me for forgiveness. Said he should have listened to me and accepted what happened with Nell and not gone after the guy. All those years, and it was the one time he didn't follow the rules."

"The rules?"

"Not to work on a case in which he was personally involved. He even asked me to have Chief Guthrie come by the following Monday so he could square it with him."

Michael stared at Sylvia as her words registered. "Oscar was a policeman?"

"A detective for nearly thirty years. His partner on the force is receiving a prestigious award tonight for a case that both of them worked on. Maybe you've heard of him. Vern Batton?"

BATTON CUPPED JENNIFER'S hand and dropped the earrings onto her palm.

Jennifer forced herself to smile. She was sitting uncomfortably close to the detective so that the camera trained on them could get the best shot of their faces.

"Who had the earring?" she asked, feeling better once he'd removed his hand.

"No one. I found the mate in Dr. Sprague's effects. When the hospital staff took his things from the room and sent them down to the morgue with his body, one of the earrings must have fallen on the floor."

"Russell didn't give them to anyone," Jennifer said in understanding. "He had them all the time."

Batton raised his glass. She clicked her glass to his for the sake of the cameraman still shooting them.

"Seems strange there's no jewelry box," she said after they had sipped their drinks. "And that it took you so long to find the mate in his personal effects."

The detective eyed her sharply. "You should be thanking me for uncovering your fiancé's murderer."

Jennifer dropped the earrings into her purse and set her glass on the table. "Nettie Quint isn't any more guilty of Russell's murder than Michael or I. And you're doing the same thing to her that you did to us. How do you think her son and grandkids feel when they turn on the TV and hear that she's suspected in a murder?"

Batton irritably waved the KSEA cameraman away.

"I don't owe you any explanations," he said. "The only reason I agreed to be videotaped with you tonight is because I'm paying off a debt to Liz. But just for the record, I didn't give anyone Nettie Quint's name."

"You know how many volunteers there are in Oncology? One. Anyone who's been a patient there, anyone on staff or a family member of a patient will know who she is."

"How do you know so much about the oncology ward?"

"It doesn't take a lot of effort to find out the truth. You really should try it sometime."

Jennifer pushed back her chair and stood.

A pleasant-faced man lumbered up to the table. "Three minutes alone with the most beautiful woman in the room and you're already chasing her away, Batton," he said. A pleasant-faced man lumbered up to the table. "Ms. Winn, I'm Leo Garapedian, former chief of detectives to this clown. You'll have to excuse him. He's a hell of a detective, but with women he hasn't a clue."

Out of the corner of her eye, Jennifer saw Liz's worried look as a newspaper photographer aimed his camera their way. For her friend, she'd play nice a few minutes more. Taking Garapedian's extended hand, she returned his smile. He waved her back onto her chair and gestured for the bartender to bring him some champagne.

"You did good, Batton," Garapedian said. "Damn if you don't deserve that eighty-five bucks the department sprung to have that plaque printed up."

"Eighty-five bucks, huh?" Batton said as he frowned at the inscription on the plaque. 'I wouldn't have guessed over twenty.'

Garapedian grinned. "Just one thing missing tonight. Oscar."

"Yeah," Batton agreed, knocking back the rest of his champagne.

"Oscar?" Jennifer said.

"Batton's partner of twenty years," Garapedian explained. "It was Oscar who took this guy under his wing when he was wet behind the ears and made a detective out of him. And let me tell you, that took some doing."

"What happened to Oscar?" Jennifer asked.

"Died last week," Garapedian said sadly. "Lung cancer."

A lot of thoughts were jumbling together in Jennifer's mind at that moment. At the top of them were the words of Preston Zahn. *One of the benefits and curses of having an unusual name is to be remembered.*

"What in the hell is taking that bartender so long?" Garapedian said to nobody in particular. "Guess I'm going to have to go to him. Sit tight, folks."

Garapedian got up and strolled off toward the bar, leaving Jennifer to stare at Batton.

"Oscar *Rubio* was your partner?" she asked.

Batton's eyes locked on hers. "You have been poking your nose into things, haven't you?"

The full implications hit Jennifer hard. Batton had known who was in the bed before Russell. He'd been partners with the intended victim.

Everyone kept saying what a great detective Batton was. But he'd been pointing the finger at the wrong people in this case from the beginning. Now she knew why. Batton had to be behind the attempt on Oscar Rubio's life—an attempt that had backfired. He was the one responsible for Russell's death.

And the look on his face told her he knew exactly what she was thinking.

"What you're feeling against your side, Ms. Winn, is the barrel of my gun. Now you're going to get up and walk out of this room with me."

"I'm not going anywhere with you."

"Yes you are. Because if you don't, this gun is going to accidentally go off and you're going to be dead."

"No one would believe it was an accident."

"I'm one of the most highly decorated detectives in the department. They aren't going to believe anything else. Now, get up very slowly and keep your mouth shut."

Jennifer rose on stiff legs, Batton right beside her.

"Hey, where are you two going?" Garapedian asked as he returned to the table.

Batton slipped his arm around her waist. "Ms. Winn isn't feeling well. I'm going to take her home."

Garapedian studied her face with concern. "You do look pale."

"If anyone asks, let them know," Batton said as he cemented Jennifer to his side and herded her toward the exit.

"Sure thing," Garapedian called to their retreating backs.

Before they reached the exit doors, Batton did a quick check of the room. Seeming satisfied that no one was watching, he pulled Jennifer behind the drapes that cordoned off the stairs leading to the second floor.

CHAPTER FOURTEEN

BATTON GRIPPED JENNIFER'S arm as he pulled her down the hallway of the Grand Hotel's second floor. One by one he tried the doors lining the way. All were locked. The only open area was the damaged ballroom. He hauled her inside.

Emergency lamps on either end spread a reluctant light across the space. Tarps shrouded the few fixtures that had not been removed. Sheets of thick plywood, fastened with heavy tape, spanned the broken windows.

"Over there," Batton said as he released her arm and waved toward a wooden sawhorse that sat beneath one of the emergency lights in a corner.

Jennifer tread carefully over the once gleaming marble floors, feeling the grit of construction debris beneath the soles of her shoes.

Self-defense classes always preached that the best maneuver when not physically restrained was to run. Inasmuch as she was in a floor-length evening gown and three-inch heels, and the man doing the threatening was a crack shot who could easily bring down a fleeing suspect, that choice didn't seem to be a good one.

When they reached the corner, Batton pointed to the edge of the sawhorse. Sitting down, Jennifer came face-to-face with his drawn gun.

She'd never considered herself brave. But she did consider herself to be practical. Giving in to the fear that clawed at her belly would only seal her fate. If she was going to survive this, she had to keep her wits.

"Who else knows about Oscar being in that bed?" Batton demanded.

"I have no idea," she said.

"How did you find out?"

Jennifer's mind spun as she sought to come up with some plausible explanation. Nettie? No, all Batton had to do was ask the hospital volunteer and she'd tell him that wasn't true. Vivian? No, for the same reason. Hospital records? She didn't have access to those and he knew it.

Well, whatever happened, she was not going to tell him about Michael, not even if it meant saving herself.

A piece of cardboard covering a gap between a sheet of plywood and the wall beside her suddenly tore loose. She shivered as a chilling wind whipped through the broken window. Deeply grateful that Michael was far away from this nightmare, Jennifer raised her eyes to the angry man before her.

"You will tell me," Batton said as he took a step closer. "Or I'll put a bullet in your brain right now."

"She learned it from me," Michael said.

Jennifer started at the sound of his voice. She whirled around to see Michael strolling casually toward them—alone, his hands in the air to show that he was unarmed. Now Batton had him, too.

Her heart sank.

MICHAEL CAME TO A STOP six feet from where Batton stood.

"Get over there with her," the detective said, gesturing with the gun.

Michael followed the command, sitting on the wooden sawhorse beside Jennifer. She'd been holding up incredibly well, from what he'd seen and heard before stepping out of the shadows and letting his presence be known. Then she'd gone deathly white.

Not surprising. For a rescue, this left a lot to be desired. If he could have circled behind Batton and overpowered him, he would have. But the open layout of the ballroom left him no opportunity to do that. And waiting in the wings while the man pointed his gun at Jennifer, threatening to shoot, wasn't an option.

Michael maintained his false air of nonchalance as he weaved his fingers through Jennifer's, gathering her cold hand into the warmth of his.

"How did you find us up here?" Batton demanded.

"I saw you slipping behind the drapes when I walked into the ballroom downstairs."

"And you came up after us, alone?" Batton asked incredulously.

"I wanted to talk to you about Oscar," Michael said casually, as though they were two businessmen who might benefit from a discussion about a product.

Michael knew that the most important thing he could do at this moment was relieve Batton's fear. Fear was a dangerous emotion—the one that lay at the heart of most aggressive acts.

"Tell me what you think you know," Batton said.

Michael considered lying, saying that all he knew was that the man's partner had been in the hospital bed before Russell. But even if the detective believed him, which Michael doubted, the probability that he would let the matter drop was slim to none.

The fact he'd pulled a gun on Jennifer proved that.

A better strategy was to put all the cards on the table and convince Batton that he had the winning hand.

"You tried to kill Oscar," Michael said matter-of-factly.

"And how was I supposed to have done that?"

"Oscar told you about Nettie's back rubs. You learned her lotions were locked up in the supply room during the day. All you had to do was see where the key was kept and take it when no one was looking. You slipped the nicotine into the peppermint lotion, leaving enough for only one application. Then you filled out one of Nettie's forms, specifying the peppermint lotion be used in Oscar's back rub that night, and pretended the request had come from his brother."

As Michael watched, sweat broke out on Batton's brow. Considering that the gap in the window was letting in the raw wind from the storm raging outside, he doubted the man was too warm.

"You knew no one would do an autopsy on Oscar," Michael continued, careful to keep his voice conversational. "When he died so quickly, it would have been assumed his breathing and heart stopped because of his end-stage lung cancer. The only thing you hadn't planned on was that his condition would degenerate to the point that they had to move him into the ICU."

Batton shook his head, not in denial but in a way that told Michael he was trying to erase the image from his mind. It was the first chink in the detective's armor. Michael took it as a good sign.

He lowered his voice, made it gentle, soothing. "You and your partner were the best of friends, close as brothers. Each of you would have given his life to save the other. I know you didn't *want* to kill him."

The detective's breath now came in shallow, audible spurts.

"He didn't leave you any choice, did he?" Michael asked.

Batton wiped the sweat off his brow with his free hand. That hand was shaking.

"No, I can see he didn't," Michael said. "It was nearly two years ago when Oscar's daughter jumped off a building to her death while under the influence of ecstasy. Oscar vowed to get the boyfriend who had given her the drug. All he had to go on was a scribbled note and an envelope. The return address printed on the envelope was a post office box. You discovered it was the mailing address for a local beauty pageant."

"You used Liz to find the guy with the same handwriting who worked behind the scenes at the pageant," Jennifer said, putting it together.

"And that was the way you helped your partner catch the boyfriend," Michael added softly. "Only instead of taking the boyfriend in, someone pushed him off a rooftop. That someone wasn't you."

"We caught the two-time loser high on ecstasy with a dealer's worth jammed in his pockets," Batton said suddenly. "We could have thrown the key away on the punk! But Oscar sends me off to get the car, and when I get back, I see them up on the roof. And I know what he's planning to do. So I race up the fire escape. But it's five floors, and by the time I've reached the third, the perp's already sailing off the edge."

Batton exhaled forcefully, trying to release the pain of a lie held in too long. "What was I supposed to do? Turn my partner in for killing the bastard behind his daughter's death? His wife had walked out on him. Oncologist had already given him a death sentence."

"All he had left was you," Michael said gently. "You had to stick by him."

"Twenty years we were together. Saved dozens of lives between us. He was the one who figured out the evidence that led me to the killer in the telemarketer case. He should have been the one who received this rotten plaque."

The detective pulled it out of his pocket and sent it sailing across the room. It smashed into the far wall.

"Oscar was going to confess what he did," Michael said. "That's what he told you when you visited him early that Saturday. He'd asked for a meeting with the chief of detectives the following Monday."

"He said he'd take all the blame," Batton confirmed. "He was even going to lie and say I wasn't with him that night and didn't know what went down. I told him Guthrie would never buy that, especially not after Internal Affairs found out that Liz had helped me locate the boyfriend. Everyone would have thought we both planned to kill him all along. But Oscar wouldn't listen. Kept saying he had to make it right."

"So you tried to end Oscar's life quickly, mercifully, before he could end yours," Michael said.

Batton nodded. "When the M.E.'s office called and said the hospital's pathologist had a case of nicotine poisoning, I thought some bonehead had autopsied Oscar. I never imagined... What were the odds that Oscar would get sent to the ICU that night? That a healthy guy would get his bed?"

"Not something you could have foreseen," Michael said, continuing to convey the sympathy he knew Batton needed to hear.

"I had to take the case," Batton said, "to be sure the evidence was controlled. You and Ms. Winn would never have been charged. Nor do I intend to give the D.A. enough to arraign Nettie Quint. I just needed to make it look like a good-faith effort had been made."

"You did a damn good job of that," Michael said. "We were convinced we were going to be arrested at any time. That's what drove us to try to find the truth."

Batton was licking his lips, assessing the situation. "You have no evidence that I did it. All you could prove is that Oscar had the bed before the dentist."

"That's right," he agreed.

"Still, I can't afford to let you go around blabbing about this," Batton said. "Even without proof, the accusation could be enough to get people to start wondering, asking questions."

His eyes strayed to the cardboard that had come loose from the window. The gap was big enough for a body to go through. In the blackness beyond lay a two-hundred-foot drop that would mean certain death.

Michael's grip on Jennifer's hand tightened. "As long as Nettie isn't charged and the matter eventually dropped," he said with all the calm he did not feel, "Jennifer and I have no reason to say anything."

"Don't give me that," Batton said. "Sprague was her fiancé."

"A fiancé who cheated on her with her best friend," Michael reminded him. "Tell me. How would you feel about someone who'd done that to you? Would you be eager to avenge their death?"

"And you're going to try to convince me that you'd let it go?"

"I came up here alone, didn't I?" Michael held up his hand, clasped with Jennifer's. "Does it look like I care that Sprague's out of the picture?"

Batton frowned as he stared at their hands. "I've got a boy. He wants to be a cop, just like me. I'm not letting anyone change that."

"Oscar put you in an impossible situation," Michael said as he lowered their hands. "You gave him your trust, your loyalty, and in return, he was about to ruin your life. He was already dying. We understand why you had to do what you did."

For the first time, Batton glanced down at the gun in his hand. Michael gauged the distance between them, judging the time it would take to cross it. He was fast, but so were a cop's reflexes.

Going for the weapon would be far too risky. Better to keep working on the man's mind, try to defuse the desperate thoughts that he and Jennifer were threats Batton had to remove.

"We'd gain nothing by accusing you," Michael said in that same soothing tone. "Jennifer's in contract negotiations with KSEA. I still have the ethics committee to get through. And if there's any more talk surrounding me, the hospital will remove me from my position and cut its losses. Think about it from our point of view."

Batton was thinking about it. And the sweat was now covering his upper lip. "So, I'm supposed to let you walk out of here, is that it?"

"You don't have the time to properly plan our deaths. If you shoot us or try to push us out that window, those scenarios are going to get you convicted of murder. You know that."

Batton's struggle to make a decision was putting a deep crease in his forehead.

"Besides, you're not a killer," Michael said with the kind of confidence that brooked no argument. "Killers are the scum you've devoted your life to tracking down and bringing to justice. You're a cop, one of the good guys. Just ask your son."

The decision was written on Batton's face even before the man gave voice to the words. "Get out of here."

That was all Michael was waiting to hear. He rose, bringing Jennifer with him. It took a good deal of willpower not to pick her up and race across that ballroom floor for the door. Instead, he wrapped her hand around his arm and forced himself to stroll casually, just as though he hadn't a care that the man behind them still had a gun in his hands. And could change his mind.

The second they reached the doorway, Michael pulled Jennifer behind the safety of the wall and wrapped her tightly in his arms.

"Hate to break this up," Ed whispered from the darkness, "but I think you two better get out of the way."

Michael looked over to see that Ed had two uniformed officers beside him. They all had their guns drawn.

"When did you get here?" Michael whispered back.

"Couple minutes ago."

"Did you hear what you needed to?"

"Enough. We've been waiting to see if you could work your magic and get yourself and Ms. Winn out of harm's way. Thank God you did. We'll take it from here."

Ed signaled to the uniformed officers to get ready.

"Careful," Michael warned. "The second he sees you he's going to know he's lost everything that means anything to him. Turning that gun on himself is a distinct possibility."

Ed nodded. "Don't worry. I'm not going to let him shoot himself."

As Michael eased Jennifer back, Ed and the uniformed officers charged into the ballroom, yelling for Batton to drop his gun. Michael heard the sound of a weapon hitting the floor. He breathed out in relief until Ed suddenly started to curse.

And that was when Michael remembered the gap in the window. And knew that Batton had gone through it.

JENNIFER SAT ON THE STEPS between the first and second floors of the Grand Hotel, huddled against the wall, Michael's jacket wrapped firmly around her. She was trembling, not nearly so much from the cold draft coming from the ballroom above as from the aftermath of fear.

Drifting to her from the floor below were the indistinct sounds of many raised voices. Outside, sirens blared. She closed her eyes, tried to shut out the noise and the awful images in her mind.

A few moments later she heard footsteps, opened her eyes and saw Michael climbing the stairs toward her. When he reached her he sat, put his arm around her shoulders and gathered her against him. As she absorbed the solid warmth of him, the trembling stopped.

"They found Batton's body at the bottom of the cliff," he told her.

"I realize he might have killed us," she said, "but I didn't want it to end like this."

"Nor did I," he said as he gently kissed her hair.

Reaching into the pocket of the jacket she wore around her shoulders, he retrieved his miniature tape machine and pushed the stop button.

"You recorded his conversation so you'd have proof of his guilt," Jennifer said. "Did you know Ed was coming?"

"I reached him by phone on my way here. I told him about Oscar Rubio and my conversation with his widow and about how Batton had used Liz. I tried calling you on your cell to tell you what I'd learned and warn you to keep away from Batton, but all I got was your voice mail."

"Everyone was asked to turn off their cell phones during the award ceremony. Michael, you were so convincing, I sincerely believed you wanted to let Batton get away with murder."

He smoothed the hair from her forehead, his voice full of that deep determination she'd had glimpses of before. "I would have said or done anything to get you away from him."

"What you did was risk your life," she said, too touched to hide her feelings.

He wrapped her in his arms, holding her close. "Jenny—"

"I've filled everyone in," Ed interrupted as he trudged up the stairs toward them. "No one wants to believe me. Hell, I wouldn't believe me, either. Both Guthrie and Zirinsky looked at me like they wanted to shoot the messenger. I'm not sure having two uniforms to back up my story is going to be enough."

Michael released Jennifer and held out the tape machine. "Maybe this will help."

"You recorded him?" Ed asked as he took the device, turning it over in his hand as though it were a priceless jewel. "Damn, I love psychiatrists."

"Sorry, I'm spoken for," Michael said as he grasped Jennifer's hand and drew her to her feet. "I'm going to take Jen home."

"Not tonight," Ed said. "I've got a highly decorated dead cop who turns out to be a murderer on my hands. There's a mountain of paperwork to get through. Don't count on being anywhere else for the next twelve hours."

"I have the ethics committee at nine in the morning," Michael said.

"Something you and I need to discuss," Ed said. "There's a female police officer downstairs who will drive you to the station, Ms. Winn. Michael, you're riding with me. We all have a long night ahead of us."

"AFTER CONFESSING THAT he tried to end the life of his long-time partner, who was suffering from lung cancer, an attempt that unintentionally resulted in the death of Dr. Russell Sprague, Detective Batton jumped to his death through an open window of the Grand Hotel last night."

Jennifer stood at the weather center podium watching Andrew read Hardrick's copy off the TelePrompTer.

The fact that Batton's confession hadn't been voluntary wasn't mentioned. Nor was the reason for his attempt on his partner's life. It sounded as if Batton had botched a mercy killing and committed suicide in remorse for taking an innocent life.

Liz and Hardrick had worked it out with the police so that the details of the story would be released gradually over the next week. For their part, KSEA got exclusive coverage during Ratings Book week. In return, the police got a chance to focus on the good things that Batton and his partner had achieved in their decades on the job before revealing that each had ultimately failed to live up to his oath to protect and serve.

Jennifer was not disappointed. What was important to her was that Nettie was cleared and the Sprague family knew both the how and why of Russell's death. Perhaps the truth would make their road to healing less difficult.

A filmed clip from the previous evening of Police Chief Max Zirinsky's glowing praise for Batton's investigative techniques and dogged determination in the telemarketer case was run next, followed by Batton accepting his award with a modest thank-you.

"Twenty seconds," the producer said in her ear.

Jennifer hadn't seen Michael since Ed had separated them at the Grand Hotel the night before. She'd been released at eight in the morning and had gotten all of four hours sleep before being called down to the TV station to discuss what she knew, and figure out how best to present her involvement in the dramatic finale to Batton's life.

The rest of the day had been a hectic blur. She'd checked her voice mail a dozen times. Michael hadn't called.

"Ten seconds," the producer said in her ear.

When she got home, she planned to contact Vivian to see if she'd heard what the ethics committee decision had been. She prayed it had gone all right.

Was Michael up in his mountain cabin now? Having dinner? Watching the news? She had to stop thinking about him.

"Three. Two."

"And now let's go to Jennifer Winn and see what the weekend forecast holds," Ursula said. "Jennifer?"

"Ursula, we'll see the last of the rain tonight, leaving the weekend sunny and warm here along the coast, with highs in the seventies, lows at night in the sixties."

Jennifer stopped to point at the weather map where she imagined Michael's cabin might be. "But if you find yourself traveling into the mountains, you may want to bring some wood for those fireplaces, because it's only going to be in the forties."

So much for not thinking about him.

MICHAEL WAITED in the shadows as he watched Jennifer get out of her car and race through the rain to her doorstep.

"Hi," he said, stepping into the porch light.

She jumped. "Michael, you almost gave me a heart attack."

"Not to worry. I'm fully trained in resuscitation procedures."

Her face was a kaleidoscope of emotions, changing too quickly for him to read.

"What happened with the ethics committee?" she asked.

He did his best to shiver and look cold, which wasn't too difficult since he was drenched. "Invite me in and I'll tell you."

Eyeing the water dripping off his forehead, she unlocked the door. Once inside, she handed him a towel from the kitchen. He shucked off his soaking wet jacket, dried his face and hands and found her studying him with a worried look.

"I didn't have to say a word," he said quickly, unable to endure seeing her unhappy even for a moment. "Ed got up in front of the committee and assured them that Batton had only told them we'd spent the night together because he was trying to cover his guilt over Russell's death."

"Ed lied about our being together?"

"He didn't lie. He merely implied Batton had. Since Batton had no right to ask us where we were that night, inasmuch as we were never really suspects, everything he learned was illegally obtained. Ed assured me he had to tell the committee what he did to avoid our filing a lawsuit against the department. Of course, he really told them because he's a good man and wanted to do right by us. After listening to Ed, the chairman made a motion to dismiss the matter. It was passed unanimously."

"Michael, that's wonderful."

The relief, the joy—it was all there in her smile. He took her hands in his. When she started to withdraw, he held on.

"I thought you were going to your mountain cabin," she said, uneasy.

"My favorite meteorologist told me I needed some firewood for the fireplace. I wanted to get some before I left. And take her with me."

Gathering her into his arms, he kissed her with all the desperation he felt. When she kissed him back with that same kind of desperation, his heart soared.

Releasing her a few breathless moments later, he said, "Jenny, I'm so damn in love with you."

Her sigh was a mixture of happiness and heartache. "I love you, too, Michael. But being with me could ruin your reputation, your profession, everything."

"That's why you've been retreating from me?"

"You've already been asked to resign as president of the California Psychiatric Association."

He smiled with relief to finally understand. "I don't care about the presidency. If they really want my resignation after all this is over, they can have it. Jenny, you're what matters to me."

"But what about your job, Michael? We could never keep a continuing relationship quiet. My face is too well known. And I can't imagine that the hospital would look the other way if one of their married psychiatrists was having such an open affair."

"They wouldn't…if I were still married. But Ben filed the papers to annul my marriage earlier this week. The judge signed them this afternoon."

"You're not married?" she said, disbelief echoing in every syllable.

"Jenny, for the past seven years Lucy hasn't been my wife in anything except name. The only reason I maintained our legal marriage was because I had no reason to end it."

Michael cradled Jennifer's face in his hands. "I fell in love with you five years ago. But I couldn't imagine someone as beautiful and amazing as you would choose to be with a man who would always be bound to his first wife. That's why I let you go that last night of the seminar. It wasn't until you met Lucy and I saw how wonderful you were with her that I realized how much love you had inside you. And I began to hope that it might be enough love for you to accept both me *and* Lucy into your life."

He wrapped his arms around her. "From that moment on, staying away from you—as you'd asked me to—became impossible. I told Ben to end my marriage to Lucy, because for the first time in seven years, it mattered that I be legally free."

"What about Lucy, Michael?"

Hearing the genuine concern for Lucy in Jennifer's voice touched Michael deeply. "Lucy will always be in my heart, a special part of my life," he said. "I will care for her as long as we both live. The court has appointed me her legal guardian."

Stroking Jennifer's lips lightly with his, he said, "I love you. I want to marry you. Have children with you. Build a life together."

Jennifer's eyes shimmered with light as she wound her arms around his neck. "Yes, Michael. Yes to it all."

Hugging her with happiness, he asked, "Would I be rushing you if we got the license on Monday, married on Tuesday?"

She laughed. "Are you trying to sweep me off my feet?"

He grinned as he scooped her into his arms and carried her toward the bedroom. "Yes. Is it working?"

Smiling, she planted a kiss against his ear. "We'll have the ceremony on the beach at sunset with just a few friends and your family."

Gently, he laid her on the bed. "Thank you for including them. They love you already. I can't wait to start our family. When I thought you might be pregnant after the first two times we were together, I have to confess, I was hoping you were. Learning you'd used the morning-after pill left me very disappointed."

"I didn't say I'd used the morning-after pill. Only that I knew about it."

"You *didn't* take it?"

She touched his lips with her fingertip. "You don't think I fell in love with you just over the past two weeks? If we'd created a baby together, I planned to keep it."

He rested his hand on her tummy, an amazed smile on his face. "You could be pregnant."

"A distinct possibility. But the odds would be better if we made love a few more thousand times. What do you say?"

His smile spread ear to ear. "I can probably manage three or four times tonight. Will you take a rain check on the rest?"

"Absolutely," she said as she pulled him to her. "But I'd better warn you. Tonight's the last of the rain. From now on, I'm forecasting nothing but sunshine."

Ordinary people. Extraordinary circumstances.
Meet a new generation of heroes—
the men and women of Courage Bay Emergency Services.
CODE RED
A new Silhouette continuity series continues
in December 2005 with
THE TRIGGER
by Jacqueline Diamond
A serial bomber is on the loose.
Bomb squad specialist Nora Keyes knows only one way to
flush the killer out:
set herself up as his next target....
Here's a preview!

Max Zirinsky knocked on the open door of Nora's office and entered without waiting for a reply. The police chief's wary expression immediately alerted her that she might not like what he intended to say.

Don't tell me you're giving the case to Sam! She bit down on the response. Running the police department was Max's job, not hers.

"How's it going this morning?" he asked.

Nora indicated the stacks of files on her desk. "I just got my hands on the records from the other murders you mentioned, the ones attributed to the Avenger. I haven't had time to review them yet."

Although murders not involving explosives lay outside her purview as bomb squad specialist, Max's mention of them had stirred Nora's curiosity. Besides, if the same person did prove to be both the Avenger and the Trigger, her familiarity with the bomb-related cases might help her spot similarities.

"Well, don't worry about those just yet."

"Really?" This seemed like a bad sign.

"Dan Egan and I decided on how we want these Trigger cases handled." Max leaned against the edge of her desk. A tall man with black hair and green eyes, he remained strikingly handsome in his mid-forties, although Nora had never felt any sparks between them. One of these days he was going to make a terrific match for someone else, though.

Feigning nonchalance, she widened her eyes to indicate interest while bracing herself. Of course one of the detectives, probably Grant, would take the lead, with Sam to assist him, she reflected unhappily.

"I know this is going to be difficult," the police chief went on, "but we've decided we want you and Sam Prophet to work together on this."

"Together?" Hearing her voice shoot up an octave, Nora strained to bring it under control. In the most professional manner she could muster, she amended, "I'm sure we can both advise the supervising detective as needed."

"That isn't what I meant," Max said. "You're both experienced investigators in your own right, and time is of the essence. We're putting the two of you in charge jointly."

"You mean you're making Sam and me a team?" She hadn't imagined anything as devastating as this.

Inquiries into serial murders involved weeks or months of intensive work, with ten-to-twelve-hour days often spilling over into weekends. They required coordination, communication and a level of closeness that Nora didn't even want to think about.

"Is that a problem?" the chief asked.

As a self-respecting police sergeant, she could only give one response. "Of course not, sir."

"Good." Max nodded at the case files. "Sam's probably on his way over here right now. I'd like you to review those together. It should help you start thinking of yourselves as a team."

"Absolutely." The word came out barely audible, because most of the air had just disappeared from Nora's lungs.

"Whatever support you two require, don't hesitate to ask." Max watched her sternly. Despite his genuine concern for his officers, he held them to high standards. "I don't need to tell you that this investigation has top priority."

"Yes, sir." She refocused her thoughts on the stakes. Three people were dead, one lay in a coma and there'd been two additional bombings, with possibly more to come. Her petty feud with Sam Prophet paled by comparison.

The chief handed her another file. "Here's the latest from forensics. I've directed that all further material be forwarded to your office."

"Thank you."

After he left, Nora sat clutching the file and staring at the wall. She couldn't believe Max had ordered her and Sam to form a team, not after their public argument yesterday.

Yet, grudgingly, she conceded that the pairing made sense from a management standpoint. The two of them had complementary characteristics, with her bursts of insight and his exhaustive attention to detail.

Moreover, they'd both accumulated a certain expertise in the Trigger's operating methods, and their training prepared them to track better than anyone else in either department. In a situation likely to attract a high profile, the city needed to employ its best talents.

A groan echoed from the walls of her small office, startling her. Nora glanced around before she realized that the groan had come from her own throat.

The Trigger presented the greatest challenge of her career. And she was going to have to battle every step of the way with a man who, she had to admit, attracted her more than he should, and irritated her at the same time.

Well, when the going got tough, the tough went to the ladies' room. Nora reached for her purse to do just that.

A large frame blocked her doorway. Although Sam Prophet stood no taller than Max Zirinsky, his presence had enough impact to dwarf the space around him. That might have been because of the thunderous expression he wore.

"This wasn't my idea," he said, "in case you were wondering."

Escape into

Just a few pages into any Silhouette® novel and you'll find yourself escaping into a world of desire and intrigue, sensation and passion.

Silhouette

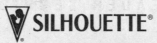

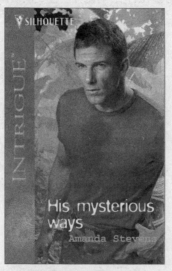

Escape into...

SPECIAL EDITION™

Life, love and family.

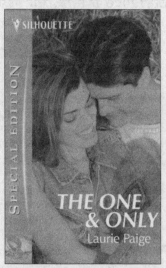

Special Edition are romances between attractive men and women. Family is central to the plot. The novels are warm upbeat dramas grounded in reality with a guaranteed happy ending.

Six new titles are available every month on subscription from the

READER SERVICE™